CENTRAL RESERVATION

http://www.willlefleming.com/

 @will_lefleming

CENTRAL RESERVATION

Will le Fleming

Xelsion Publishing

For Morwenna and Daniel

For Henry

And for Abigail: *lux et umbra*...

February 2001

1

On a grey Thursday morning Holly lay in bed, staring at the ceiling, and wished her sister would die. Five hours later her wish came true.

It would have been harder to deal with, Holly thought afterwards, if it had been the first time she'd made the wish. Having that prayer so swiftly granted would have been seriously disturbing, apart from anything else; and then there would have been the guilt. She felt bad enough as it was. If it had been the first time, she'd never have escaped the sense of responsibility, and that would have been yet another way in which Yvonne kept a hold on her.

In fact she'd been hoping for Yvonne's death for almost a year before it happened. It had started the day after their thirteenth birthday; the day Danny Blake had shown her his penis. Danny had a large head, pale blue eyes, and, in Holly's opinion, confirmed criminal tendencies. He was raw and bony, and seemed to enjoy hitting people in the face, skinning his knuckles against their teeth and chins. He'd never hit her, but for some inexplicable reason he did enjoy telling her she was a faggot, saying it with relish and looking around for approval from his mates. As some kind of twisted birthday present, Yvonne had decided to tell everyone that Holly fancied him. Holly thought she'd never have forgiven her, even if Danny hadn't responded to the news by exposing himself.

He'd been waiting for her at the end of second period. She'd seen him ahead of her in the corridor by the changing rooms and just as she reached him he'd opened his grubby trousers to reveal a tiny wrinkled brown thing like a dry slug. Holly had felt a clear burst of rage at the injustice of a world with Yvonne and Danny in it, and had surprised herself by acting without any thought at all and instead kicking him as hard as she could. His hands had taken some of the blow, but she'd connected well enough to drop him to the ground. His henchmen had whooped and cackled as he'd writhed on the floor. She'd walked away, head down, her heart beating heavily, and found an empty classroom. As soon the door had shut behind her she'd leant back against her hands and begun to fantasise about the death of Yvonne. She'd pictured her being sucked into an industrial turbine, ripped and ground into progressively smaller pieces until she was reduced to shreds no bigger than confetti, a mass of gaudy scarlet scraps to be scattered by the wind.

For a while the rush of it had been amazing. Holly had luxuri-ated in the sensation: savoured the thick, meaty taste of hatred, felt the false pulse of malice thrum in her palms. Then, with no warning, she'd been hit by the aftermath – a sudden acid surge of remorse. She had never let herself hate Yvonne before. She couldn't hate her twin. It wasn't normal. Not that she pretended to be normal, but even so. Yvonne had stupid nostrils and bright pink skin and was mostly unkind but Holly couldn't want her dead, not really. Could she?

It took her a long time to answer that question. Eventually she'd realised that she didn't want any harm to come to Yvonne, exactly. She didn't want her to eat a poisonous mushroom, or bounce rag-gedly under the wheels of a car, or slide beneath the slick surface of an icy lake, even though she did picture all of these things happening sometimes. She just wished that Yvonne had never

4

existed. Or even that either one of them had never existed. Holly thought she could cope with the idea of oblivion. Oblivion was freedom and unknowing and silence and absence. The one thing it wasn't was proximity: the unbearable sense of a togetherness from which there was no escape.

2

The day Yvonne died was cold and wet. Holly had been woken by the rain, and felt the chill air from her open window on her skin as she allowed herself to wish for her sister's destruction. The silent intensity of her plea was broken by the arrival of her mother. Belinda kicked open the door, not to break it down but because her arms were full of laundry, though the way Belinda kicked open doors it was hard to tell the difference. She hurled the clothes onto the floor, yelled, "Clothes!" and marched out.

Holly listened to the noise of her departure echoing in the air for what felt like minutes. Belinda always did everything at top volume, no matter how early it was. Though for her seven o'clock wasn't really early, Holly supposed. In fact there was probably no time that counted as early for Belinda, unless it was the day before. She started the milking at half-past-five every day, and had always been awake long before that, even when Daddy was alive. Perhaps she slept on her feet out there in the dairy parlour, her hands automatically fumbling the clusters onto the line of udders. A somnambulist milker, Holly thought. She loved the word somnambulist.

As usual on laundry day Yvonne came to Holly's room to extract the clothes she wanted from the pile. Holly watched her, head turned on the pillow, the eiderdown by her face damp and warm from her breath. They didn't speak. Yvonne ferreted through the clothes silently, as stealthy as one of the dogs when it had stolen

6

food from the kitchen and didn't want to be seen eating it. Holly didn't know why, Yvonne must have known she was watching. That was just the way Yvonne did things.

Although they were twins, they didn't look anything like each other. Yvonne often said it was strange, how dissimilar they were, eyeing Holly uneasily. She also often said that this was a good job, and she didn't know how Holly coped. Holly used to feel a deep dull unhappiness when Yvonne made comments like that, but ever since she had allowed herself to hate her, she felt secretly pleased: every act of unkindness was justification, made her feel less evil. Yvonne was right, though, the difference between them was strange. Yvonne was long and willowy with fair hair, lots of it, fine blonde hairs covering her arms and extending out beyond her hairline. Holly was pale and dark and had been short for most of her life though she'd got tall, this last year, nearly as tall as Yvonne. They still looked like strangers though. Sometimes Holly thought that one of them must have been adopted. Perhaps they both were. She couldn't imagine Belinda having babies – little about her gave the impression that she was really a living, breathing organism. Her face was craggy, her hair like gorse, her frame as tough as wood: she was more of an outcrop than a person.

After Yvonne had sidled out with her armful of clothes Holly got up to look at the day. Outside it was just getting light. Drizzle ran down the glass and the line of trees that divided the overgrown garden from the hump of Back Field stood straight and bare in the mist. They lived on a farm about a mile from the nearest village. It was reached by a narrow lane that ran between high green hedges and ended at a five-bar gate. After that the lane became a track, laid with broken pieces of concrete that banged on the bottom of ordinary cars as they lurched along. It was hard to reach the house in anything less than a pick-up, which was one of the reasons they had few visitors.

Holly stood for a minute, shivering, smelling the air. Then she stuck her hand through the window, brought it back in and inspected it. Her fingers were cold and white and her hand was wet. Acting on impulse, she bent her head and licked the rainwater from her palm like a cat. There was a noise at the door, and she turned to see Yvonne watching her. "You're weird," she said, picked up a stray sock, and left. Holly looked thoughtfully after her. There didn't seem much point disputing the fact. Downstairs she could hear Belinda making breakfast. If they'd had any neighbours, they'd have been able to hear Belinda making breakfast too.

"Holly, do you want to do it with me?"

A pause. She knew it wouldn't last long.

"Holly? Do it. You know?"

Holly sighed, and tried to shuffle pointedly even further away from Danny Blake. It was the school's annual outing to the All-County Amateur Rugby Sevens tournament, and he had decided to sit next to her on the coach. Holly had never understood why the whole prep school, all 42 pupils, had to attend a rugby tournament, but it seemed to be the highlight of the year as far as their headmaster Mr Cockburne was concerned. He was standing at the front of the coach, his hairy head bobbing as he talked to the driver. Probably telling him to hurry up in case they missed the first game. Danny snickered in follow-up to his comment and Holly gave him a withering look. At least, she hoped she did. She'd been practising the expression in front of the mirror. Yvonne had caught her doing that, too. She had an uncanny ability to turn up just when Holly was acting in a way that would reinforce her Holly-is-weird theory, which was maturing nicely after 13 years of observation.

"Holly? Do you?" Danny persisted. Holly gazed out of the window with determination. From long experience, she knew they were approaching a critical moment. This had been Danny's subject of choice, on and off, ever since the penis incident. It generally worked, making his henchmen snigger. Today, though, even they had stopped listening. Their lack of response meant he'd either have to abandon or escalate his campaign. The latter was more likely.

She tried to concentrate so hard on the view that Danny would entirely disappear from her perception. They were overtaking a livestock truck, and the yellowing fleeces of sheep were stuck through the slats of the lorry like tufts of stuffing. Count them, Holly told herself, try to work out how old they are, anything. The inside of the truck was too gloomy to give her many clues, though even from what she could see it was obvious they weren't looked after properly: they were packed in, and some liquid was leaching down the side of the vehicle. Good job Belinda wasn't on this coach, she'd probably insist they pulled over and gave the driver a talking-to. They were passing the cab now, and Holly could see his face: rough and stubbly and unkind-looking. Not very different from how Danny would turn out, probably.

From the back of the bus she heard a shriek of laughter. Yvonne's position on school trips was the central seat of the back row, where she held court among the popular boys, an assembly of goons and sport-playing savages. Holly wondered crossly what had prompted Yvonne's shrill mirth. Probably someone telling her that he fancied her. Yvonne said everyone at the school fancied her, and though at first Holly hadn't believed her, the claims were increasingly backed up by practical experience. Holly knew this very well, because after Yvonne's first kiss (Nathan Osgood) she'd come straight to Holly to tell her, and since then it had been a post-snog ritual. She'd skip up, ostentatiously wiping her face, to tell Holly exactly what they'd done with their tongue, and increasingly, their hands.

Holly didn't enjoy this for lots of reasons. Firstly, Yvonne was unsubtle in drawing out the moral of her stories: that the scale of sexual attractiveness was drawn between her at the pinnacle of desirability, and Holly at the nadir of repulsiveness. Second, the mere fact of Yvonne's success made Holly feel stupid and clumsy and naive. And third, most painful of all, Holly loathed herself for falling victim to the first two. She ought to rise serenely above such quotidian anxieties – quotidian was another of her favourite words – but her flesh was weak, it squirmed under Yvonne's gloating, her stomach knotted with anxiety despite the fiercest instructions from her brain not to care.

Through the coach window Holly could see the marquees outside the stadium where the tournament was held. She looked at them feeling an irrational but complete certainty that life was never going to change. She remembered the moment, because it turned out to be only a few seconds before her life changed forever.

3

Holly replayed the next moments in her mind over and over again. She went through it so often, partly remembering, partly imagining what had happened, that the episode became like a film in which she was only a character. She could see herself, near the back of the bus, looking away from Danny. He reached out a hand, curled bony fingers around the back of her neck, pulled her towards him, with his mouth wide open and his tongue already stretching out, and she experienced her first kiss.

At that moment of slippery bruised-lip sourness, what was happening elsewhere? The driver was slowing down for the wrong entrance and Mr Cockburne was telling him off for it. Holly imagined him saying something peevish like, "No, you fool, cars only. Coaches round the side. Come on, man, come on."

Perhaps the driver wanted to teach him a lesson, or perhaps he just didn't like school parties, and wanted these little ponces off his coach so he could see if any of them had got chewing-gum stuck on his upholstery. Either way, in a surge of irritation, he pressed down hard on the accelerator. At the same moment, after its driver had argued with the car park attendant about correct change, a battered Landrover reversed abruptly back out into the road. It slipped neatly into the path of the coach, which, it was eventually established, had just reached 40 miles an hour.

The coach hit the Landrover square-on. In her remote, impossible memory of it all Holly saw the coach driver lurch forwards, and his forehead bounce back from the rim of the large steering-wheel, leaving blood. Mr Cockburne, who'd been standing in front of a sign telling him he shouldn't, was lifted from his feet. His head hit the large windscreen, which remained intact, but crushed his skull. His body folded upside down against the wide sheet of glass.

Holly had pushed Danny away before the impact, hard, and he'd fallen into the central aisle. He had just stood up as the collision happened, and was flung forwards. As he travelled down the aisle, airborne, it must have looked as if Mr Cockburne was staring back at him between his legs. Then Mr Cockburne began to slide down the glass, leaving a bloody trail, and Danny curved in the air, landed on his back on the ridged plastic floor-mat, and skidded along. Above him, Holly wondered if he saw a flying angel, its hair spread in a fan, a surprised expression on its face. Even if he did, Danny probably didn't have time to recognise this vision as Yvonne, because his head hit the stanchion of seat six and his neck, which had always looked thin compared to his large skull, snapped. Meanwhile Yvonne's flight was curtailed by the moulded plastic back of the same seat. Her head and neck telescoped together, and she collapsed abruptly onto Danny's body.

All along the coach, Holly's classmates catapulted into the seats in front of them, and collapsed backwards, blood streaming from smashed noses, fragments of teeth glinting white. Near the back Holly, who was twisted in her seat from the effort of pushing Danny into the aisle, opened her eyes to find that she alone was unhurt. But more than that: she opened her eyes to find, for the first time in her life, that she really was alone.

Afterwards, Holly sat shivering on the verge. By herself. She'd been one of the first taken off the coach. People had bustled all around her, their hands pushing her toward the backs of ambulances and lifting her hair and peering at her neck and prodding her ribs until she winced. But when the hands found no sign of serious injury, they'd moved on. A thick burly man from St John's Ambulance had given her a lemon sherbet from a damp paper bag, wrapped her in a blanket, and left her.

She looked around. The daylight hurt her eyes: it seemed too bright, like coming out of the cinema in the afternoon. It was cold and windy and there were flecks of rain in the air. She could feel wet grass soaking through the blanket and her heels were slippery on the muddy ground. In several places on the road the tarmac gleamed darkly with blood. All these things registered remotely. She felt as though she had fallen away from the world, was regarding it all from a great distance.

Everyone apart from Danny and Yvonne had been taken off the coach now. There were a lot of injuries, but no-one had died apart from those two and Mr Cockburne and a woman in the car they'd hit. They'd taken Mr Cockburne away already to make room. The dead woman was still there, but they'd raised barriers to shield her from view. As Holly watched, she realised they were bringing Yvonne and Danny out: men were awkwardly trying to fit two covered stretchers down the crumpled steps of the coach. She pushed herself slowly to her feet, her fingers and toes feeling icy, her side aching. The stretchers were taken through the crowd, and she followed, the blanket awkwardly around her shoulders. The men put the bodies into an ambulance parked on its own, a little distance away from the others. She watched them pant as they manoeuvred the stretchers inside. She expected them to drive off, but they pushed shut the double doors and left. The ambulance sat unattended, going nowhere. No hurry, Holly supposed.

She walked up to the side of the ambulance, laid her hand gently against its cold flank. No-one seemed to have noticed her. She didn't know whether she wanted to look at the bodies or not. She told herself the door was probably locked, anyway, but the handle gave under her touch, and the door swung back towards her, greased and heavy. She pulled herself up and let the door close against the back of her legs.

Inside it was dark and cramped. The two rounded bundles lay side-by-side, a mass of fine blonde hair emerging from one of them. She looked at it for a moment. How many times had she gone into Yvonne's room and found her just that way: sleeping, only her hair visible? Except this time the hair was coarsely sprinkled with red drops. Holly tightened her throat, expecting to feel sick, but she felt nothing. She shuffled closer, in between the two bundles, and reached out a hand to the blanket covering Danny. She breathed deeply, and pulled the heavy cloth back to reveal Danny's head and chest. His head was twisted to the side, his shoulder stuck high up against his ear.

"You're dead, Danny," Holly said to him, not knowing why she was talking. "You died."

She looked at his blank face. He had no menace left. She remembered his tiny wrinkled penis, and realised with remote surprise that she was feeling pity.

"I'm sorry, Danny," she said, meaning it. She might have said more, her brain was making her do all sorts of strange things, but before she could, there was a rattle at the back of the ambulance and the door was thrown open. She turned fast and hit her heel against the wheel of the trolley and stumbled backwards. One hand pressed against something soft, and she knew without looking that it was part of Yvonne. She fell hard against a metal ledge.

A voice said, "Jesus Christ!" and from under the trolley she saw a paramedic at the open door. "Sorry, but God, you gave me a shock, love," he said. "What are you doing here, eh?"

Holly tried to speak but from where she was lying in the corner she could see the top of Yvonne's head. It was matted with dark blood and flattened and lumpy. Holly regarded it blankly for a moment. Then she felt a great lurch inside, as if she was being sick and her whole stomach was going to emerge glistening like a pearl. All of a sudden she was sobbing.

4

Belinda took a deep breath in, hating it. Hospital air: dense and warm and sickly. She sat opposite the doctor, who spread his hands over the surface of his desk.

"So. Ah… yes," he said, after a pause. "There it is. Again, I'm so sorry."

She looked at his hands, not his face. He couldn't have enjoyed being the one to give her the news, and he'd been kind enough, but she didn't like the idea of meeting his eyes. Seeing his obvious thoughts: poor woman, to lose her husband and now her daughter. And one of twins. It shouldn't happen to anyone. Seems to be coping but you can never tell. Should put a note on her file.

She stood up stiffly, feeling the knee that always complained complaining. It was a little room, yellow light, shiny plastic posters on the walls. She wanted nothing more than to be out of it and out of the hospital and in the open. He was telling her that support was available, and automatically she shook her head and muttered that she would go about things her own way, thank you very much, even though the conscious part of her – the voice, the part that was really her – was deep inside her head looking at the darkness and not saying nor even thinking anything.

This was how it had been when Paul died, she remembered. The outside world muffled, nothing clear, nothing sinking in, and a feeling that her real self needed to be alone and to think about everything properly and then it would all make sense and the muffled feeling would disappear, just as long as she had some time. But when she was by herself it didn't happen. She just ran around in circles in the darkness inside her head until she was tired enough to stop thinking. And when she woke up or got out of the tractor the world would be as remote as ever.

Even months later, when gradually and imperceptibly the gap between the world and her real self had narrowed, almost anything could suddenly send her spinning back into that far internal distance: his suits on their hangers, his shoe polish, a man in the distance with the same angle of jaw and neck. In that one instant she'd be lost again, alone inside herself again for hours, even days, until the darkness ebbed away once more and returned her to what she supposed was life: the blur of the present moment.

They were standing by the door now, and the doctor was fidgeting, which meant she should get out. They both reached for the handle at the same time. He dropped his hand quickly and she opened the door and there was Holly, on a seat halfway down the corridor. Holly looked up and their eyes met. Suddenly, to her surprise, the world rushed up on Belinda and the corridor became bright and real and she was feeling something sharp – and she knew what it was: it was a pulse of fear. Her thin fierce child who always wanted to be alone. Now she was. It was as if this had been done by her force of will; as if she had made it happen.

As soon as Belinda had the thought, she saw Holly's face change. Holly was looking at her with an adult expression of worry and sympathy alongside a pale, closed-in panic. Belinda's fear disappeared and she felt hollow instead. The way Holly was looking at her; that concern, that understanding she was showing; in her whole life Yvonne had never looked like that, not once, and now she never would, and Belinda felt she couldn't bear it. She was suddenly helpless, and the helplessness was enough to stir her into action. She walked briskly down the corridor. Time to get

17

home. No point hanging around here. Whatever had happened wouldn't change the fact that every day, things needed doing, and it wasn't as if anyone else would get them done.

★ ★ ★

Holly looked out of her window as she and Belinda drove home. It had been getting dark by the time they'd left the hospital, and as they drove along the lane leading to the farm, the open hillside was lost in blackness. Then the hedges rose up on both sides of the lane, so close that their branches rattled on the windows, and Holly looked instead down the tunnel of green that enclosed them, pale and washed out in the headlights. Belinda was smoking a cigarette. She normally pretended she didn't smoke in the pick-up even though Holly and Yvonne – Holly's throat closed and her chest hurt, it had always been Holly and Yvonne, but not anymore, now it was just plain Holly – could smell smoke the minute they got in, and wouldn't have minded. Belinda started smoking faster as they approached the gate and Holly knew why, because this was where she and Yvonne always argued over whose turn it was to get out and open it. As the pick-up slowed Holly knew she should say something wise and gentle and kind, but she couldn't think of anything. So she just got out quickly and tried to seem invisible as she let Belinda drive through.

When she got back in she saw that Belinda was crying. The spot of a tear stained her cigarette, and her face glistened. Somewhere dark inside, Holly realised that she was the only person who might be able to help Belinda. She shrank into her big wax coat, covered in dog hairs, and stared into a long bleak future. She had no idea how to begin; how they would ever properly talk about this. They hadn't really talked when Daddy died, though that was different because Yvonne... Holly swallowed. Because Yvonne had been there too. Now it was just her. Holly told herself that it had to be possible, there had to be some way she could find to comfort Belinda; and she tried not to think about who that left, if she ever needed comforting herself.

They reached the end of the drive. As they turned into the yard, the headlights passed over the front of the house, and Holly stifled a cry. Yvonne was standing by the huge front door. Holly couldn't breathe. The headlights passed on, and left the porch in shadow. For a moment Holly felt better, it had been her imagination, that was it, it was only to be expected, anyone might... but before she could convince herself the outside light clicked on and this time she could see Yvonne clearly. She looked exactly like she had that morning, except all around her was a thick outline of dark purple, like the edge of paper soaked in ink. It was as if she had been cut out and stuck back onto the world.

Feeling a deep, sick anxiety Holly opened the passenger door and stepped out. Belinda was already halfway to the porch. In a few steps she walked up to Yvonne, then past her, or through her, it was impossible to say. Holly followed slowly, and stopped outside the porch. Yvonne was only a foot away. Holly meant to say, "Yvonne?", but for some reason she didn't understand, she said, "Mummy?" She hadn't used that word for years. Belinda banned it when Daddy died. "I have a name, and now that you'll need to grow up, I'd sooner you used it," she'd said gruffly at his funeral. So Daddy remained forever Daddy, but after that day Mummy was gone.

"Mummy?" Holly whispered again. Belinda didn't hear, she was already walking through into the kitchen. Yvonne didn't react either. Waves of distortion rippled over her face, and although Holly could have touched her, she seemed far away and remote. Holly felt a powerful rush of distance, like vertigo. She also felt perfect certainty. She knew what Yvonne intended. They had never really been alone. Why should that change now Yvonne was dead? Her ghost wasn't going anywhere.

Holly stared at Yvonne's face in dismay. Beyond her the open door of the house led into darkness. The light had never worked in the hall. Holly wanted to scream, to faint, to be carried to bed and given soup and have warm fresh pillows and a duvet and a bedtime story and a kiss on the cheek and a long soft arm around her always in the night. For the first time since the ambulance she felt tears sting her eyes. Then she walked past Yvonne's ghost, knowing without looking that it had turned and was following her into the cold dark house.

5

The Family arrived three days after Yvonne's death. Holly sat on the stairs to watch them come in. Yvonne sat next to her, but whether or not she was watching, Holly couldn't say. One of the first things she'd discovered about Yvonne's ghost was that she was the opposite of the Mona Lisa: no matter where you stood, her eyes didn't follow you around the room. It was impossible to see her properly even if she was right in front of you, which is how Holly had woken up every day since the crash. First she would become aware of a weight pressing against her chest; then she'd open her eyes, stiff and unmoving in a breathless clutch of wrinkled sheets, her hands by her sides, as if in a vice, staring into the face of her dead sister from inches away. She hadn't screamed, not even the first time.

Belinda must have heard the Family's car negotiating the drive, and marched into the hall. When she saw Holly on the stairs she stopped abruptly, then nodded without saying anything. Outside car doors slammed and the footsteps of the Family gritted on the yard. Belinda didn't stride to the front door and pull it wide open and wave. Instead she lifted a foot, then put it back down again, like a horse being shod. She turned back to Holly and this time smiled, a hard crinkle in the corner of her mouth. *Smile back*, Holly told herself, and did.

Over the last three days, this was the change Holly had observed: Belinda had become hesitant. She seemed as if she was in the wrong house, the wrong life altogether. It was only a subtle change, because Belinda had daydreamed for as long as Holly could remember. In the parlour at evening milking, when Holly and Yvonne helped, she often used to disappear to a strange place: gazing into an unknowable distance, running her hand absently along the cobbled ridge of a cow's back. Yvonne used to say she was thinking about Daddy. Holly couldn't begin to guess where she went at times like that. The two of them would just get on with their tasks, attaching the clusters or dipping the teats and trying not to let disinfectant slop onto their overalls, until an argument broke out. That would bring Belinda back with a fierce snap and a tremble of her hair.

"Come on, you two," she'd say, wading in between them as if between calves, her hard hands separating them. "What's this sillybuggers?"

Now, though, she seemed to go to that place more easily, and take longer to come back. A lot longer. The first day after the crash Holly had got out of bed, wincing at her side, which was tinged a dull yellow, and gone downstairs. Vic and Douggie had been in the kitchen with Belinda. Douggie hadn't been able to look at her, staring fixedly at a mark on the lino floor instead. He was quite young and Scottish and hadn't been at the farm very long. Vic had nodded gravely, not saying anything, but quietly expressing pity. Vic had been at the farm for years and Holly must have known him for most of her life, though she didn't really know anything about him. He was maybe 40, or older, and he had a calm still face and never smiled. Sometimes they shared bags of sweets, and then he would talk, a bit, and ask about school and games and all those ordinary questions, taking sweets solemnly in his thick fingers.

Holly had stood quietly by the counter and listened to them awkwardly talking about some disease and what they would do if it spread, and she'd seen that Belinda wasn't really there. Normally she'd be striding around, her hand chopping the air, and Vic and Douggie would frown as they tried to keep up, following her from room to room, even out onto a tractor. This time there had been long slow pauses and Belinda had looked vaguely at the kitchen without recognition. Holly had felt the chill of understanding: this was how it would be from now on.

That cold insight was the change she had noticed in herself. Since the crash Holly seemed to see everything. Sometimes this ability was swallowed up by a feeling: an aching sensation, a kind of lonely dread, that she guessed must be shock or grief, or whatever she was supposed to feel about what had happened. She refused to surrender to it, though, whatever it was; refused even to think about it or whether or not it was the same feeling as she had when Daddy died, and when it came, she lay still and filled her mind with the same few notes of music, or anything at all to distract her brain, until at last the dread receded like the tide going out and all that was left was the keen edge of observation, rigid and precise, cold in her throat and heart as if she'd swallowed a sword. It cut through the soft fuzziness of the world. Holly knew what people were thinking. The police and doctors and social workers: they were tired and sympathetic and embarrassed and sometimes full of what seemed to her barely concealed delight at the awfulness of it all. A few parents of classmates had visited. They'd nodded with pale smiles and told Belinda it would be all right in time, and as Holly watched them walk off, she could see their whole bodies quivering with relief that it was Belinda and not them; they had not had to look down at the purpling steel-tabled corpse of their child.

So Holly sat by Yvonne and watched Belinda with this new cold sense of understanding. As the footsteps crunched louder she glanced at Yvonne. When Daddy had been alive, Holly and Yvonne had sat on the stairs sometimes and listened to him and Belinda shouting at each other in the sitting room. In some ways it was a good memory, because although the shouting was horrible and made Holly dizzy with thinking about what would happen if it never stopped, in the end the anger always blew itself out. The shouting would be just as loud but faster, and then the door would fly open and Belinda would march out looking exasperated but forgiving and tell Daddy his children were on the landing. He'd come out and climb the stairs, peering around, pretending not to see them. They'd grab a leg each and he'd pull them upwards, dragging them along the carpet, calling down to Belinda that they must have been taken by fairies and to break out the champagne because they were free at last, which always made Yvonne squeal, and Daddy would look down with surprise and tell Belinda to put the champagne back on ice, he'd found them, and bend down and pick them up one by one and...

Holly shook her head. That was their ritual, was all. Which meant that now Belinda must be looking at Holly and seeing Yvonne next to her in her mind's eye. *Look at us*, Holly thought intensely. *Concentrate. See her. She's still here*. But it didn't work. She'd known it wouldn't, right from the first morning when Belinda had walked through Yvonne several times without a flicker. She was so unaware that Holly had had a wild flare of hope: maybe Yvonne's ghost wasn't actually there at all. Maybe it was an illusion, a sign of madness. The trauma of the crash had turned her schizophrenic, or psychotic, or just generally mental. Holly found the idea quite comforting. The dogs had forced her to abandon it, though, because they could all see Yvonne too. They didn't bare their teeth at the spot where she stood or whine or raise their hackles, or any of the things Holly had read about. They just ambled towards her ghost and stood patiently, expecting to be stroked.

Holly watched with despair. When nothing happened the dogs wandered away phlegmatically. Yvonne remained. There was something about her uncaring stillness that made Holly feel sick. But the more fear started to rise inside her, the more she knew what she had to do: she had to fight it. Her heart racing, Holly had walked slowly and deliberately towards Yvonne, one hand reaching out to her. Yvonne seemed to recede as Holly approached, but she felt colder and colder until she must have been standing on the same spot as the ghost, even though Yvonne still seemed far away. Holly felt surrounded by a cold, slick slipperiness like liquid or raw meat from the fridge. She endured it for a long moment until she felt Yvonne move, and then she stood still, breathing hard through her nostrils like a horse, trying to think about nothing but the raucous passage of warmer air. It worked, but only for minutes at a time. She knew she needed to find something to murder thought for much longer.

Because Belinda remained in the centre of the hall, caught between the act of moving forward and, probably, if she was feeling anything like Holly, the desire to run away, the Family had to let themselves in. This was straightforward, as the hall door usually stood ajar, even at night, admitting dogs, the breeze, dead leaves. And now ghosts, of course. Or had there always been ghosts, Holly wondered? Saxons and Tudors and Victorians? She hadn't seen any. Perhaps everyone who died became a ghost, and she could only see Yvonne because they were twins. Perhaps...

The heavy door swung forwards. Malcolm, Holly's uncle, held it with a burly forearm, but her aunt Eva wriggled eagerly through. Hungry for a taste of the tragedy, Holly thought. The children remained outside, backlit like angels. Eva stopped dead when she saw Belinda with what Holly could tell was deliberate melodrama. Eva would have planned this entrance carefully; she planned everything carefully. Holly watched her closely from over her mother's shoulder. For a moment there was a pause. Belinda and Eva faced each other down the length of the wide hall like gunslingers, and Eva's sympathetic lip-stick smile twisted nervously.

Then she stepped forward and the false moment disappeared in noise. Bay, the collie, poked her head around the door that led out to the workrooms and began to bark with half-hearted suspicion, a bit too late to do much good, but then Bay always ran on her own timetable. Eva had recovered her poise, the last thing she was ever without, and covered the distance to Belinda with her arms outstretched while Malcolm squatted and said, "Hello! Hello then!" to Bay, who promptly barrelled into his arms, yelping obsequiously.

There was a hitch when Eva and Belinda came within touching distance. Eva was very polished at greetings, as Holly had often experienced. She'd seem to hug, but would keep her hands on her victim's shoulders, her arms bent, ready to thrust away if necessary. Then her head, tiny within a fragrant nest of hair, would push forward, a heavily made-up proboscis. For a moment it would linger next to another human face; a deep breath of perfume and the tickling of the outer ringlets; then she would withdraw, with a red smile that expressed sympathy for everyone less gorgeous than herself. Or maybe than her thirty-year-younger self, Holly surprised herself by thinking. She waited for a flash of guilt, but none came. Yvonne's death had had that advantage.

Trouble with this routine was, none of it ever worked on Belinda. Holly couldn't imagine any kind of embrace between the two of them, not even Eva's artificial version. They were like matter and anti-matter: contact would probably cause the end of the universe. At least, Eva's carefully built universe. So when they came close to one another Eva made a squeamish grab at Belinda's wide shoulders and looked into her face with lips compressed.

"My dearest thing," she said, then nodded, and that was it. Suddenly, before Holly had had time to prepare, Eva was past Belinda and making her way towards her. Holly couldn't help shrinking back. What would Eva do in these circumstances? She might keep Holly in the hair and incense cloud for so long that she'd start to suffocate… but no, instead she stood at the bottom of the stairs, respecting Holly's grief, and looking up at her with a brave and encouraging smile that had evidently been pre-planned. Not even a flicker of awareness of Yvonne, Holly noticed. Eva seemed so like a witch from a fairy story that Holly had half-hoped she would have 'the sight', or whatever it was called. But her face showed nothing apart from generous approval.

Behind Eva Holly saw Malcolm take Belinda in his arms and hold her tight. He was one of the few people who had the capacity to do that. Malcolm was tall and strong-framed, he had rough sandy hair and a high forehead and never seemed afraid of anything. Already the hall seemed full because he was in it, and yet there were still three more dogs and three children to go.

6

Holly couldn't remember when the family had become the Family, or even whether it had been her or Yvonne who gave it the capital letter. It was partly in honour of the fact that the Family were more or less the only relatives they had. Holly's grandfather through Belinda had died before she and Yvonne were born, and Daddy's parents died before she was six. That just left Gran, who visited about twice a year and presided watchfully over meals that always included boiled potatoes and peas. She was family, but not Family. The Family was odd and dangerous and exciting. Malcolm was Daddy's brother and when they went there Daddy was another person. He got drunk, in fact everyone got drunk, even Belinda, who swayed and creaked like timbers and smothered Holly and Yvonne more and more often with her rough one-handed embrace. Sitting at dinner with the Family, Daddy and Belinda had seemed to Holly to glow, as if a different kind of light was shining on them. She remembered thinking that it was because they were remembering their other lives, before she and Yvonne were born, and she remembered being proud of having the thought, and full of curiosity about what that life had been like. But that was just before Daddy died, and the light that came from that former life had been switched off forever.

For as long as she could Holly stayed at her observation point on the stairs. She wanted to cling to an advantage when the children came in. For a while, at their most intimidating, they'd been the Children, but Holly had made a conscious effort the last time she saw them to make them only children again. Julia didn't want to come in, and Holly could tell she was scared. Julia must have been 14 already because she was nearly three months older than Holly. She didn't really seem older, though, maybe because she was the youngest of the children and was always unsure and eager for praise. It should have been Salome's task to shepherd her in and smooth everything over with an adult gloss, because Sal was the oldest and had always had an easy kind of assurance. For a while, though, Holly had noticed her drifting away: away from Family obligations, normal social behaviour, life in general. She had stopped smiling and the last time they'd met Holly had been sure she'd stopped blinking, too. She'd left school so must have been 18 or 19 now, and seemed more detached than ever as she undulated slowly in. So Ben had to bring Julia in with him. Holly felt a dull thick jolt of anxiety when Ben came in. He was 15 and 7 months and six days and she felt guilty even admitting to herself that she knew that down to the day, practically the hour. Yvonne had once said she'd kissed Ben, though Holly suspected she'd been lying. She hadn't replied, just waited until the savage bitter rage had died down enough for her to be able to breathe again, which had only taken an hour or two.

They had tea in the kitchen. By this time all the dogs had arrived. Malcolm and Ben and Julia spent a lot of time playing with them as Belinda ransacked cupboards for mugs. Occasionally one of the dogs emerged stiff-legged from the festivities and wandered around beaming, looking for wider approval. Not from Eva, though. Holly watched Eva and the dogs go through their usual encounter: a moment of cocked-head wariness on each side, with their respective thoughts so apparent as to be almost visible. Eva telepathically instructed the dogs that she'd have them shot if they laid a single paw on her dark, slinky outfit. In response the dogs were more quizzical than hostile. Holly had read somewhere that dogs saw as much through smell as sight, which would explain their expression: in scent terms, Eva must have been a one-woman tornado. Eva turned to Belinda once satisfied she'd quelled any canine opposition.

"Let me help, darling," she said. Belinda gave her a savage look that only Holly noticed then handed her the stained metal pot, which Eva took carefully, not showing distaste.

"Thought I'd let you know the rule," Malcolm said to Holly at the table, a dog grinning under each large hand. "No-one's going to ask if you're all right, ok? And no-one's going to offer to do things for you. But whatever you ask, we'll do. That sound bearable?"

Holly swallowed and nodded. Malcolm smiled gravely. He wasn't like everyone else: she couldn't see the artifice of what he was doing. He was too big, and acted too fast. He didn't have everyone else's caution. She wished she'd hugged him when he came in, but it was too late now.

"Have you seen anyone from school?" Ben asked, after a pause. "That's what I'd hate, if I was you."

Holly shook her head. She meant to answer properly, so they wouldn't think she was finding it hard to speak, but the strange sword in her throat had swollen and she couldn't. Ben's hair was black like Eva's and his eyes were dark. He seemed much older than the last time they'd visited. Julia smiled at him to congratulate his insight and touched his arm. That was new, Holly thought.

They didn't used to touch. She cleared her throat. You can do this, she told herself.

"Be famous, now," she said, hating the unevenness of her voice.

"Yeah, horrible," Julia said. "People staring and everything." Her skin was shiny but she seemed earnest. She looked at Ben and smiled again. "I know exactly what you mean," she said.

But not how I feel, Holly thought. Julia had always got on well with Yvonne, which had been reason enough for Holly not to understand her. In fact Yvonne was standing behind Julia now. Holly looked at her flatly. Meals had been the worst, since Yvonne died. Her ghost stood mournfully by the table like a waiter and watched. Holly and Belinda didn't say much, but Belinda still made plenty of noise: she banged plates on the table, and the room echoed with the acid scrape of cutlery.

Julia was bigger than the last time Holly had seen her. Really Julia was Ben and Salome's half-sister, and Holly's only true cousin. Ben and Salome were what Eva brought with her. Presumably they were the children of her first marriage, and did have an actual father – though they never talked about him and called Malcolm Dad – but Holly sometimes suspected Eva had spawned them single-handed because they looked exactly like her. They had the same dark hair and skin, the same distance between themselves and the world, though they didn't exploit it like Eva did. Eva seemed to Holly to spend a lot of time and effort trying to be enigmatic. Ben and Sal were just effortlessly mysterious. At least Ben was mysterious; Sal was whatever was on the other side of mysterious, and had been even before she'd retreated so far into her own private distance. The old Sal had smiled a lot and had been good at making people laugh; but even as she'd smiled, her eyes had always been very still. Meeting her steady gaze sometimes made Holly feel as if she was being exposed on a hillside. Sal's look was coolly appraising: she gave the impression that she was capable of scanning the far reaches of the universe, so anyone wanting to talk to her had better have something pretty important to say.

Julia, on the other hand, looked like Malcolm, which was unfortunate because Malcolm was rough and broad and strong and it didn't really suit her. Her shoulders and hips were wide, and her whole frame was solid. In fact she looked, Holly realised, like a proper farm girl. Despite this disadvantage she was wearing black embroidered with cobwebs and clearly had a very different idea of the kind of person she thought she was: contained and slender and feminine. Alongside this she also had a look of defiance, because she must already have known that person would never exist.

"How are the… the herd, and everything, darling?" Eva asked Belinda, who shrugged.

"Getting by," she said.

Eva looked pained. She never seemed to realise that Belinda was curt with everyone, not just her. Or at least this never seemed to stop her taking offence. Malcolm intervened.

"Has the news affected you yet?" he asked.

Holly looked at him. What news? She wanted to know, but not enough to risk trying to speak. She realised faintly that Yvonne would always have been the one who asked. Before Belinda could reply Eva stepped forward and touched her arm for a moment.

"Oh gosh darling, of course, I completely forgot. The foot-and-mouth thing. How horrible. But surely, dear," she added, looking at Malcolm, "It won't affect Belinda, it's nowhere near here, is it?"

Malcolm smiled with a trace of tightness and Belinda muttered something about how it was too early to tell and seeing what came of it, which led to an awkward silence. Holly frowned. That's what Vic and Douggie and Belinda had been discussing earlier.

She hadn't listened that carefully. She'd heard of foot-and-mouth but not in the same way that she'd heard of TB or anything else they'd always really worried about. She didn't know what it was or what being near it meant. She wanted to ask but could hardly do that in front of the children – if she had any defence against them at all it was being a wise country girl with all sorts of odd but important knowledge about farming and the moon and things like that, and confessing ignorance was unthinkable. Belinda didn't seem unduly worried but then that might just have been her recent manner, it was hard to tell. Malcolm didn't push it, anyway. After a moment he stretched hugely.

"Good to be out of that bloody car, anyway. I forgot what a pig of a journey it is. We haven't done it for some time, have we?"

Holly looked at him quickly. Everyone did. He seemed genially unaware, as always.

"No," Belinda said simply, hitting the kettle, which started working again. Holly wondered what would happen if she waded into the conversation and said, no, it has been some time, two years actually, I remember quite well because it was Daddy's funeral. Whose death will prompt your next visit? For a dizzy second she thought she was going to say it out loud, if only because she'd have liked to see the look on Eva's face, but then the moment receded.

"It's so lovely having you to stay at ours, that's all," Eva said. "We like being able to give you some TLC, don't we?"

She followed this up with a darting glance aimed at Malcolm but clearly designed for general consumption. The glance managed somehow to express that while she found being in the countryside and especially on a farm and most especially on a dairy farm repugnant, she had done her duty by issuing frequent invitations instead. No-one could accuse her, said her heavily mascara'd lashes, of abandoning this poor withered offshoot of a family and tending just her fertile, chubby and flourishing brood (only Julia really fitted that description, Holly conceded, but at least all parents and siblings were present and correct and alive, which gave Eva a substantial edge in rearing terms over Belinda. Unless you included cattle).

"Darling? Didn't you?" Holly realised Eva was saying, looking at her sweetly. She had no idea what the question was about. Didn't you sounded like it needed a yes, though, so she nodded dumbly. Eva wrinkled her eyes in fellowship and understanding.

7

After tea no-one seemed sure what to do. Belinda didn't start a procession upstairs as she normally would, bags being dragged up step by step and dogs everywhere underfoot, so they all stayed in the kitchen nursing cold mugs. Malcolm frequently started talking to Belinda, but was overridden by Eva, whose high-register interventions left lingering silences in their wake. Ben looked at Holly with comfort. Julia looked at her with curiosity. Neither Sal nor Yvonne looked at anyone, both were consulting a troubled internal landscape instead. Eventually after a particularly random remark from Eva Malcolm rose convulsively, and went to the back door.

"It's so good to be out of town," he said, stooping to get a view of the sky. "Lovely day. You lot ought to be outside," he added, gesturing to Ben and Sal and Julia. "Get some fresh air into you. The kind of ruddy outdoor sensibility that children used to have in the 50s, or whenever the good old days were. What do you reckon to giving them a tour, Holl?"

Holly looked up, confused, from a close study of the scarred table surface, which she'd started as a distraction from the awfulness of everything, but which had become genuinely absorbing.

"Give them their country legs," Malcolm said. "Actually, that's sea legs, I suppose. But you take my drift?"

"Oh. Er…" Holly trailed off. She had her reasons for not wanting to go outside, but she couldn't share them, and she couldn't think of an excuse. "If they… if you want to," Holly said.

Julia's face fell, but she looked at Ben, who shrugged and nodded in the same gesture.

"I would," Sal said, which made Holly jump. It was the first time she'd spoken since arriving. Her voice was deeper than Holly remembered.

"Take the dogs," Belinda said. "Don't…"

"Let Horace get tired, take them into Top Field, I know, I know," Holly said.

The dogs were getting up with puffy resignation, a long-retired squadron accepting new orders without protest. Horace was a grizzled arthritic Labrador with a prodigious appetite and an air of careless command, who supervised the others with incompetent benevolence. Bay, the collie, was slightly less antique but substantially more eccentric; she had a gap-toothed smile and a perpetual eagerness to be put to work, combined with an inability to learn how to do anything. Then there was Gin, half-whippet, half-Jack Russell – mostly warm-hearted but occasionally neurotic – and finally her daughter Dizzy, the only one with enough energy to disobey orders from Wing Commander Horace. Dizzy was already in the back porch, clattering on the stone with scrabbled enthusiasm. Now that the dogs had got the idea, there was no putting it off. It had to be done sometime, Holly supposed – had to be put to the test. Now was as good a time as any.

Going outside was Holly's last hope of escaping Yvonne. Over the last few days, her strategy for dealing with this… this thing, this phenomenon, had been to establish parameters, find out how it was going to work. She'd discovered that Yvonne was elastically tied to her, more or less. Whenever Holly moved, after a few seconds' delay, Yvonne followed; whenever Holly stopped, the ghost did too. Doors and walls were no barrier. The only advantage Holly had was that Yvonne moved slowly, so if she ran, it would take the ghost a while to catch up. She worked this out by standing in the kitchen, waiting till Yvonne came in, then running back past her, through the huge chilly sitting-room and into the hall and up the stairs and back along the corridor to the bathroom. If she was quick, it gave her more than a minute. It still meant that Yvonne would be there while she used the toilet, though. Holly didn't know why that upset her so much. She wasn't squeamish; Yvonne had never given her a chance to be. But to be sitting so exposed and to see Yvonne's form drift into the room and just linger there, right in front of her... Holly couldn't stand it.

Her only chance, she had decided, was that Yvonne would not be able to follow her everywhere; that something about the wide blowiness of the outside world would defeat her dogged determination. After all, the ghost hadn't appeared till she got home – so maybe it couldn't leave. Holly hadn't yet dared to test this idea. Too much was at stake. If she was right, then she had a chance of sporadic freedom at least. If not, if Yvonne was on her tail forever, then... well, that wasn't worth thinking about. Because if Yvonne could follow her outside, she'd be able to follow her to the Reservation, the only place Holly had ever had to herself; and if Yvonne got that, Holly couldn't see much point in the future, really. Not that she had any option, she supposed. Suicide hardly looked like it would be an escape.

Holly took the others into the back porch, bumping her knees against the dogs, who circled with clumsy enthusiasm until she lifted the iron latch and let them out into the yard. As they filed out she half-saw, half-sensed Yvonne leave the kitchen and follow on their trail. The moment was here, and her heart was beating heavily, its thud breathless and dreary.

37

"You'll need boots," she said to the others, indicating a mud-encrusted line. Most of them were long-unused and dusted with spider-threads. Julia looked at Ben, who was taking his shoes off without complaint, and did the same. When the others were ready, though, she still hadn't found any that fitted her.

"What about…" Julia started to say, indicating the pair that had stood next to Holly's, before everyone had the same thought.

"Oh I don't…" she started, just as Holly said quickly, "That's fine, no-one else needs them."

They both stopped. Julia looked for Ben again but he turned away. He wasn't up to this. Holly didn't blame him. How could anyone ever be? Sal was outside already.

"I couldn't," Julia said. "I mean…"

Holly felt a spasm of annoyance run through her body, and then remorse, because it wasn't Julia's fault. There was a kind of static ballet of awkwardness, which for Holly was almost unendurable: there wasn't enough room in the back porch for all of them, so Yvonne was muddled in the air between them, and the reek of her was on Holly's skin. Ben and Julia didn't notice anything, but Holly had to get outside. Julia said lightly she'd be fine without boots and Holly said her shoes would come off otherwise, as gruff as Belinda, and all the time Ben turned so his back was to them and Holly felt so sorry for him, because she knew how much he must want to be cool and in control, and how smothered and helpless it felt not knowing how to be.

After what felt like an eternity Julia suddenly said of course it was fine and began tugging on Yvonne's boots, her face flushed bright pink. Holly felt her new insight fail her momentarily, then she understood. Julia thought Ben was angry with her for making a fuss, and that was important enough to endure wearing dead girl's shoes. What this closeness to Ben meant, Holly had no idea. Well actually she did, immediately, have an idea, which she put straight out of her mind, because she knew it was impossible. Mostly knew it was impossible. When did her mind become so prone to assumptions like that? Why was that her first thought? Anyway, Julia was just defining herself through Ben, that was all. It was a stage she was going through. Holly knew all about going through stages, because it was one of Yvonne's favourite ideas. Yvonne had planned various stages for herself, dismissing Holly's cautious objections that she might be slightly missing the point. Not that she had got to experience many of them, as it turned out.

As Julia bent over and heaved, Yvonne's ghost fluttered about her. Holly had a sense that it was exuding petulance, even though it hadn't actually changed, was as remote as ever, so she was probably just making it up. But if it was somehow aware of the real world, maybe it was feeling selfish, angry that its things were being used by others. No change there, Holly thought, and then felt tears come immediately to her eyes, which she blinked crossly away. It was always her bitter thoughts about Yvonne that made her cry, even though Holly had promised herself not to forget Yvonne's faults just because she was dead. *Come on*, Holly thought. *Obsess over the boots. Hear the voices from the kitchen. Remain.*

Julia had got Yvonne's boots on now and Holly led her and Ben outside. The dogs were clustered around Salome, looking up at her and wagging their tails with a pleased air, as if they'd invented the world and were hoping Sal would like it, but her gaze was fixed on the far horizon. Holly didn't look behind her and didn't wait. She set off past the block of empty stables on the right, down the track of corrugated concrete covered with crusty patches of dirt, and on towards the gate. Vic and Douggie were working on the fertiliser spinner in the little yard beyond the stables. Vic nodded as usual, and Douggie looked more nervous than ever, probably because he saw all the children following her. He wasn't good with strangers – it had taken him about two months to say anything to Holly after he arrived. Holly hadn't spoken to either of them properly since Yvonne died and she knew she ought to talk to Vic and tell him she was all right but not now. She kept walking with her head down to the gate and opened it to let the dogs through. Gin and Dizzy bounded ahead, the others following more slowly. Holly watched the dogs sniffing the turf. Then she looked at the grass trying to work out how it was coming along for the time of year, and then up at the messy white sky, and then at the low trees along the line of the hedge blowing in a chilly, damp breeze. She tried to control her breathing. This was it. Once the others had come through the gate she'd have to turn and shut it; and in turning, she'd know whether or not Yvonne was with them.

8

Holly had some moments before her fate was sealed, because the others were looking thoughtfully at the mud-churned arc on the other side of the gate where the cows had stood, and plotting a way through. Ben leapt experimentally from dry hillock to dry hillock and made it across unscathed. He turned and gave them an ironic bow. Holly half-smiled. Even while she was fastening her mind in prayer and begging God or Vishnu or even Satan, why not, to keep Yvonne in the house, she knew that someone had to break the atmosphere of caution and reserve, and Ben was the only one who could do it. He seemed to know it, too, and cleared his throat.

"So. We've got news, by the way," he said.

Julia was picking her way with wide-legged sturdiness through the mud. "Oh... should we..." she said doubtfully.

"What? Not tell her? Why not?" Ben said.

"Just... is it the right time, that's all," Julia answered quickly.

"Probably better to ask her that rather than talking about her," Sal said. Even though she was joining the conversation she managed to sound unconnected, as if she was musing on a completely different subject. She'd coasted past the mud by sticking to the edge and once she'd made her comment she turned to face the breeze and closed her eyes, looking elfin with her long arms and hair blowing.

Holly stayed by the gate and looked at Ben and Julia. Whatever this was, it was delaying the moment when she had to turn.

"Tell me, then," she said. "What is it?"

"Our father," Ben said. "Don't worry, I'm not praying," he added hastily. "Though we probably should. Our father, see, has been fired from his job. We are going to be thrown on the mercy of the state, he says. Which isn't what Mum says. You can probably imagine what Mum says. Has been saying. A lot."

"Oh," Holly said. For a moment she couldn't think what Malcolm did, then she remembered. He was a history teacher at a secondary school. Head of history, actually, or deputy head teacher, or something.

"He hasn't been fired," Julia said indignantly. "He's resigned."

Holly registered with remote half-interest that Julia was prepared to contradict Ben if Malcolm was the issue, but she didn't have the energy to wonder why. She could feel nothing on the back of her neck; no tingle, no presentiment. Did that mean there was nothing behind her?

"Yes, resigned," Ben said. "Sorry. I forgot the approved version. He has resigned in protest. He has not, I repeat not, been fired for beating up two sixth-formers."

Sal turned back from the wind, her face stained a little with cold. "You shouldn't say that," she said impassively. "You should take it more seriously."

"Why? Dad isn't."

Sal shrugged. "You don't know whether he is or not," she said. "That's his way. Maybe it's to stop Mummy worrying."

Ben made a face. "Not working brilliantly, is it?"

"Don't joke about it," Sal said. "That's all. Not to anyone."

"Not even Holly?" Ben said. "She's hardly going to be a witness for the prosecution, is she? Are you?"

Holly shook her head, and smiled tightly. The others were through the mud and waiting. Dizzy was a hundred yards on, and Horace and Bay were looking back at her enquiringly. She couldn't lean on the gate any longer, it was already as if she was auditioning for the part of a yokel. She turned, pushed the gate to, busied herself with the tying of the knot, then looked up. Two yards away Yvonne stood watching her, rippling a little in the breeze.

Holly felt a little fracture inside her throat. She gazed calmly into Yvonne's face, knowing she had a choice. She could scream, and if she started to scream she wouldn't stop, and Malcolm and Belinda would run out of the house and Eva would teeter after them and Ben would be next to her, too awkward to touch her, and Julia would be shaking her head and saying tearfully she couldn't bear it while Sal told Julia to shut up. And then what would happen? Once she'd started screaming she could keep doing it. She could scream and cry and thrash around in the bed they'd have to put her in, and doctors would come, and social workers, and people would talk about her worriedly downstairs, and eventually they'd have to take her away and do something to make her quiet and maybe that would go on for a long time, and that whole mini-future was a choice she could take, right now, standing ankle-deep in cold mud, leaning on the gate, looking at her sister's ghost.

Or her other option was to compress the scream inside her and turn back and arrange things so that the fracture sort of stuck together and no-one realised something had broken, and ask them what had happened to Malcolm. For about three seconds she stood still and just thought about the choice. If she didn't scream they'd go for their walk and come back to the house and have more tea – it was a seven-times-a-day ritual at the farm, at least – but after that she had no idea how to go through the rest of the day, and the next, and the funeral, and going back to school, and the infinity of daily life. That was scary, but at least there was the possibility of some kind of change, whereas in the warm room they'd take her to, not a lot would ever happen; how things were now, they would probably remain. And that had to be worse.

So in the end she'd decided before she felt Ben's hand touch her arm. "We can go back," he said. "If you want?"

Holly shook her head, took a deep breath, then released it. She turned and picked her way through the mud.

"Who did he beat up, then?" she asked.

9

Holly got the story the long way round as they went up the track towards Top Field then turned down, past the copse, along the path that led towards the End. Sal stayed a little way ahead as they walked so her sources were Ben and Julia, who argued over every detail. In the end, as far as Holly could untangle his exaggerations and her denials, it seemed that Malcolm had separated two boys who'd been fighting, and one of them had been hit in the face by his elbow.

"So... he complained? The boy?" Holly said.

"They both did," Julia said, fiddling with some grass she'd pulled up. "Said Dad hit them both."

She shivered in her coat, and dropped the grass, then looked at her hands, which were dirty. They looked right that way, she was a natural at the agricultural life. Maybe there had been a mistake: maybe it had always been Julia's real destiny to have been brought up on the farm, and Holly should have been the product of Malcolm and Eva's bohemian disorder in Guildford. Though that was hard to imagine. Holly tried to picture what it would be like, always being in the same house as Eva. Eva in a dressing-gown; Eva in the shower; Eva putting the rubbish out. No; it was impossible. None of these Evas could really exist.

"And people believed them?" Holly asked, leading them on again in a wide sweep through Beeches.

Ben shrugged, kicking a hard lump of mud along the tractor

rut. "No. Not really. But the head teacher said he'd have to be suspended while it was investigated, so Dad decked him, too."

"Ben!" Sal said, with two syllables and reverb, overhearing that.

"That's what everyone is saying, though," Ben said to Holly. "He's like the Hulk, he's out of control, he's a fighting machine. It's quite, you know. Cool."

"Dad said he'd resign if he wasn't supported, and they didn't support him, so he resigned," Julia said. "Mummy says he'll get his job back, though."

"Well, that's half true," Ben said. "She says he must get his job back. Or there'll be hell to pay." He said the last words in an odd sing-song voice, then said, "Name it?"

Holly looked at him blankly. Julia said, "Is it Clint Eastwood?"

"No," Ben said, his voice full of mock-disgust. "It's... well, I don't know. Luke Skywalker's dad. Adopted dad. Star Wars. Name that film," he said to Holly, who nodded. She'd be rubbish at this, she knew already. Probably not worse than Julia, though.

"As if he wants to," Sal said. "Get his job back. Why should he? He hates it anyway."

"What you need to know is that this is a Situation," Ben said. "Between Mum and Dad. So don't be surprised if they don't talk to each other for about a month or so, it's normal."

"It isn't, I hate it," Julia said. "Coming here is bad enough without..." She tailed off.

"God, Julia," Sal said, then walked off fast, clapping one hand against her leg to summon a dog. Bay was the only one who responded, bounding forward eagerly, then looking disappointed when Sal had no more complex instructions.

Ben sucked his teeth. Holly carried on a step or two, then turned and looked at Ben and Julia, who'd stopped moving. She didn't know why they were reacting like this. It wasn't such a bad thing to say, was it? She didn't care if Julia hated it. No-one could really enjoy coming to a house where half the people were dead and the heating didn't work properly. Anyway, it was hardly such a revelation: Julia had looked miserable about being here from the moment she walked through the door. And most fundamentally of all, why should she care what Julia felt? Holly wondered if she was allowed to say that. Probably not; the others would think she was attacking Julia, and then there would be arguments, and Julia would apologise profusely, and finally there would have to be moving acts of forgiveness overseen with both saccharine and steel by Eva. None of which Holly could particularly cope with.

"Holly, Julia didn't mean..." Ben started, but Julia interrupted.

"You don't have to speak for me," she said fiercely. "I don't hate it here. I mean... I hate it because of them. Dad and Mummy. They fight about coming here. They have for years, and then we get here and they just don't talk and they look at each other like... and I hate it."

"Oh," Holly said. "Because they don't want to come?"

Julia said, "Well..." but Ben shook his head.

"It's not that, it's..." he broke off and looked after Sal, who had got a good distance ahead and was listening to the wind again. "She said we shouldn't ask you about it," he said, indicating Sal with a jerk of his head. "But you might know."

"It's because of what happened," Julia said significantly.

Holly was confused. "To Yvonne, you mean?" she asked, and cast an involuntary glance behind her. Still there. No change. No chance.

"Oh no," Julia said hastily. "Please don't start thinking about... all that. This is something else. It's... it was your Dad. We think."

Oh right, Holly thought, that's fine, I mean he's been dead forever, we can talk about him without a care in the world. She

47

knew that was unfair, but she was feeling sick and leaden and didn't much care.

"Daddy? What about him?"

"We don't know," Ben said, bending over and playing with Gin. "Something happened. Sometimes I think Sal knows, but if she does she won't say."

"Like... an argument?"

Ben and Julia exchanged a glance. "Yeah, probably," he said, unconvincingly.

Holly scowled, she didn't know whether it was because they were lying or because they thought she wouldn't notice they were lying, which was only a small difference but meant a lot to her. The second one was much worse than the first.

"Anyway, since about four years ago, whenever we come there's issues," Ben said. "Even when your Dad, you know. Was ill. And everything. Especially then."

Were there? Holly couldn't remember issues. She could just remember a kind of half-lit existence in which Daddy spent his time in hospital and Belinda spent hers in the yard and she and Yvonne were in the house talking to each other a lot about diagnoses and prognoses and all the other things the doctors said, which started out with bright remarks about survival rates as long as the cancer hadn't spread and then turned into strained remarks about life expectancy now that the cancer had spread. She could remember a lot of everyone lying to each other, Daddy lying about how he felt and Belinda lying about what the doctors said and she and Yvonne lying almost every time they were asked anything – You aren't too sad, are you? No! and Are you helping your mother with everything? To which they said yes, though everyone knew Belinda would never accept any help with anything. Holly also remembered Daddy smiling when it hurt, and Belinda holding his hand and looking at his face with an expression so different from

Holly's experience of Belinda she looked like another person. But she couldn't remember issues, exactly.

"Oh," Holly said, after a while. "I didn't know anything about that. Yvonne might have done, she was good at knowing things about people."

Julia made an odd crumpled noise, but Ben just nodded. "Well," he said. "That business – which is what Mum calls it, by the way, as in 'we aren't talking about that business' – and the firing and how long we're staying are kind of the main subjects of conversation, that's all."

"How long are you staying?" Holly asked, looking at both Ben and Julia to make sure her voice was balanced and not pleading. They both shrugged.

"According to Daddy, as long as we're needed," Julia said, and Holly nodded slowly. She was thinking about a house with talking, and people asking each other how they were, and events to fill up time. There was consolation in that, quite a lot of consolation. She saw Yvonne out of the corner of her eye. If she was really never going to be alone again, then other people were her only hope.

10

Halfway through the circuit of the land – the inner circuit, which was about two miles – they got to the End. Most of the names on the farm were official, and old, appearing in faint grey lines on a map of the parish that used to hang in Daddy's surgery. But for some areas Holly had her own private names, told to no-one. The End was one of them. Despite the name, the End was halfway along a field. It was an imaginary line, running north to south, from the tall thorn bush in the south hedge of First Hill, to the thick, lonely oak tree that stood in the middle of the field, whose base was swathed with tall grass in summer where the mower couldn't get in to cut it, up to the barbed-wire gap that led to Beeches, and on through all the other fields.

It marked a change in the land. On the farm side of the End the ground was tussocky and uneven, rising behind the house to proper hills – they lived on the edge of the Downs, long bare mounds of land that continued for four or five miles and cut them off from Ledborough, which was the nearest town. On the other side of the End the ground changed: it became smooth, and sloped down and away in long sheets for about quarter of a mile as far as the Motorway, which ran along the valley. A thick grey bar that marked the edge of the farm.

Holly had drawn this line across the fields because she'd decided that this was where the farm world ended, and the Motorway world began. Beyond the End, if she ran, the farm world could never get her back, because she picked up speed all the way down the shallow incline until she got to the wire fence and the hedge, and beyond that the embankment, and then down to the Motorway itself. And most importantly, the Reservation. The frontier of her life. When she was at the Reservation she was no longer at the farm, and she wasn't anywhere else. She was in the Motorway world, and party to its laws and its laws alone.

The Motorway had been part of her life even before she discovered the Reservation. The distant hiss of traffic was a constant on the farm. When machinery was running, or the TV was on, the sound was no longer audible, but Holly loved the way it was still there – just temporarily overlaid by something else. When the machine rattled to a halt, or when the house fell silent at night, gradually her ears would start to pick it up again: a static background hum, rising and falling in cycles, like the operation of a much larger machine, one that never stopped. And because they were on the side of a hill the Motorway was nearly always in sight, too. Holly loved it, especially after dark. There were no overhead lights on this section of the Motorway but it was lit by the sweeping arcs of headlights, and it reminded her of the patrolled fence of a prisoner-of-war camp. The farm was on the inside, a guarded place on which some unknown agency bent its mind. Outside was freedom and all that entailed: loneliness and threat and fear, lost behind enemy lines, nowhere to go.

"How many cars every hour, do you reckon?" asked Ben, watching the road.

"Such a waste," Sal said, sighing.

Holly made a complicated gesture that involved non-committal agreement with Sal, though she didn't seem to need much of a response, and ignorance of the answer to Ben. He looked thoughtful.

"Does it ever stop?" he asked, looking at Holly. "At night, I mean?"

Holly had turned and was checking again for Yvonne. Still there. Ready to watch if Holly wanted to go to the Reservation; ready to follow; ready to invade this last place, the only thing she hadn't had while alive, but dead would take with ease. Holly wondered what the others thought every time she looked over her shoulder. Did she seem mad? Luckily now they had got this far the dogs were as often behind them as in front, which gave her cover for these frequent revolutions.

She turned back to Ben. "Oh... I don't know," she said, apparently carelessly, even though she knew the answer better than he would ever guess (it did stop, yes, in the small hours; the maximum gap Holly had observed being 74 minutes no traffic in either direction, 119 minutes empty northbound only, and the current winner, 201 minutes southbound, though she thought she might have fallen asleep for part of that so couldn't be certain).

"We've never been down there, have we?" Ben said. "I mean, when we were here before. You must have been, Holly?"

Holly felt her breath shorten, but just shrugged. "Maybe, a couple of times. It's grim," she said.

"Yeah, but it must be kind of thrilling, right?" he said. "We could go and be like Railway Children, wave pants at all the cars." That was the kind of random idea that might enthuse Julia, Holly feared, but she didn't know how to stop him talking. "Shall we, then?" he asked.

Holly pretended to think about it so that he wouldn't know the vehemence of her opposition then said they couldn't because of the dogs, which he accepted, but reluctantly. She could tell he would, soon, go down to the Motorway. Which wasn't a problem – as long as he didn't know what she did there. As long as no-one did.

The dogs realised in their vaguely telepathic way that Holly had spoken about them and bounded up with unhelpful energy, given that they were supposed to be her cover. Dizzy charged into Ben's legs like the idiot she was, then ran off sheepishly trying to pretend it had been deliberate.

"What's that one called again?" he asked.

"Anything," Holly said, which was true. Dizzy was the only dog to have been born when she and Yvonne were old enough to know much about it. Daddy had suggested they have a competition to name her, which he probably regretted immediately, since a spirit of deadly rivalry set in. Holly had suggested Dizzy, Yvonne went for Amethyst. Daddy never got a chance to adjudicate properly because that was when they found out he was ill. So she and Yvonne just stuck with their own suggestions, each of them (and Holly knew she had been equally guilty in this at least) trying to brainwash the puppy into responding better to their own favourite, until the poor thing was in a state of visible mental confusion.

Now, Holly supposed, she could officially claim to be the winner of that particular battle. Trouble was, Belinda had got into the mix too by using neither of the names Holly and Yvonne had come up with and calling the dog Dolly instead, to which Dizzy responded best of all, probably because Belinda was the dispenser of food, and therefore her pronouncements carried more weight.

She explained all this to Ben. "Wow," he said, looking at Dizzy, who had wandered back again and was gazing up at him with tongue-lolling devotion. "Maybe we should say it's open season. What do you reckon?"

Holly shrugged. They were walking parallel to the Motorway now, close to the turning back up to the farm. She pointed out that the poor dog, which was extremely simple even for a dog, might disintegrate under the stress, and get schizophrenia or something (she couldn't help looking round to check for her own personal badge of madness as she said it. Still present and correct). Ben suggested Jafaar the Grand Vizier, and Holly said maybe as a second name, so Dizzy became Dizzy Jafaar, which they both agreed would be a good name for a bad band.

While they had been talking Sal and Julia had gone ahead, but now they were standing still looking across the valley. When Holly and Ben caught up with them Julia pointed.

"Look," she said. "There's someone over there. Miles away, but you can see him all right."

They followed her arm. On the other side of the Motorway there were several wide open fields, and there was a tiny black figure moving across one of them.

"You never see people like that," Julia said. "Just... walking. In the middle of nowhere."

"It's Will Sadler," Holly said.

"Who?" Ben asked, and she shook her head in bafflement. Holly had only met him maybe three times in Ledborough but she couldn't imagine not knowing of Will Sadler, not having Will Sadler stalk across the edge of your imagination.

"He's..." she started, then stopped. How could you describe Will Sadler? "He's kind of mad," she went for in the end. "I mean, he's famous. He shoots things."

"Really?" Ben said with delight. "Like?"

"People's dogs and cats," Holly said. "Apparently. He always has a shotgun. Unless he's in town. And people say he shoots at things that aren't there." Her voice slowed as she said that. Like she looked at things that weren't there.

They were all watching him march across the field. Even from this distance the way he leaned forwards, and the angularity of his walk, made him seem unnatural, like a walking tree. But behind him...

She started towards the road.

"Holly?" Ben said.

She turned. "Er… it's like you said before. Let's go down to the Motorway," she said.

"What about the dogs?" Julia asked, but Holly didn't care, she had done explaining enough, she didn't even care that Yvonne was going to follow and get closer to the Reservation than she'd ever been. If it was what she thought, it was worth it. She ran to the End and then down the slope, her knees hurting, the wind in her ears. *Come on*, she told herself, *before he gets to the corner, before he starts back up the track, come on*. Halfway to the Motorway she stumbled, took two or three flying steps, then slowed, looked up, and burst out laughing and crying at the same time. She was still a long way from the hedge and the embankment; Will Sadler was still several hundred yards off, and walking away from them now; but it didn't matter. She could see clearly enough. Following him, matching his uneven walk – a ghost was trailing him. He was being haunted, just as she was; he was being pursued.

She could hear the asthmatic groan of dogs who'd run when they should have known better and the thud of footsteps as the others got closer and she had no idea what she was going to say when they caught her up, but she didn't care. *This was something that happened to other people too.* It was a problem, that was all, an unusual problem but even so. Problems had solutions. Will Sadler reached the end of the track and disappeared, the ghost following him with an imbecile obedience that Holly recognised all too well. He was mad, he had a gun, people said he kept vicious dogs and she didn't know if anything he said to her could help, but she could sense the slow advance of Yvonne behind her, and knew she'd risk a lot more than dogs and madness and gunshots to find out.

11

The funeral was the next day. Holly woke up early and lay still in the dark, next to Yvonne, thinking about how she would get to talk to Will. It wouldn't be easy. Apart from anything else, she had to work out how to get onto his land, because it was all on the other side of the Motorway. Technically it was possible to run across: there were occasionally gaps in the traffic, it was how she got to the Reservation. But running across the whole road was out of the question. For one thing, it would mean leading Yvonne across the Reservation, allowing her into that place, if only for a few seconds. Holly wasn't prepared to let that happen. And even more than that, she rebelled against the whole idea of crossing the Motorway. It was against her philosophy. The Motorway was the edge, the frontier. It marked the end of the farm, the end of her world; it was Styx and Rubicon. That was what made the Reservation – what was it? Liminal, that was it. That was the whole point. Somehow, though, she would find a way. She was going to see Will Sadler, and he was going to explain what was happening.

After lying awake for what felt like hours she heard people getting up, and went downstairs in the huge ancient cardigan she used as a dressing-gown. No-one else was dressed yet either and no-one seemed to know what time they were supposed to be anywhere. They had a chaotic breakfast and then everyone went off to get ready as if they were going to a party but without any of the fun. Holly shut her door on the noise outside and laid her funeral dress on the bed, with Yvonne watching. The dress had been for Daddy's funeral – she and Yvonne had been bought an outfit each. In fact, had Malcolm bought them? They all went to get them together, Malcolm and Eva and Belinda, that was right, and Eva had spent all her time with Belinda, one hand on her arm consoling her, so Malcolm had been with Holly and Yvonne. Holly remembered, because prompted by some insane impulse he had suggested they get the same outfit. Holly and Yvonne had stared at him with equal horror in a rare moment of unity. Then Yvonne started explaining forcefully why that wasn't a good idea: she was three inches taller, everyone would think Holly was a dwarf, how could anything possibly suit them both. Malcolm had held up his hands in mock-surrender and let them get what they liked. Yvonne had got a black suit with a skirt, like a business suit, and a white shirt. At the wake she looked like a waitress. Holly had looked at dresses for a long time, which had made tears come to her eyes, because a few months before she'd told Daddy that she didn't like dresses and was only going to wear jeans from now on and he'd nodded solemnly and said it was a judicious decision of which she should be proud. She'd refused to let herself think about that and just taken something long and green into the changing-room without caring much, and although Malcolm had looked pensive when she came out, it was what they ended up buying. If Yvonne had been a waitress, what would she have looked like, she wondered now, looking at the dress on the bed; but she knew the answer. An awkward little girl, that was what this dress must have made her.

She made herself stop thinking about Daddy and tried to put on the dress, but it was hopeless. She didn't think she'd grown that much, but clearly she had. She felt a sudden sharp incision of grief. Maybe the Holly who had gone to Daddy's funeral was as dead as he was, swallowed up by her monstrous new self; which, in turn, was only waiting to be consumed by further remorseless expansion, until she was some adult woman with children and the Holly she was now was not even a memory… But she shook her head. That would never be true. Whatever the future held, she would not allow herself to forget: she was sure of that.

She folded the dress carefully away and ended up just putting on a black T-shirt and jeans. When she went downstairs Eva's face rippled like a flag in a high wind.

"Oh, darling, not today," she said. "Hasn't she got anything else?" she asked Belinda. Holly could have told her this was a mistake: Belinda hated talking about clothes, especially non-farm-clothes. The shoulders of her black jacket had plucked-up tufts from the hanger and smelt of mothballs. It was probably the first time she'd even looked at it since Daddy died.

"Wear what she likes," Belinda said gruffly. "Not a bloody school photograph."

That didn't stop Eva disappearing upstairs and coming down ten minutes later with a black suit. Holly had to look at it twice before she realised what Eva was holding.

"What about this?" Eva said to Belinda, who shrugged, not recognising it. Holly felt her heart start to race because she realised she was about to say something she was actually thinking.

"You want me to wear my dead sister's clothes to her own funeral?" she said unsteadily. Malcolm had come downstairs now, his shirt collar up like Elvis, fiddling with his tie. Eva brushed down the jacket.

"It's respectful to make an effort," she said.

Malcolm stared at her in disbelief, which gave Holly the courage to say, "Maybe what she's wearing now would be better, it's not too late, you could still get it out of the coffin." She could hardly breathe, speaking her thoughts was making her feel giddy

58

with the sense of release, and she only realised too late that she had to follow up something like that by walking out.

"Holly, don't be nasty," Belinda said, and she turned round and ran upstairs.

She heard voices coming from Sal's room and found all three children inside. They went quiet when she came in.

"Are you all right?" Ben started to say, but trailed off, because the answer was obvious, Holly supposed. She wasn't crying but couldn't speak. Sal stood in front of her and looked at her inscrutably for a moment, then put her hand on the side of Holly's head and held it there, then made her sit down. They all carried on getting ready but weren't talking, so after a minute during which Holly just tried to slow her heart rate, she thought she should try to kill the silence somehow. Ben was sitting on Sal's bed in a shapeless suit. He had a black funeral tie on.

"Did they give you that?" she said, pointing at his tie. He looked nervous.

"It was your Dad's," Sal said in her low voice. Holly nodded slowly. What with Yvonne and Daddy's wardrobes going spare they could open an outfitters. Julia had the wardrobe door open and stared at herself critically in the full-length mirror.

"I can't believe I've got to wear this," she said, pulling at a too-tight black shirt, the buttons straining.

"It looks all right," Ben said. "It's not... you know. It doesn't matter."

"Yeah, but this was Sal's like four years ago," Julia said.

"Eva wanted me to..." Holly started to say, then stopped. She hadn't criticised Eva to any of the Family before. Was it allowed? Probably yes, today of all days, but it didn't feel right.

"What?" Ben said, smiling, but Holly just shook her head.

"Nothing," she said, and he looked away, and Holly kicked herself without knowing exactly why.

They all gathered in the kitchen, including Yvonne, which Holly supposed was fairly ironic in the circumstances. Malcolm asked if Belinda wanted a drink and she shook her head silently. Holly had eventually been told to wear her school trousers under her black top, which made her look like a mime artist, but it had shut Eva up. Sal was silent with an even greater intensity than usual and Holly wasn't surprised that Eva, who was in her line of sight, was shifting awkwardly. Even if you were her mother that look couldn't be easy to face down. Ben asked if he should make tea and they all talked about when they ought to leave and whether there was time, until there wasn't, and they all went out to the Family's car. Yvonne drifted after them, a shimmer of air and dark purple passing through the front door. Holly suddenly thought about the journey. Maybe Yvonne wouldn't be able to get in a car! That was her first thought, and her heart beat hard, but a sardonic voice in her head immediately followed this thought with another. *She'll get in all right, and there won't be room*, the voice said. *You'll end up all mixed in with her.*

Holly didn't know whether to push forward or hang back when the car doors were opened. Malcolm got Belinda to sit in the front. The others all stood around, Yvonne amongst them. Holly watched her narrowly. She was between Ben and Julia, who both moved through her every now and then without any sign of discomfort. Sal was keeping her distance, which might have been her natural isolationism, or might have been some feline instinct. Holly wouldn't have been surprised if Sal had instincts.

Once Malcolm and Belinda were in the car there really was no prospect of delay. Holly took a deep breath and climbed into the back seat. Eva and Sal followed her, with Ben and Julia in the fold-up seats in the boot. Ordinarily Holly would have been dismayed at this division, but she already had much worse to deal with on the seatmate front. She really didn't have any luck with this, she thought, remembering Danny on the bus. As they all got settled Holly concentrated on her seatbelt, then looked to her left. She was pressed against the fragrant edge of Eva, who was sitting in the same seat as Yvonne, forming a joint entity. What a package, Holly thought, and actually laughed slightly. She tried to turn it into a cough, but she ended up sounding like a mad person, and she sensed Eva exuding sympathy.

Malcolm turned to them all and seemed about to say something, but thought better of it, and pulled off without a word. They swayed and shuddered down the track.

"Darling, do drive sensibly," Eva said.

"I am driving sensibly," he said irritably. "You try getting down here more sensibly than this."

"Fix it one day," Belinda said, staring out of the window, as the exhaust grated.

"He didn't mean that," Eva said quickly. "Did you?"

"Keep it, I would," Malcolm said. "If I had my way we'd have one of these. Give people a bit of a challenge."

12

The church was full. Everyone from school was there, many of them with white bandaging taped to the middle of their faces and the dull green spread of bruising underneath. Danny was having his funeral afterwards, so most of them were in for a long haul. They met Gran outside. Malcolm had offered to collect her but she had said he shouldn't bother, she wasn't going to be a nuisance, she'd get a friend to drive her. Gran lived on an assisted housing estate near Bristol, but she used to live on the farm, even when Daddy and Belinda were married. She left after Holly and Yvonne were born. Holly knew this because Daddy used to call them his magical princesses and congratulate them for having got rid of the wicked witch. Holly didn't know about that, she liked Gran, whose main quality was to be totally unimpressed by everyone and everything, even, apparently, her grandchildren. This had been crushing for Yvonne, but Holly quite liked it. Once you realised she really wasn't interested you could sit with Gran in companionable silence, or play card games, or listen to her talk about Grandpa. Gran had never liked the farm, she told Holly, but she had put up with it for him.

"He was such a merry lad, your Grandpa, all his life," she said, with a flicker of a smile.

"Merry with everyone," Daddy had said later, after Gran had left. Belinda had told him to shut up, and he'd laughed, and Holly had curled up inside the delicious pleasure of that sound.

The church was the first time Holly had seen anyone from the crash. She flinched under the steel rods of their wide-eyed stares, but met them anyway: partly out of determination, partly to see if anyone showed any recognition of Yvonne's presence. Nothing, though, as far as she could tell. No-one said anything as they went up the aisle, Malcolm escorting Gran, looking like a giant next to her. Holly had always felt that people didn't know what to make of their family, out on the farm. Maybe it was because Daddy had been a doctor and had known embarrassing things about people, or maybe it was just because they came from the country, which for most people in Ledborough was a strange, savage wilderness full of vanishing footpaths and barking dogs and dark looks and legend.

The front pew was reserved, but it must have been Danny Blake's family who arranged it for their funeral afterwards, because there wasn't enough room. He can't have had any relations, hardly, Holly thought, as they tried to work out what to do, being watched by the ranks of eager mourners.

"I'll stand at the back," Malcolm said. "I'm sure if you budge up…"

"Please don't go," Holly said involuntarily. They all turned, surprised to hear her speak. She was surprised, too.

"Well…" Malcolm said, looking at the others.

Eva said, "In that case we'll stand," with surprising ferocity. "Come on, Benedict."

Holly wanted to exercise her grief veto there as well and send off Julia instead of Ben but Eva was looking dangerous, and she didn't dare.

Belinda said, "I'm going for a cigarette," and marched down the aisle. Now it was just a disaster. No-one felt they could be left behind, so they all trooped out of the church again, as if they'd had enough and weren't staying, while people rustled and murmured.

Poor old Yvonne had only just drifted up the aisle and had to drift after them again, an uncertain presence at her own funeral. Surely if she was going to respond to anything it was this, her own send-off, Holly thought; but Yvonne's ghost was inscrutable as always.

By the time Belinda had had her cigarette and they all made their ceremonial re-entrance the vicar must have cleared out the next pew for them, too, and Holly ended up sat in the front row with Belinda and Malcolm and Gran, the others sitting behind. The coffin was on trestles just in front of them. The box looked quite big and the legs not steady enough. Belinda's hands trembled holding the hymn-book and she cried without making any noise. Holly stared at the coffin, not looking to her left where Yvonne's ghost sat, and wondered what was happening inside it. Would Yvonne's face have gone grey? Would she be stiff with rigor mortis, or did that wear off? Had they put on make-up? They did on telly.

Was this what she'd done when Daddy died, she wondered? Sat in the church and looked at his coffin and tried to work out if he was rotting yet? She couldn't remember his funeral at all. She didn't think she'd remember this one, either. It went very quickly. There were hymns, which Eva sung loudly, her quavering voice rising from the row behind. Holly didn't sing, even though she liked singing normally. At first she had just stood quietly, but she saw the vicar looking at her sympathetically so she started mouthing the words, angry with herself for being weak.

The vicar didn't say much about Yvonne. He was probably scared of Belinda shouting at him. He just said that no-one could imagine what Holly and Belinda must be feeling now, which was certainly true, Holly thought, her skin cold where her sister's ghost sat next to her, shoulder to shoulder. At the end no-one had arranged what was happening, so it all fell apart again. As soon as the vicar stopped Belinda got up and walked down the aisle, fast. Holly was still staring at the coffin. Malcolm nudged her and she looked and got up but by the time they followed she was ten yards behind, which meant she had no-one to shield her from the attention. Most of the parents smiled with faint sympathy but everyone from school stared. The ones with bandages taped to the middle of their faces looked like they had snouts.

13

It was the empty time that Belinda hated: time filled with nothing but jawing. After the church she marched straight for the car, but of course it wasn't that simple, nothing ever was, and they had to stand around and make conversation and decide who was coming back for the wake. They only got moving in the end because Eva started bleating about how nothing would be ready. Stupid thing to say: Vic's sister-in-law was at the farm preparing and she was hardly incapable of sticking some sandwiches on some bloody plates, Belinda said, not meaning to sound so aggressive but not being able to help it. Eva stood her ground, as usual, which was one of the few good things you could say for her.

On the way home Belinda kept looking at Holly in the rearview mirror. She was sitting hunched up against the car door and staring out of the window. There had been a shadow in her face ever since the accident and the worst thing, Belinda knew, was that people would always look at Holly and see that shadow: see the absence of Yvonne. She had no idea what Holly was supposed to do about that, though. By the time they got to the lane all the cars had bunched up and they led a cortege along to the gate. It wasn't a long cortege, though if Belinda had had her way there wouldn't have been anyone. She didn't begrudge them the urge to commemorate and to be supportive, and she didn't want to be mean-spirited, but the idea of being talked at by people she hadn't seen since Paul died made her feel ill.

As they approached the farm Holly spoke for what seemed the first time in hours. She said she would do the gate and wait till everyone was through then walk up to the house. Belinda thought it was an excellent idea, give the girl some time to herself, though Eva was immediately tutting. However, when they turned the last corner they saw the gate was already open and a van was parked between the posts blocking access. Micky Newton, the vet, and another man with him. Belinda had no idea what Micky was doing there, it was hard enough to get him to come out in an emergency, let alone when she hadn't even called. She might owe him money, she supposed, but asking for it on the day of the funeral would be bad taste even for him. Douggie and Lizzie, Vic's sister-in-law, were there as well on the other side of the van. Douggie didn't look up but Lizzie seemed relieved to see them, waving wildly as soon as they came into view. Malcolm stopped sharply and Belinda got straight out.

"What's all this, Micky?" she said, marching across to him.

Lizzie started speaking fast and now she was closer Belinda saw that she was crying, but she held up a hand and Lizzie stopped.

"Ah, look, Belinda, I'm sorry about this, I am," Micky said, not seeming it, but then he had a sly type of face that always made him seem crooked, whatever the circumstances (Belinda had never made up her mind whether this was a fair reflection on him or not). "It's bloody awful timing, but there's nothing we can do."

Belinda was aware of Malcolm next to her and the others just behind and vaguely of car doors opening down the lane and heads emerging.

"About what," she said, her voice with too much bite, she knew, but it was obvious now what was going on.

"Confirmed case this morning on Oaklands," Micky said. "I was there myself, along with Stuart here." He indicated his companion, who nodded, his face blank. "From the Ministry," Micky added unnecessarily, you could spot a MAFF clown a mile away.

Belinda felt her teeth clench hard against each other, and the familiar soft darkness begin to cloud in her mind and draw her away from the world, but she fought it; fought to stay in this moment and survive.

"They're saying no-one can come in and I've done everything ready and it'll all be wasted," Lizzie said shrilly through her tears, but Vic had come up from his car now and he and his wife Beth took her to one side, thank God. Douggie was staring pleadingly at Belinda as if to say he hadn't done anything and she nodded at him, then looked evenly at Micky.

"That'll have been in his sheep, then," she said, her voice sounding like someone else's. Micky nodded. "Well then," she said. "We've had no contact with his animals, we've got no sheep any more in any case. No livestock in or out of here in the last six weeks at all. So what the hell are you doing?"

"Mrs Jones, foot-and-mouth…" the MAFF idiot started to say, but Belinda cut him off and told him that some people at least were old enough to remember the last time and if he was going to tell her how serious it was, he had better be prepared for the consequences.

Micky smiled like a shark. "Look, Belinda, every farm within ten miles gets a Category 'D' surveillance notice. That's all it is."

The darkness surged, soft and mushrooming. She took a deep breath. "Three things, Micky. First, it's ten kilometres, not ten miles. I've read the directive, even if you haven't. Second, I'm not convinced Oaklands is that close. It's probably 12, 13 miles from here, let alone ten kilometres. And third, I've just buried my daughter, and we're all going inside to have a drink. If you want to talk to me you can come back tomorrow."

The MAFF man cleared his throat and started to take out a

folder and as he did so Belinda felt the most powerful urge she'd ever had to hit someone, hard, to see blood; and as soon as she felt it she knew it was too late. She'd hit people in the past, but it was always before you thought about it. Once you had the thought the moment was gone.

From that point on it turned into a bloody farce. Stuart, the MAFF idiot, said that of course they didn't want to disrupt the event but did the farm have sufficient disinfecting equipment to clean all the cars on the way out and with the greatest sensitivity might it not be a good idea given the inadvisability of movement at this critical stage to change their plans. Malcolm breathed heavily and asked in a very even voice whether Stuart had always been this much of a prick, or whether it was a recent development, and Eva said, "God" a lot. After a while Belinda stopped really being aware of the details of what was happening. She knew she was pushing her way past Micky and Stuart and marching up the drive, and she knew that Holly was next to her. With a huge effort from within the dark cloud she reached out and put an arm around Holly's shoulders. Holly leaned against her as they walked and the other children came with them, and Belinda told herself to be glad of that, of their instincts, these kids, to stand together – even though all the time she was receding, receding.

Malcolm stayed by the gate and made compromises and spoke to everyone in their cars and explained the situation. God knows what Eva did. Lizzie followed along saying over and over again how sorry she was, though Belinda didn't know what for. About half the people in the line of cars gave Malcolm their apologies, in the circumstances, but the other half came. They didn't stay long, just stood around in the sitting room in awkward groups of three or four till they felt they had done their duty. At least it stopped people telling her it was all going to be ok, because it was perfectly obvious it wasn't. Belinda went outside often for a cigarette and watched it all through the glass. Julia stayed in the kitchen with Eva, who was faffing around trying to help Lizzie and mostly getting in the way, and Ben and Holly carried trays of sandwiches to the guests. Even from outside she could see Ben with a sad smile and people touching his arm and being comforted; and she could see Holly doing the rounds, her narrow face set and drawn, and people not knowing what to say to her, so saying nothing. Apart from Malcolm, who mostly stood to one side with Sal but made sure Holly came over to him every now and then and talked to her quietly in the corner.

Eventually it was over. They sat in the kitchen with tea looking at the trays of food that no-one had eaten: softening crisps and Lizzie's sandwiches with the bread curled. Eva was clearing her throat and umming and aahing until Belinda couldn't stand it anymore, so she told her what she evidently wanted to know. Category D meant that they couldn't move the animals off the farm but they hadn't been planning to in any case; and it meant that they were all free to come and go as long as they disinfected their clothes and their car every time they did. Eva did her best not to look relieved that they could leave whenever they wanted. Salome sat by the window looking out and thank God Ben put on the television and started watching it with Holly and Julia, talking to them all the time and laughing about whatever rubbish was on. Belinda sat and waited for the darkness to close in, but there was still light left in her mind, and in it she could clearly see the future. If it came. In her mind's eye she saw the cattle penned in the small yard and the slaughtermen taking them one by one into the crush and putting the gun against their foreheads and firing the bolt through bone into brain, and the twitch and sag running the length of the back and shuddering through the belly of each animal and the smell of it and the panic and it happening time after time after time until all of them, every single one, were dead. If it came.

14

Holly thought that life would stop, but it didn't. The milking carried on and the milk was still collected. She listened to Belinda and Vic and Douggie having dark conversations, when Douggie was there, which was less and less often. Vic said that people had been muttering that the government had something to do with this. Belinda said she thought that was bollocks, which was a word Belinda used a lot. Vic said that he'd been told the works yard at the railway had been rung up weeks ago to ask about railway sleepers. Why, Holly asked, and everyone exchanged glances and he said awkwardly that when foot-and-mouth disease was found they had to slaughter animals and then burn the bodies and the railway sleepers were used for the fires. Holly nodded faintly and tried not to think about the scale of that, of those huge timbers used as no more than kindling. Vic also said that beaten-up old trucks had been seen transporting livestock all round the area and people were saying they'd been spreading the disease. Belinda asked why on earth anyone would do that and Vic smiled a little and said he granted that was a mystery, but Holly was thinking: the truck she'd seen on the road before the crash; the filthy sheep...

After they got the news Holly thought it might be all she was able to think about, but it turned out her mind was capable of worrying about the farm and gnawing at her to find Will Sadler and do something about Yvonne at the same time. She had worked out a way to get to the other side of the Motorway, if she could face it. The only problem remaining – apart from the whole issue of facing a mad person with a gun – was opportunity. Before the Family arrived there had been endless empty hours after school, and whole days at weekends, when she could do anything she liked as long as she didn't mind Yvonne being there. Now the house was full of people and everything she did had to be explained and discussed – there was so much more talking than before. And noise, too: noise being made by someone other than Belinda. The Family produced a din all of their own to complement her crashing and slamming. Two days after the funeral Holly lay in bed waiting for the rhythm of doors opening and banging and footsteps thundering up and down the corridor to die away. As soon as there was a lull she got up and opened the door, hoping for clear passage to the bathroom, but just as she was about to make a run for it Julia slipped in like an eel, so she went downstairs instead. Ben and Sal were in the kitchen. Holly smiled then stopped on the threshold. Malcolm was rooting through the fridge, his back to her, naked. His back was wiry with blond hair, which darkened on his buttocks into a deep and awful chasm between them. Holly tottered. Ben was reading a cereal box and Sal was chewing toast, both of them unaware. For a wild second she thought it must be a ghost who looked like Malcolm. Then Ben noticed her.

"Holly," he said. "Dad!"

Malcolm turned round. He was holding the milk and had a white moustache from it on his lip. Holly concentrated on that as hard as she could, willing her eyes away from the shock of pendulous fuzz further down.

"Oh bugger," he said. "Sorry, Holly, love. Thought you were out with Belinda. Avert your gaze, and I shall recover my dignity."

Holly turned around and faced the wall. Malcolm passed her in

73

the doorway. "Put the coffee on, Ben, I'll be down in a second," he said, as he went.

Holly glanced after him with awful fascination. His buttocks seemed enormous, like the haunches of cows. How could anyone be that big? How could anyone be that naked?

"Sorry, Holly," Ben said.

She turned back. "Does he… is that normal?" she asked.

"Yeah, fraid so," he said. "Pretty much standard."

Standard, she thought. That? "So… all the time? Or just sort of special occasions? And… I mean, we never knew about this, so… has he always…"

"Apparently," Ben said cheerfully. "He used to be a bit more discreet, you know. You'd just run into him on the way to the bathroom. Nowadays he does it all over the place. Weekends, evenings, kitchen, sitting room. Whatever."

Holly shook her head. She tried to imagine it if Daddy or Belinda had ever walked around naked. She didn't think they were all narrow-minded or anything but the whole idea defeated her. She couldn't decide what to ask first.

"Sitting room?" she said eventually.

He nodded. "Watching TV. If we're there he doesn't come in and sit down naked. Not usually. But you find him like that some-times."

Sal stirred, still on the same piece of toast. Sal's languorous rhythm reminded Holly a lot of Yvonne, but it didn't annoy her. It seemed more natural, somehow.

"Shame is more primitive than nudity," she said. "As Daddy says."

"Yeah," Ben said laconically. "Mum doesn't, thank God. Tea or coffee, modom?"

"I'll do it," Holly said, feeling like she had to be the host for some reason, and joined him at the counter.

"Took some persuading not to do it in front of, like, friends," Ben said in a mock-conspiratorial whisper. "We told him he'd get done as a paedophile, though. That convinced him."

Right, Holly thought. Of course. But even while her mind boggled at the idea, and most of her hoped she would never be faced by that sight in the morning again, she couldn't help feeling an obscure glow of pride that he would do it in front of her. It was as if she was part of the Family; as if she belonged. That nakedness was a badge of membership felt pretty disturbing, but still. She'd never once thought while Yvonne was alive that being surrounded by people would be so important, but already she couldn't imagine what it would be like when the Family left. Being alone with Belinda and the silent ghost of Yvonne and that just continuing, the three of them, for years and years: the idea suddenly seemed impossible.

Given the life that had taken over the house, Holly thought she might have to wait days for her chance to make the journey to Will's, but in the end the opportunity came sooner than she expected, because Eva proposed a group outing to Ledborough.

"A trip to the shops would do us good, darlings, we all need to take our mind off things," she said sweetly, and although Belinda's face made inviting her unnecessary, Malcolm got roped in. Holly tried very hard to make it seem like a great idea about which she was really excited. Then on the morning of the trip she said she felt ill, looking down at her lap so anyone tempted to ask would realise this was a sign of grief and must therefore be respected. Eva made a big deal about doing exactly that, being very sensitive and saying that Holly must be sure to look after herself. Eva would congratulate herself on her thoughtfulness later, Holly knew. She really didn't envy the others the trip.

When the car had disappeared and Belinda was in the yard with Vic Holly scraped her hair back into a pony-tail and clipped it up flat and shrugged on her wax coat and pulled on her boots and set off, giving Bay and Horace – the others were out with Belinda – her stern look, which by now they knew to obey. They subsided with a groan, and she was free, walking through the cold wet clean air with only Yvonne for company.

She deliberately didn't think about what lay ahead until she got to the End, and was on the down slope to the embankment. Then, with the Motorway close in front of her and the noise of traffic surging in the air, she allowed herself to imagine what might happen. For all the jokes people told about Will Sadler she knew it might be properly dangerous. The times she'd seen him in Ledborough he'd been mumbling to himself and wild-eyed and seemed genuinely ill. She didn't really think he'd shoot her but she would be trespassing, and he might point a gun at her or let a dog run at her and either one of those seemed fairly real and scary. She remembered him bent-backed against the apparition on his heels, though, and knew there was no choice in this. She had to go through with it.

She eased through the barbed wire fence at the embankment, and was about to turn right along the line of the Motorway, then decided she should allow herself one good look at the road first. She scrambled a couple of steps up the steep loose soil, pulling herself up by the thistly grass, until she was at the top of the slope that led down to the tarmac. Looking out from there was as magical as ever. The shudder of the passing cars on her skin and hair, the reverberations of tyre and exhaust, the faces glimpsed so fleetingly, all so varied, some gazing unblinking at the road ahead, but nearly all of them careless: fiddling with something in the cockpit, the radio, or eating a sandwich, or talking on the phone, or driving with one hand and looking idly around as if they were waiting to meet a friend, not hurtling along in thin metal shells a blink or a sneeze or a cough away from obliteration.

When she just looked at the road, it reminded Holly of watching the sea or clouds in the sky: something so vast and massy it made her feel like a bird in a gale or plankton billowing among the waves. But sometimes she fixed her eyes on one car as it approached, and tracked it along, watching the driver: a person, just as real as she was. By keeping her eyes on that person, she got a real sense of the speed – at the moment the car flashed by, it hurt her eyeballs to keep up, that was how fast they were going. Speed like this was a drug to Holly. What would happen if you put a brick wall in front of a car driving at 80 miles an hour? A completely immovable wall? Surely the car would become instantaneously flat, would be transformed into something two-dimensional in less than a heartbeat. Or what if one of the drivers put their foot on the clutch, and put the car in reverse? Would it be torn in two in a shower of metal dust and fire? And most of all, what would happen to her if she took maybe twenty steps down the slope and stepped from the hard shoulder in front of a lorry?

That was what she used to wonder. She felt tears come to her eyes. She'd always liked to think a death like that, so quick, so complete, would maybe cheat whoever kept count; maybe her soul would be knocked out so fast it would become free. Standing on the bank next to Yvonne, though, she knew she had been wrong. Whatever death was, it was pretty clear that freedom never came into it.

15

After Holly had breathed the oily shifting air of the Motorway long enough, she slid back down the embankment and started walking. The path wasn't easy, pushed in against the barbed wire fence, but she hurried as fast as she could. She had a lot of ground to cover before she got to the tunnel. Her way across.

The tunnel was about half a mile beyond their farm on Colin Thomas' land. Holly wasn't worried about trespassing on his property, he was a little jolly man who drank all the time and waved at Holly if he ever saw her in town. He didn't have any guns as far as she knew and only one dog, which was as tiny and happy as he was. However, the tunnel itself was a horrible place. She'd only been there once and had tried to dare herself to go inside, but it was made to let wild animals cross under the road and wasn't really high enough for a person to go through easily and she didn't like the look of it at all. Also there had been a smell coming from it, dark, like old meat, and as she'd been peering into the entrance she'd thought she'd seen movement and she'd scrambled up the gully and away so fast her hands had stung where she'd torn clumps out of the ground.

This time she had something much more serious to worry about and she told herself the tunnel would be easier. No-one passed the message on to her brain, though, and when she came in sight of the dip in the land that marked its position she felt her heart beating faster. The dip was enclosed by a fence, then steep slopes led down to a concrete trench. It was at least five foot deep and wide as a person, so it was like a long narrow grave. Looking down she saw the floor of the trench covered with an unpleasant shiny many-coloured liquid, even though it had been dry for days. The liquid was surrounded by a rim of algae or maybe something worse. Where the trench went under the Motorway there was a white square arch of concrete, flat and blank.

Everything in her felt this was a bad idea, but she forced herself not to pause, and went over the fence and started slipping down the gully in one movement, not giving her mind or body a chance to resist. Even when she got to the trench she swung her legs in and dropped down but then, with the concrete walls either side as high as her head and Yvonne drifting down behind her blocking her way and nothing but the gaping hole in front of her she had to stop, and fight to control her breathing.

She stared into the tunnel. There was a bright rectangle of light at the far end but it looked impossibly far away. Now she was low down the noise of the Motorway had taken on a new register, bass, echoing. Just look, she told herself, take as long as you like, but she knew that wasn't true, if she didn't move forward soon there was no way she'd be able to do this. She jerked convulsively and took a step forward, then another, looking at her feet. How many steps would it need, fifty, eighty, and she'd be through? That was all it was. Suddenly she was at the mouth itself and the effort of keeping going was so hard she let out a muffled noise as if she'd been hit but she kept walking, ducking her head, not looking at what might be hanging from the roof of the tunnel and ready to catch in her hair or at anything apart from her feet, but in only two or three paces it became very dark, and besides she realised she hadn't breathed for a really long time, so she stopped, and breathed in.

The smell was bad, but not as bad as she'd feared. It was mostly damp and fungus and fumes - not sour and meaty, like last time. The whole tunnel was shuddering with sound, like a gigantic hoover roaring overhead, and it was so loud that she felt anonymous and invisible, which gave her the confidence to look up. Although the rectangle of light wasn't nearly as close as she'd hoped, it wasn't so far either. She took a step towards it then stopped. The funny thing about the rectangle was that it wasn't actually a rectangle at all. The sides and top were straight but the bottom was humped and uneven. Go on, she told herself urgently, and started walking forward, keeping her eyes on the hump as she felt the knowledge rising in her throat that it must be something, must be maybe a growth, or... or...

She was closer now, and still walking despite the thudding in her ears, and she knew what she was walking towards, because she could see an edge of bristly hair outlined against the brightness beyond. Some kind of animal. It was maybe ten yards in front of her – and behind her was Yvonne. Holly paused, breathing fast through her nose, and told herself there wasn't any animal that wouldn't run if you were big, if you pushed your shoulders back and shouted. Cows had run at her a hundred times and she'd done that and they always turned and fled. But cows didn't have dens and young to protect. Cows weren't dogs or wolves or whatever this was, because it was big enough to be either. She knew that if she turned and saw Yvonne and saw how far back it was to get out of this place she'd scream, so she didn't turn, she just stood still and looked at the animal. Either it would move or courage would come to her or something else would happen – it had to, otherwise she would be here forever.

It was actually nothing happening, though, that made her move. After nearly a minute standing motionless as the traffic thundered overhead, keeping her gaze fixed on that bristled flank, she realised it hadn't stirred, not even for breath; and after a minute more she knew it was dead. She didn't mind dead animals, even ones that had been torn about or were foul-smelling, but even so she felt a deep sick unease. Carefully, slowly, she stepped towards it. It was a dead badger. There was something so ungainly about its shape, lying on its side like a sack, swollen and ridiculous. But its face and muzzle were sleek and gleaming. For a moment she forgot where she was, and Yvonne following her, and where she had to get to, and just looked at it. It was very beautiful, up close. So perfectly still.

She wished she could watch what would happen to it. Not in detail or anything, but from a distance, like on nature programmes – time-lapse photography. Over months and years this beautiful glossy creature would break down, its flesh would boil away, leaving clean white bones. Holly loved bones, they were some of her favourite things in the Reservation, and although she was afraid she was getting too old for it, staring into the eyes of the Skull still made her shiver. The idea of having an entire badger skeleton was so seductive that for a second she imagined coming back with a rope and pulling the badger out and burying it somewhere, then, later, sifting the naked bones from the soil. But that 'later', that one year or two years, was beyond her. What if she forgot, and left the bones in the earth forever, mouldering, unremembered?

And while she was thinking about that, and wondering how the badger died and whether it would be safe to step forward and gently touch its face, it suddenly got dark, much too fast, and she looked up and saw that the square of light ahead of her was gone and in its place was the outline of a man, stooping, filling the entire passage, and Will Sadler was coming down the tunnel towards her.

16

Ben sat in the car on the way to Ledborough, just looking forward to time by himself. He liked being alone: going to the cinema or reading in a bookshop cafe, free and self-contained. Especially at the moment, given the way he was feeling. He knew that what had happened to Yvonne was terrible and unimaginable, and that things didn't look good for the farm, and then there was the way Mum and Dad were, which he didn't mind as much as Julia but which was pretty tiring all the same – but none of it seemed to matter. He felt light and alive and as if he had air in his veins not blood. He also knew what that probably meant, but he didn't care, not now, he just wanted some room to move in and breathe, and a town with shops and lights and life to explore. It was a shame Holly hadn't come. If she had he'd have stayed with her, if she wanted, instead of being alone. Partly because she was dark and secret and often surprising and he really liked being with her, and partly because while she seemed to be holding herself together, he'd never seen someone looking so lonely.

Thinking about it, though, she'd always seemed lonely, even before what had happened. And… something else. Not wise, ex-actly, though that was part of it. It was more that she seemed somehow full. Full of thoughts and life and the kind of person who didn't always talk but whenever they did it was always worth hearing. She also seemed much older than the last time he'd seen her. Her sister dying a couple of years after her dad might do that, he guessed, but she was also just... older. Before she'd had quite a wise face but apart from that had seemed like Yvonne's little sister – compact and clumsy like all girls were between about five and ten when they could have been any age, as far as he knew. Boys too he supposed. Anyway, now she was much taller and thinner and just more like a person and less like a kid.

When they arrived in Ledborough his opportunity for solitude evaporated, though. After they parked the car Dad said he and Sal were going for a coffee and the crossword. Ben didn't know when they'd arranged that; he'd figured Sal would get roped in to some female shopping excursion. Mum seemed pretty surprised by it too and gave them a sour look as they sloped off. Then she turned back and said with that edgy sort of brightness, "Right, Julia, let's see what this place has to offer, shall we?"

Julia looked at him pleadingly. He nearly managed to resist and strike out for freedom anyway, but she seemed so desperate, and besides, what the hell, how bad could it be, so he smiled and said, "I'm in."

They went to a department store, not a proper national one but some kind of local outfit where the floors were all dimly lit and the staff were old. He'd thought that at least Julia and Mum would look at clothes and he could be semi-detached but almost as soon as they walked in Mum said, "So how are you feeling, today, darling?" and followed it up with a significant look and he realised they were going to be trapped into another rendition of the only conversation they had any more.

"Fine," he said, looking at her and nodding a lot so she would know he meant it. "You know. Chipper. OK. All right."

Mum gave one of her smiles, all teeth and crinkle. "If you want to talk about... anything, you know you always can, don't you?"

He turned away. Julia had already found something she wanted to try on. Her ability to do that was amazing, it only ever took seconds and she had an armful of about 15 different garments. She said she was going to the changing rooms and Ben knew he might actually be in trouble.

"I know," he said. "I do. I really do. I just don't think talking about it will help, is all." He pulled a shirt off the rack that was clearly meant for an old man but was actually quite neat. Maybe he should take a huge pile of clothes and go and hide in the changing rooms himself.

Mum was smiling even harder now. "Not talking about it isn't really a permanent solution, is it?" she said.

It was the cheeriness of her voice he couldn't stand; or rather, the desperate effort at cheeriness. "God, Mum, are we on permanent solutions already?" he said, feeling the bite in his voice. "Permanent? Really? If we're talking permanent solutions we're really bringing suicide into the mix, aren't we? Is that what we're doing?"

He meant it as a kind of joke and half-laughed as he said it but without warmth, he realised, from her reaction. Her face shrivelled and her smile faded and he knew he'd screwed up. He said he was sorry, touching her arm, and he genuinely was, but it did mean the conversation was over for now and he couldn't help feeling relieved.

For a while he just sifted racks humming and Mum looked at her own stuff in frosty silence, then Julia came out of the changing rooms.

"What do you think?" she said.

He tried not to wince. It was armless and Julia's arms at the top looked like other people's legs. "Nice. Just… I'm not convinced by how it is around the shoulders," he said.

She looked down at herself on either side and said he was probably right and smiled at him so gratefully that he realised being here was probably worth it. Just. She told him to wait because she needed to show him the next thing. Both his sisters said he was good at looking at clothes. All girls did, in fact. Even... well. Her. He suddenly felt a surge almost like being sick, but he swallowed it back down. He wasn't thinking about that. Not now, not ever.

17

Holly stood very still, trying not to think about the fact that she was now on the wrong side of the Motorway. A few steps ahead of her stood Will Sadler, talking to the air, as if holding a conversation with a missing partner. Not his ghost, though. His whole body was twisted away from it, everything about him seemed to deny its presence. Holly glanced at it again, still amazed at the sight of a dead person who wasn't Yvonne. It was an old woman, wearing thick layers of clothes like Belinda. Will's mother, Holly guessed. She was mostly bald, with only wisps of white hair. As Will kept up his half-monologue Holly realised it might all have been wasted effort; she might not even be able to get him to look at her properly. Still, it could be worse, she thought. She wasn't in the tunnel anymore and he didn't seem to have a gun. That was something.

When she'd looked up and seen him blocking the far end of the passage, her first thought had been to run, right at him, force him back, so that whatever he planned to do to her at least wouldn't happen in that dark little tunnel... but then he had beckoned her forwards. It was creepy being summoned like that, but she hadn't had much choice, so she'd stepped over the dead badger and walked towards him. He'd backed away and disappeared. She'd paused just before the opening to the tunnel in case he was waiting outside to grab her, but then she saw him a few steps away, talking to himself. She'd stepped out into the light, and almost into his ghost, which had made her stumble away. Being surrounded by the smell and feel of a ghost who wasn't Yvonne was somehow even more repulsive.

Since then she had waited for her heart to slow to its normal rate and for Will to say or do something, but he just kept on mumbling to the air. She realised that to get anything out of this she'd have to take the lead. She stepped towards him, Yvonne following obediently, showing no awareness of the other ghost (Holly had half thought that they might be able to interact, but they both remained impassive, blank, heedless). She was close enough to touch him now. The first thing she noticed was the smell: the sweet rank odour of unwashed hair and clothes. It wasn't so bad, though, and he didn't look as dirty as she remembered. His lips were moving but even standing next to him she couldn't make out any words.

Holly swallowed. "Please…" she said, and pointed at Yvonne. Will turned, but looked at her, not at the two ghosts.

"You know what I mean," he said abruptly. "Know you do. Yes. Theirs. You'll see that. Not ours."

Holly shook her head. "I don't understand. Just look, please. See?"

She pointed again and this time he did look straight at Yvonne, and that on its own was enough to make her throat and heart swell after living so long with this unacknowledged shadow. He frowned, and seemed about to speak, then turned jerkily and started walking, so fast he was almost running. Holly hurried after him, aware they were heading further and further away from the Motorway and her way back home. She had to engage him somehow, make him listen. She stopped running, took a deep breath, and called loudly, "Mr Sadler – who is she?"

At first she thought it hadn't worked, but then he hesitated, and stopped altogether. He turned and faced her, still twitchy. Slowly and deliberately she looked straight at his ghost, then pointed at it.

"I can see her," she said. "Tell me who she is."

"She…" he said, as though it was the first time he'd ever said the word. "She…" He broke off, and looked at her doubtfully.

"Please," Holly said. "I'm just trying to find out what they want. Why they're here." She felt tears starting. "I just need to know… why she's doing this to me."

There was a pain in the roof of her mouth that meant she was about to cry properly, and if he didn't understand her now, she didn't think she'd be able to speak again. He nodded sharply several times.

"I'll tell you," he said. "I'll tell you." She looked at him mutely, and after nodding again he stepped closer. "Forty years," he said. "Forty years. Dead, but not dead, no. Not dying, not going, not dying, not going. Not going. No."

Holly stared at him. Forty years. So it was a life sentence, then. His face was working, and she could see him trying to slow down his brain, to put thoughts into real spoken words.

"It shouldn't… it shouldn't happen," he said eventually. "Not allowed. Not… right. Can't…" His expression was anxious and pleading. Holly felt that he had much more to say, and that if she could only find the right question she could unlock the answers she needed. But before she could ask anything else his face suddenly showed fear, real terror, and he began to twitch and shake worse than ever. She looked over her shoulder but couldn't see anything that might have caused this. Then she heard a noise: a low growling surge, coming from the ridge at the side of the field. A truck making its way up the lane. In a moment the cab and the top part of the body appeared above the hedge.

"What is it?" she asked, turning to Will. He'd fallen back a step. "Who's coming?"

"Not… not now, no, now, no," he said, trembling.

There was something much too real about his fear, Holly felt scared by it herself. When they were afraid adults normally disguised it with anger or laughter or something else, but Will was showing fear like a really small child might show fear and she hated it. The truck stopped about twenty yards away, most of it still hidden by the hedge. It was a dirty livestock truck, rusted and battered, like the one she'd seen the day Yvonne died. In fact – was it the same truck? She couldn't tell, but it seemed very familiar. Micky Newton was in the passenger seat. Holly felt a cold rush of anger, even though she knew what was happening wasn't his fault. He wound down the window and called, "All right, William?" Will flinched next to Holly, he didn't seem to like Micky either. A door slammed. The driver must have got out on the other side, but Holly couldn't see him.

"Made a new friend, have we, William?" Micky said. Will didn't reply; he was hunched and moaning and had a hand to his head.

"Mr Sadler," Holly said urgently. "Why is he here? What's happening?"

He didn't answer. Holly turned back and suddenly, as if water had been thrown in her face, she was hit by a dizzying feeling. A man's head was visible over the hedge. The driver of the truck. His head was big and seemed very high up. How could he be that tall? The feeling intensified and Holly doubled over like Will. She felt as if she were in a vice; some kind of percussive pressure was being exerted on her, a soundless drumbeat throbbing in her ears.

Part of her mind was able to focus on what was happening, and she wondered if this was a symptom from the crash. Brain tumour, stroke, something. But as the driver started walking along behind the hedge, still looking at them so his head was sliding sideways, cut off from his too-tall body, and as the waves of pressure in the air thumped in her skull: she knew. He was doing this – the driver. Something about him was oppressing her. And Will Sadler, too. Which meant…

She forced herself to look up. The man was staring at her. As she watched, he calmly turned his head and looked straight at Yvonne. She was sure of it. Then back to her and he grinned mirthlessly, baring his teeth. *God, god, god* she thought, the word thumping in her mind like her pulse. *He knows.* He whispered something in Micky's ear. Was he telling him too? There was a loud rattle from the back of the truck, and the gate fell with a bang. As if in a dream Holly saw men jump down from the inside. They were wearing plastic overalls pulled only to the waist and in their hands… guns. They all had guns.

"Them," Will said suddenly. "That's them, see? Got to go, get away, go away. Now, now…"

Holly knew he was right. She didn't understand what was happening, but she knew for certain that she couldn't bear it. With effort she straightened herself.

"I'll come back and see you?" she said, but he was walking away from her, and away from the others, at an angle, as if he was striding out towards freedom – though she knew he wasn't escaping them. She turned and started half-walking, half-running.

"Not on our account, I hope," she heard Micky Newton say, and laugh. "We don't need her, do we?"

She looked over her shoulder at that. The driver and one of the other men were shaking their heads. Others were starting towards the house, pulling up their overalls. And one last man was getting out of the truck… Douggie. She froze. He lowered himself to the ground, looked up, and saw her. For a second they just stared at each other, then Holly ran. Soon the sound of the Motorway was louder than the voices from behind her and she concentrated on it until it was all she could hear.

18

Two days later Holly stood in her room, trying not to think. When she'd got home from Will Sadler's Belinda and Vic had been in the yard and she'd thought they might have been looking for her, but they'd been staring down the valley across the Motorway. Holly had realised that faintly on the wind you could hear the sound of gunshots.

"They're slaughtering at Lower Marsh," Vic had told her. "Will Sadler's place." Holly had wanted to say she knew and it was maybe something to do with ghosts and please God why couldn't they all see that Yvonne was following her everywhere she went… but all she did was stand next to them looking up at Belinda, whose face was set and dark.

After a moment Holly had asked where Douggie was, which seemed a safe way of finding out if they knew he was involved. They did.

"He's over there, most likely," Belinda had said gruffly and Vic had explained that so many animals were being killed across the country that they'd brought in the army, and when the army couldn't cope had just asked for volunteers and Douggie had signed up. He had no idea why, he'd said, it was horrible work but Belinda had said if things went on like this it would be the only work to be had for fifty miles then she turned and walked away. Holly had looked after her filled with a mixture of pity and fear and a desperate desire to tell her what was going on. To tell someone. But she'd known it was no good. How could she even begin?

Since then she hadn't worked out what to do next and mostly lived in fear of the slaughtermen coming and that man, the tall man with the large head and bright eyes who knew, on his way to find her. Because what if, she couldn't help thinking, what if Vic had been right about the trucks? The livestock lorry at Will Sadler's could have been the one she saw on the day of the crash. What if this was being spread deliberately? What if that man was working for the government and they were bringing this disease wherever they found people like Will and her? Will had said something about ghosts not being allowed, and he talked about 'them' as if there were people in charge – and then 'they' had arrived.

Holly mostly knew that this was ridiculous. Foot-and-mouth was everywhere, across the whole country, so that would mean ghosts had to be everywhere too. Besides no-one could organise something like this unless there was an enormous government conspiracy and ghosts were discussed by the police and the army and the Ministry and none of that was really possible, she was sure it wasn't; but that didn't stop her thinking it. The slaughtermen could be here any time. And almost worse than the thought they might be here tomorrow was the idea that they might wait until the Family had gone; until it was just her and Belinda to stand against them with no Malcolm and no Ben to help.

As if in answer to the thought of him Ben appeared in her doorway. Holly felt her face redden. Blushing, she thought, really? But then he hadn't been in her room. No-one had.

"We're summoned. There's an announcement," he said, and grinned. Holly was about to smile back when, as ever, Julia appeared next to him. She put her hand on his side, and he dropped his to her shoulder.

"Have you told her?" Julia asked, looking up at him. As though they were about to announce their engagement, Holly thought sourly.

Downstairs Eva was hovering at the door of the kitchen. There was no way she could actually help while Belinda was in there, it would have been like entering the workings of an industrial machine, but she had to be seen taking some of the burden of cooking. Malcolm was standing by the fire with a glass of whisky. Holly looked at it with a jolt of memory. The only time there was whisky in the house was when Malcolm visited and he and Daddy would stand together, light glinting off the rich red in their glasses, their breath fiery smoke when they laughed.

"Ah, good. We have a quorum," he called to the kitchen. Salome was on the sofa reading one of Daddy's books. He'd had shelves of dusty Penguin paperbacks, with lurid covers of snarling men and dishevelled women. Yvonne used to flick through them eagerly, though she was generally disappointed to find they weren't as explicit as they looked. When Malcolm spoke Sal uncurled herself and put it down. Belinda came through from the kitchen with a dishcloth over her shoulder and a glass of wine, Eva flapping in her wake.

"I think you lot should be sitting down," Malcolm said to Holly and Julia and Ben. "Don't worry, only for the solemnity of the occasion. I feel I need a grave and oratorical air."

Holly and the others sat dutifully. "Unaccustomed as I am and all that," he said, waving his whisky glass liberally, "I have a proposition to make. I mean, we all do, but… Anyway. As I'm sure you agree, you three are the luckiest people in the room, certainly much luckier than Sal, because you all go to school, and everyone knows your schooldays are the happiest of your life."

"You don't have to make a production of this, darling," Eva interrupted, in her sweet voice.

Malcolm inclined his head to her ironically. "Sorry, my love. My classroom air. You didn't get to see it much. Anyway, my point is this. My recent liberation from the shackles of employment has had the unforeseen consequence of making life quite tricky for you two," he said, indicating Ben and Julia. "As you know, you are technically allowed to go back to West Hill, but things might be a little hair-raising if you do. In the circumstances."

"Dad, it'll be…" Ben began, but Malcolm put up a hand.

"Let me forestall any rash and noble statements, Ben. If you go back you'll enjoy an uncomfortable notoriety, which I'm sure you'd handle admirably. Thing is, Holly is in the same boat. I don't want to speak for you, but the idea of school can't be much fun?"

Holly shook her head. Why couldn't she say something debonair like Ben would? She felt tears close to the surface, and looked away.

"Quite," said Malcolm. "And we haven't mentioned the possibility, remote as I hope it remains, that further restrictions will be in place on all our movements. All of which factors lead to my proposition. I offer you three my services. Well, ours. Sal is going to teach you English." He waved a hand airily. "I propose to take on the rest of the syllabus."

"Like… tutors?" Julia said.

"Good heavens, no," Malcolm said jovially. "We are talking the works. Home schooling. Guaranteed to achieve top exam results and abnormal socialisation, but then, there's a risk to everything. Do it and come what may, is my motto." He half-turned to Eva, and went on, "And before you say anything darling, you are right that recent events have put a dent in that aphorism, but a man must live by his principles. Anyway, that pretty much sums up our proposal, I think. Right, Sal?"

She nodded with languid amiability from her sofa. How would

she teach English, Holly wondered absently, given that nearly all of her communication was non-verbal? Perhaps they would appreciate the masterworks of literature through the medium of willowy mime. Her head was spinning. She hadn't even got beyond the day the Family would leave, to the day she'd have to go back to school and face the beady curiosity of classmates. And now Malcolm, like some Arabian genie, was going to make both those days, and the empty years that followed them, disappear in smoke and let her spend four years in a room with Ben. Well, two. If he did A-levels. Assuming they would stick to the standard school curriculum, which obviously they wouldn't, her brain scolded her. But even so. Even though Julia would be there. Even though, Holly swallowed, Yvonne would always be there – she was standing in front of the fire now, looking down at it, the flames distorting through her inky outline as if through gas – still, to be rescued from school and from the prospect of solitude like this felt as if she was being plucked from a vast ocean, a drowning ant fished out by the cheery red clatter of Air Sea Rescue.

"What do you say, gang?" Malcolm said. "And yes, that kind of cheesy patter will come as standard."

Holly saw Ben shrug and nod and Julia watching him and nodding after he did, and it was all she could do not to barrel across the rug and butt into Malcolm and throw her arms round him and start crying. In fact the temptation was so great she almost started getting up but then she noticed Eva's appraising eyes on her. She'd love that, the transformative power of her husband redeeming the lonely lost bereaved little girl, and Holly was determined not to give her that satisfaction. She held her chin up high and looked at Malcolm and nodded, but her determination couldn't stop the scramble of tears in her eyes. He smiled at her without seeming to notice, and Holly felt a deep lurch which she realised, almost with surprise, was love.

19

It was amazing to Holly, given how afraid she felt a lot of the time, that when she was with Malcolm and the others she felt all right. In fact part of her felt more than all right, felt somehow glowing. For all the anxiety looming over the house and for all her own personal worries about who might come up the drive and why, at least days now took on shape, purpose, togetherness. They set up a classroom in one of the old workrooms that stretched out from the house in an L-shape, like a bent arm. One morning they went around the house looking for anything vaguely academic to use as decoration. There was a relief map of the Urals with all the writing in Russian, and a poster of a whale leaping out of the sea in spray that Holly had been too embarrassed to have on her wall for a year, but Ben said that taste's loss was natural history's gain and they smiled together and then Julia appeared in the doorway with the plastic light-up globe from Yvonne's room and a toothy smile and asked Holly using a voice as curdling as Eva's whether she could cope if they used it, and surely Yvonne would like the idea? Holly felt a sudden crazy urge to say that Yvonne was standing right next to her and Julia could just ask, not that she was likely to get an answer. But it probably wouldn't achieve much. She felt such lightness of heart that she even pretended to think and then nod bravely and smile, and Julia bounced off delighted.

If Holly was honest Malcolm wasn't quite the perfect teacher she hoped, at least not before lunch, when he had a tendency to brood and set them to write essays or go through textbooks while Ben did revision for his exams. And probably because he had been reminded of exams Ben wasn't quite as radiant as usual either, more sober and serious and engaged, though he'd look up now and then and catch her eye and smile a little. Malcolm's other pre-lunch routine was to give them to Sal, who eschewed the homemade classroom and taught them English in a den she'd made around the sofa in the living room. She'd asked Belinda in her low murmur for soft furnishings. Belinda had arrived carrying two single mattresses, one under each arm, standard lamps and ornaments falling like axed trees in her wake. Sal found an armful of throws that Holly hadn't seen since Daddy died and sprayed it all with some kind of incense or perfume and that was where they sat and read. Because they only had one copy of everything, they read different books then swapped them over before having discussions about how the books made them feel, led, which wasn't the right word, by Sal. This meant reading speed was on show, and Holly, who read fast, was determined to finish her book first, even though she knew deep down that this was a pretty sad way to try to impress Ben.

However, the afternoons were completely different. After lunch Malcolm came alive, especially if it had been his turn to make the food. Eva and Malcolm took turns and her lunches were all steamed vegetables eaten in silence, especially from Malcolm, who forked them around gloomily and sipped a glass of wine with frozen restraint. His, though, were wild sandwiches thrown together while he drank huge tumblers of kitchen wine. Then lunch was brilliant, dazzling, and Holly and Ben and Julia spent half the time laughing helplessly at some story from Malcolm about the locals he met on the way to the shops, which would even make Sal smile, while Eva glared at his untouched table wineglass with suspicion. And afterwards, Holly loved the lessons. Malcolm

98

leaned against the desk they'd dragged in to the classroom and taught them everything. Really everything. One day he taught them Wittgenstein, the next nuclear power, the next the history of Afghanistan. And it was teaching not lecturing: he made them do it all. Mostly this involved role-play carried beyond the realm of absurdity, which he orchestrated, lips twitching, like a National Theatre director.

"Where do you go? Where do you go?" he roared at Julia, who was playing an electron. "You are a cloud of possibility. You are here and you aren't here. I don't even know if you're real. Emote quantum uncertainty, that's your job."

Ben and Holly laughed at the way he flicked his hair and so did Julia, usually, but not that time. That time she shivered then cracked, bursting into tears and running out of the room. Holly leaned against the wall, not knowing what to say. Malcolm met Sal's eye – Sal had been sitting in a chair reading and nominally playing a nucleus – and they shared a significant look that seemed to Holly to suggest this wasn't Julia's first tantrum. Eventually Malcolm sighed and said, "Prisoners to our hormones we are all," and sat down heavily, which left Ben as the one to go after her.

Afterwards Julia's outburst seemed to Holly to mark the end of the good days when there was no sign of the slaughtermen and noise bubbled around the house like a kettle boiling. She supposed it couldn't have lasted, anyway. No matter how much people felt it would be all right when they were together, when they were alone everyone must have been afraid, and at night Holly sometimes felt a kind of terror that Yvonne had never given her. It took maybe a week for the anxiety that slithered beneath everything finally to emerge. She was lying in bed half-asleep, the covers pulled right over her shoulder and her face buried in her pillow so she had the least chance of seeing Yvonne, who was faintly visible even in the dark, when she heard a sound she hadn't heard in ages. Her eyes opened wide, and immediately her heart began to hurt each time it beat. For a while, nothing; then again, and this time unmistakeable. Shouting. Belinda, and a deep reply, Malcolm; then suddenly the shrill sound of Eva.

For what felt like half-an-hour Holly lay and listened. Her long experience had made her an expert in this, like an Eskimo with snow. Back when it would have been Daddy and Belinda, she would have called this an *altercation* – about halfway up the scale. Normality. Still scary, though, like any storm: there was always a moment when although you knew it would come to an end and everything would have survived, you were suddenly afraid that this time it wouldn't.

Since she could first remember, Holly had thought of shouting from downstairs as a thing. An object. She'd wake up, not knowing what had woken her, then the *thing* would be there. It was a low, jumbled thing rising from the floor, like a mountain range emerging from the sea, just the peaks visible: voices breaking the surface in jagged little summits. For a while she would just listen, and the thing would stay down by the floor; then suddenly it would rise up, like someone had pulled a rope hard, and it would get big and soar up into the room and all around her the beats of the words would flap like the wind snapping sails: you *never* can't hear can't hear I'm *not* going to let you *stand* there and can't hear can't hear how *can* you you *stupid* can't hear can't hear…

And that was when, struck again by the fear that this time the world was ending, she'd creep to the top of the stairs and Yvonne would be there and they would hold their vigil. As she lay still, listening to this new, three-voiced shouting, Holly's heart beat harder and the pain was in her throat now and she was nearly crying. Because… because… the only reason she would allow herself to consider was because she had no-one to go to the top of the stairs with. Despite everything did she miss Yvonne that much? She opened her eyes, feeling them stinging, and without lifting her head looked at all that was left of Yvonne, standing inscrutable by her bed. That was too much, so she pushed back the covers and put on her cardigan and went down the dark corridor and sat at the top of the stairs anyway, Yvonne following her. Holly leaned into the wall and cried, silently, as the rhythm of the fight developed, not even bothering to measure it against her scale. She felt a more complete misery than she could ever remember before: a boundless sphere that started in her and had no end. She was frightened by the completeness and the never-endingness; in fact the more she thought about it the more panicked she felt; but just as she was thinking she might start shouting, too, she heard footsteps behind her. She had time to think *please God not Julia* then she felt a hand on her shoulder and knew without looking that it was Ben, which felt a million times better and somehow even worse.

He took his hand away and sat down quietly in exactly the spot Yvonne was hovering. "Are you… sorry. Of course you're not ok," he whispered.

Holly stayed bent towards the wall. She didn't want him to think she was crying over some stupid fight, but because – because of everything else; but she didn't know how to say it. He'd think she was some…

"You must miss him," he said. It was such an amazing thing to say Holly forgot to cry for a second. *Him.* "And Yvonne, too. But I guess you used to do this when your Mum and Dad were fighting, right, and now… now they're both gone."

Holly turned her face to him, speechless, wiping her cheeks. *Daddy*, she thought; but she knew she couldn't let the thought continue, and with a huge effort closed down that part of her mind. Still… Ben had *known*.

He shifted. "Sorry, I don't know if… I just remembered sitting like this in our house, and just thought…" he tailed off. With all the courage she had Holly pushed herself away from the wall and leaned against him instead, and his arm went round her shoulders and suddenly she knew this was what tonight was all about.

They sat together without talking for a long time. Then Ben straightened suddenly. "I thought they'd start talking about it," he whispered.

Holly had stopped crying now and looked up at him. She'd been so overwhelmed that she hadn't been listening to the fight, it had receded into the far distance.

"What?" she whispered back.

"It," he said. "The thing. You know, the reason they hate to come. Listen."

Holly did, intently. Belinda and Malcolm and Eva were in the kitchen, which was a room and two closed doors away, so it was almost as hard to hear the detail as upstairs. Eva was talking, had been for a while, she realised. Then Malcolm answered. His voice carried, and she straightened, too, because he was talking about Daddy. She heard his name, twice, but nothing else.

"See?" Ben said. "I think…" He stopped. Whatever Malcolm had said, it had an effect. Eva was shouting and it was carrying much more clearly. Holly realised she must have walked out of the kitchen, which meant…

"Come on," she said urgently, getting up. "They're coming."

He held back, but she pulled his arm, and they just made it round the corner when Eva threw open the door. The light spilled into the hall downstairs and flared up the wall.

"Wait," Ben hissed, and Holly did, because Eva wasn't heading for the stairs, but the front door. They heard a heavy tread and Belinda said, *"Malcolm!"* sharply but he came into the hall after Eva and suddenly they could hear his voice clearly.

"You and Paul, you and Paul, you and fucking Paul!" he shouted. "It's futile! Why the hell do you…"

"Malcolm… children," Belinda said. "I'm sure Holly has heard all this before, but the others…"

Holly felt Ben look at her and shook her head in the darkness. She didn't know what Belinda meant, unless it was just that Holly would be used to shouting.

Malcolm said loudly, "They had better bloody get used to it," but Holly could tell he wasn't really arguing. "If she… oh, sod it. I'm sorry it always goes this way."

"Don't be," Belinda said softly. Holly marvelled: she sounded like someone else entirely.

Malcolm sighed. "I'd better go and get her," he said.

"She can hardly get lost," Belinda said, which was more like her usual self.

"No, but that's why she's gone, isn't it? So I'll follow. It won't take long. Those heels, and the dark…"

They went together to the front door and their voices faded away. Ben stood a foot away from Holly on the half-lit landing.

"Fuck," he said, but Holly wasn't listening. "I guess that explains the shitty moods when we come here. I mean, if my Mum and your Dad… Jesus."

Jesus, Jesus, Jesus, Holly's mind rang like a drum. *Jesus. Shit.* All the words in the world could not do this justice, and it was nothing to do with Daddy and Eva – *Daddy and Eva!* her mind registered briefly, but not now, not now – because right now, she was looking at Ben, and *not at Yvonne.* Yvonne wasn't there. She wasn't on the stairs and she wasn't in the corridor. She'd gone.

20

Belinda would have ignored the idea if Eva had suggested it, but in fact it was Malcolm, so she supposed it might be worth trying. "A psychologist?" she said doubtfully. "Don't think Holly'll like that." She wouldn't, Malcolm agreed, if they suggested it as an option, but she might accept it if they presented it as a fact.

"Just tell her it's the done thing. That's not lying, it is what people do nowadays."

Belinda didn't have much experience of psychologists. She had half an idea of a psychiatrist, a bald man in a book-lined office looking like Sigmund Freud and sounding like a pompous arse, but psychologists and therapists, no sense of them whatever. There was some kind of alternative therapist in Ledborough, who used to put cards on various mournful notice-boards containing parish announcements and yellowing lists of sale items. She was just the kind of woman who would be a therapist, frizzy-haired and hopeless. Malcolm guffawed with exasperation.

"They might very well be hopeless, but that's not the point. The point is they sit there so unthreateningly that you can tell them everything. Which is what might do Holly some good. Who else is she going to talk to?"

Belinda conceded the point, not that she thought Holly put much store in talking through anything. Malcolm told her to find someone through the doctors. Harford was her chap, an old friend of Paul's, though since Paul died she'd hardly seen him.

She didn't like the idea of going into his poky little surgery, past all the chronic coughers and shrunken old people, never had; but Malcolm kept asking till she made an appointment, and she even arrived more or less on time. Harford was terribly enthusiastic about the whole idea, in the same way that he was terribly enthusiastic about everything.

"Now what about *you*, Mrs Jones," he said, once he'd found details of a clinic attached to St Mary's Hospital and written the number and address carefully on a card for Belinda to take away. "How are you coping with your loss?"

He looked at her hopefully through his glasses, as if this was a reasonable question to ask and not a fatuous insult both to Belinda's experience and her common sense. She wanted to tell him exactly what she thought: that he was talking absolute bollocks. Loss, damn stupid thing to say, she'd thought that when Paul died too. So what, she'd *lost* a husband, now she'd *lost* a daughter? As if they were objects she'd misplaced, games that hadn't turned out for the best, never mind, better luck next time? Like it was about what had happened to her? Nonsense. She was alive and Paul was dead and now... Now they were both dead, plain and simple. What was the point in stupidity at a time like this? Rest a while, that was what her sister said she should put on Paul's stone. Only sleeping. Crap. He was extinguished, extinct, destroyed. Only thing left of him was rubbish. Clothes, papers, his name on letters, that wasn't anything. You lived and you died and when you were dead you didn't linger, all the things you left gave no sense of you, they were only reminders of how absolutely you were gone.

But she knew Harford wouldn't understand and was basically kind in his own incompetent manner so she said, "I deal with things my own way," and followed it up with a glowering look that made him shuffle papers. She'd given him a speech once about

105

how she was sorry his expertise was in categories but she wasn't prepared to let him put her in one, so he could stuff his units per week and his free help to give up smoking, and since then he'd always been quick to retreat from confrontation.

Eva also thought it was a terrific idea, so Malcolm suggested they tell Holly fast – before she could – and when Eva wasn't there. Belinda said she was sure it wouldn't matter, though she thought it probably would, but it seemed impolite to acknowledge in the open what a pain in the arse Eva was capable of being. Malcolm was definite, though.

"Ah, if it came from Eva I think Holl might be tempted to be contrary," he said. "Not without reason, mind you, but still."

In the way of these things, despite the urgency, there didn't seem to be a moment to broach the subject. Belinda sometimes wondered what happened to time. She spent whole days and never saw Holly on her own, they just passed each other in rooms on the way to places they had to get to. There was never a chance to talk, so she'd just pat Holly's shoulder, because that was mostly what she meant to communicate anyway.

The next morning, though, she was by the tractor and Malcolm was saying he could go to the cash-and-carry if it would save her time and Holly came out of the house, with that habit she was developing of looking over her shoulder as if she expected some-one to run after her any minute.

"Just the woman!" Malcolm said, clapping Holly on the shoul-der with exactly the kind of jolliness she hated, except her face was transformed with pleasure because it was him who'd done it. That was Malcolm's trouble, he could get away with anything, he always had.

"Got something to tell you," Belinda said more sharply than she meant, wondering why her manner was never easy like Malcolm's.

Holly's reaction was pretty much what Belinda expected. "So you think I'm crazy, then," she said, defiant but not confrontational, simply leaving it to them to do the work, which was one of her more disconcerting abilities.

"A nut-job," Malcolm said, nodding. "As a hatter. Loony-tunes. Absolutely. Whereas your Mum and I, of course, are absolutely normal."

Holly smiled and that was how easy it was, Belinda realised. She wasn't persuaded yet, but from that moment on she was prepared to be.

"Don't take any nonsense, I shouldn't, if you do go," Belinda said.

Holly said, "No Belinda," very gravely, and for an odd moment it was like the good times when the girls used to tease her, laughing together, and she'd have to smother her own laughter while they did it.

Holly wandered off saying she'd think about it and Malcolm said, "I think that went pretty well, don't you, all things considered?" Belinda smiled and then, as usual, there was Eva tottering out of the house in her ridiculous shoes. Eva crinkled her whole face in fellowship when she saw them, and Belinda thought, not for the first time, that she knew exactly what Eva was thinking. Because of what had happened, she always would.

"How are we, then, dears?" Eva said, and Belinda wondered why she found it so hard simply to respond with some pleasant banality, but somehow it was beyond her, so she swung herself up onto the tractor and said to a space in the air between Malcolm and Eva, "Do the cash-and-carry if you don't mind. Holly will tell you what we need."

The noise of the tractor starting saved her from Eva's response, which doubtless would have been disappointed but understanding, and she revved the engine hard, mostly because it was increasingly needing it, that was another thing that wanted doing, the tractor and about four other machines were all overdue a service. Not that there'd be anything to pay for it if the bank manager kept up his stupid way of behaving. But if by revving the engine Eva also understood that there was work to be done and it was hard and serious and smelt of diesel, then that wasn't the worst thing in the world.

Once she was halfway down the drive Belinda relaxed, a little, the tight grip she held on her mind. The cab of a tractor was the perfect place to do that. It was the right size, and full of instruments she knew exactly how to operate. The psychologist Holly might see would probably say it was a sense of power. The machine giving her the illusion of control, propping up her insecurities, whatever they were. Unresolved grief issues, some rubbish like that. They'd probably be right, too, but so what? Being able to describe why something helped didn't mean anything. You needed to do it, over and over, until it worked. Maybe she'd ask Holly to take out the little Massey Ferguson and plough over one of the patches on the hill. Might help, couldn't hurt.

She climbed out to do the gate at the turning into North Field. After she'd closed it behind her she paused before getting back into the cab, and looked out over the shallow dip in the land leading down to the valley. From here she could see the fields they'd had to sell the last time things had been bad: nearly a hundred acres spreading out to the north and east. Colin Thomas had them now, not that he had the first idea how to look after them properly.

She felt the old ache of loss. The same every time she looked at land that had been hers and now had nothing to do with her. It was a constant in her life, had been ever since the first sale when Dad was still farming. Land that had been her world, a wide expanse of earth and sky that took every ounce of effort and desire and work to coax into life every year, gone forever. Like an amputated limb, Paul had said, which wasn't right, but showed that he'd thought about it. Even if it wasn't understanding, it was an attempt to understand. That was why she'd loved him. He tried, as much as you could hope; and if that turned out not to be enough, he never got frustrated like most men. He just accepted there was a difference there, and got on with it. Couldn't ask for more. Not really.

21

Holly stood at the top of the embankment, feeling the beat of her blood in every single vein. She felt sick but certain. Apart from anything else, it was too late to change her mind. She squeezed Ben's hand. His palm was sweating; hers too probably.

"Are you sure about this?" he asked.

Holly took her time. She half-turned and looked back up the long sweep of the fields to the house. Still no sign of Yvonne. Judging by last time she might have half-an-hour, or even more. And then again the elastic pull might re-assert itself and Yvonne might discover them together – and discover the Reservation; but she had to let life happen. *Do it and come what may*, she thought. She turned back and looked down at the road. The air gasped, swirled, push-pulled in the passage of traffic, and the smell of oil coiled around them. Protection. At last she turned to Ben and smiled. "Trust me," she said.

He chose not to make a joke, which was just another way in which he was perfect, and she watched the road, her eyes keen, feeling like a kestrel surveying the ground. Then she saw it: the Gap. The one. Unless the red car was going to move into the fast lane and pull forwards and fill the space... but no.

"Now," she said, and together they ran down the bank.

A lot had happened in the last three days to bring her to this point: running towards the tarmac, about to share freely the only place in the world she'd ever had to herself. It had started with that first departure of Yvonne. Ben must have thought she was mad when it happened. They'd gone to his room to talk about what they'd heard on the stairs and it was everything she could do not to hug him and dance around the room and tear down the curtains and wear them like a ball-gown. Yvonne had gone and the liberation had made her giddy. Was that it, she'd thought over and over again; was she free?

She hadn't been – at least not for good – but she'd had long enough to savour the joy of it, the feeling of light and air and hope. Ben had talked about Daddy and Eva, seeming surprisingly bitter. He said he knew that Eva was all over men, that's what she did, but he hadn't thought it meant anything. Though Derek – his real father, whom Holly had never met – Derek had said that she was a bird that couldn't be caged. Yes, like a vulture, Holly thought to herself, so full of glee she had almost laughed aloud. And after all she'd had an affair with Malcolm, that was how their marriage started, Ben said. Holly had been nodding and listening but as the first euphoria of Yvonne's departure started wearing off she'd been too delighted by the idea of being in Ben's room to say anything very clever or insightful. He'd found a lamp from somewhere instead of the cold overhead light and there was a guitar and clothes over everything and a smell Holly breathed deeply, remembering it from visits to the Family's house: slightly spicy, like incense, probably just deodorant but like no-one else's room she'd ever been in.

Then Ben had asked what she thought about the idea of Daddy and Eva together. Holly had tried to consider it properly. Part of her instinctively felt furious with Eva, but then she always felt pretty furious with Eva. Really, she supposed, Eva was very like

Yvonne. Yvonne always got what she wanted, and maybe it was that simple: Eva had decided she wanted Daddy, so it had happened. Just as she'd been trying to think of a way of saying this that wouldn't make her sound like a heartless aunt- and sister-hating crone she'd looked across the room and seen Yvonne standing with her back against the door. Watching her. As if she had never been away.

The only good part about Yvonne's return was that Holly hadn't been able to help crying and Ben had come over to the bed and put his arm round her again. Looking back Holly could remember that feeling even more clearly than the exultation of Yvonne's departure. She'd leaned against him and wondered what it was that made him so... special, she guessed. Though that wasn't the right word for it. The most important thing about Ben was that he wasn't a boy, at least not in the ordinary Danny Blake sense of the word. Ordinary boys had always seemed awkward and ungainly to Holly, unable to understand what was going on around them. Their clumsiness was scary: they moved with a kind of spastic rage, and were so quick to anger and cruelty and unkindness, even though people seemed not to mind half the time, as if it was understood that they didn't really mean it. People also never seemed to mind when boys walked into a room and ignored what everyone else was doing and started to talk loudly about something everyone already knew. She'd even seen them *congratulated* for doing this at school – for 'taking part' – as if it was some kind of feat not just to slouch into the room and snigger and slump into a corner. As if not doing that was worth a prize. If Holly had been in charge she wouldn't have congratulated them, she'd have given them a quiet warning not to speak again for the next five years, and if they'd broken it she'd have had their tongues removed. Painlessly; she wasn't a monster.

Holly had known for sure that Ben wasn't a boy, not in any way she understood it, the last time they'd all visited the house in Guildford. He had two or three guitars in his room there and he'd been playing one quietly, almost silently to himself, but before that could seem cool and off-putting, Sal-style, he'd looked up with a grave unspoken sense of welcome. When she went in she'd noticed all the team pictures on his walls. He was brilliant at hockey apparently and had trophies everywhere. He'd seen her looking and said ruefully he was pretty embarrassed by them but not enough to hide them. There was something so open about him, so gentle, so wry, so warm, and she'd stayed there without talking for almost ten minutes before Yvonne had come in and ruined everything.

Anyway. This was the amazing person with whom, ever since that night on the stairs, Holly had shared a secret. She hadn't known whether he would tell the others or not, but the next morning he came to her room and said he thought they shouldn't. She hadn't been able to help the smile on her face. After a moment he'd come in properly and walked around looking at her stuff. None of it was real treasure, she kept that in the Reservation, but all the things he particularly noticed were her favourites. He ran his finger over the blackened silver skull ring that she'd thought was the most amazing thing ever to be created in the world when she was eight, and he picked up and hefted the polished onyx ashtray, as heavy as a murder weapon. He didn't say anything, just nodded, and she felt like she was a collector receiving the approval of a connoisseur. She glowed as he walked away and wondered how anyone could want anything but to fall into step with him and let him lead them to a new destiny.

After that Holly had already half-decided to tell Ben about Yvonne and Will Sadler and everything that had happened, but it had taken the trip to the psychologist to make up her mind. He'd been a nice man called Dr Gould, neat and dapper, with close dark hair and glasses and greying stubble. His face had looked kind but then that was no surprise, he'd hardly look like a Bond villain if he spent his life telling people not to mind so much that members of their family were dead. He had sat across a low table from her and said she could tell him anything and for a long moment she had wondered if that was true. She'd even asked, in a low voice, what he would say if she told him her sister wasn't dead but was standing in the room watching them both. He'd half-smiled and it wasn't a patronising smile of disbelief, either, and he'd said that there were more things in heaven and earth than were in most people's philosophies, and that no-one really understood the effects a loss like Holly's could have, and whether it was a way that her mind was using to deal with the situation or some other kind of phenomenon it was certainly something she could tell him about and she shouldn't worry about sounding crazy.

Holly nearly did, and even the prospect of it had given her an incredible sense of release, but just before the words had come flooding out she'd asked one more question: what if other people could see her sister too? He'd been making a note as she said it, and for half a second it seemed like his pen stopped, just the end of it, as if he'd been struck by a thought, but then he kept on writing and said she could tell him anything at all. Holly had paused for a whole minute and then she'd realised what had just happened. If she told him that this wasn't some little fantasy, but that as far as she was concerned it was real and physical and actually existed, then for all his nice words about it not mattering, it would matter. He would shift his expectations. He would think that she was properly ill: that she had delusions, that she was acting on her delusions, that they might get worse. She knew what would happen next, too. He wouldn't mention it again, he'd let her talk, but his pen would be moving, and he'd have written something in his notes that could change her life forever. She'd felt the thrill of understanding something that she'd have missed when she was younger. He'd looked at her quizzically and like an actor or a spy she'd shrugged and said it just felt as if people were watching her sometimes, and she'd seen that wariness leave him. He'd nodded confidently again and told her that what had happened scared people, she should be under no illusions about that, and from then on it was easy.

On the way home afterwards she'd realised two things. First, she had to tell someone: the sensation of relief when she'd been about to tell Dr Gould had almost overwhelmed her, and she couldn't go much longer without letting her guard down. Second, Ben was her only possible option. That realisation grew in her mind in the pick-up on the way home and when they pulled into the yard she saw him sitting outside the back door in a patch of sunlight writing in a notebook and knew she was right: she could trust him with anything. The dogs had come out because of the car and as soon as they'd barked dutifully at it they ran to Ben. For a moment he sighed and tried to continue with his notebook, but then he put it down and grabbed hold of Dizzy, who yelped and turned round and round looking so happy that Holly wouldn't have been surprised to hear her laugh out loud. Horace watched sadly, knowing his turn for such delights had passed, but then Ben reached out to him, too, and he preened his stiff back in the warmth of Ben's attention and Holly thought, *Bring him. Take him to the Reservation. The next time Yvonne goes... if she goes... share it with him.*

22

When their feet hit tarmac Holly laughed aloud in the certainty that this was right. She felt Ben pulling back, wanting to slow down, but she knew how to do this. They ran straight towards a car and she saw a flash of a face turned towards the window, registering surprise, and then it was snatched away. Their feet gritted on the hard shoulder and they crossed the rumble strip, which was the point of no return, and were running on the Motorway itself.

"Fucking *hell*, Holly," she heard him call out over the noise of the cars that had just passed, and then they were in the Gap, when the traffic parted like the sea and you had one moment if you didn't trip to make it across. They reached the middle lane and Holly pulled them sharply right because she wanted to step on a cat's eye, which was what she did, crossing the lanes, when she felt really happy. The rubber depressed under her foot and sprang her forwards. Two last huge steps and they were at the Reservation. She let go of his hand and jumped over the barrier into the only world in which she'd ever been alone.

He stopped, she'd known he would, the barrier was so much higher than it looked from inside a car.

"Holly, what are we doing," he said, shouting over the noise.

"Showing you something," she called back. "Climb over, come on."

She looked up the hill towards the farm. Still nothing. Yvonne had disappeared twice since the first time, once for as long as an hour. They might get away with this. Ben gingerly climbed over the sharp corroded edge of the barrier and she pulled him into the long brittle grass that filled the Reservation, making him duck down so that it gave them cover. She could feel him shaking from the adrenaline that she felt coursing through her own body too.

"Jesus," he said. "Look at it…"

She did, for a long moment. In the few seconds that they both stared, dozens of cars thrummed past, transporting a hundred different human beings to a hundred destinations. The air shook as if it were solid, as if it were a rug being beaten and they were feeling its ripples against their skin.

"I thought you never came here?" he said.

"I lied," she replied, simply, liking the way it sounded.

"So… you come here and just watch it all?" he asked.

"There's more than that," she said. "Come on. But stay low, all right? If too many people see us they might call someone."

Not that it would really matter, she knew. She loved this place because whatever people thought, it was already too late. By the time they realised what they'd seen they were hundreds of metres away. Once she thought someone might have called the police, because she'd seen the flash of a police car in the fast lane and the driver had been looking at the Reservation. As soon as they'd gone past she'd quickly buried the Things and waited her moment and run back across the road and up the embankment. She'd been right, too, because the policeman had come off at the next junction and come back the other way. No good, though, he was too late. And that was that. They'd looked for her, but they would never find her. In the Reservation she was safe.

They scrambled along for a few metres towards the Clearing. On this stretch of Motorway the Reservation was about three metres across, with barriers either side. There was a tangle of grass and spiky weeds in between, covered with a grey film of dust, with vivid flashes of bright metal and plastic half-buried among the yellowing roots. At the Clearing the grass and nettles parted to reveal a brown oval of dry, crumbling earth, mottled with iridescent patches of oil. At the heart of the Clearing Holly had buried the tin chest that contained the Things: her most treasured possessions. Chief among them was the Skull, a fox's skull, the bone as thin as china, the missing snout dreadful, the gaping eyes all-seeing. Before she had brought it to the Reservation, she'd talked to it. Once she had it here, where it clearly belonged, she prayed to it.

She led Ben, still stooping, into the Clearing, and they sat on the soft dry earth. In summer it teemed with ants and lazy wasps and tiny quick spiders skittering into the cracks but now it was bare and cold under their hands. He looked around, nodding slowly.

"So… is this like a kind of ritual thing?" he said.

That was it, Holly thought. She should start talking now. Yes, exactly, it's a ritual. Let me show you. And she should start digging in the earth, splitting its dry surface, uncovering the box. He'd watch, fascinated, as she dusted the earth from its surface like an archaeologist; he'd help her tug open the lid against the weight of soil, and one by one she would reveal the Things.

Somehow, though, she felt unable to do it. Partly it was the thought of Yvonne arriving halfway through. The idea of her finding this place at all was bad; her finding it with the Things spread out like goods for sale made Holly feel sick. And yet, even while she told herself that was all it was, she knew there was something else. He'd smile, of course he'd smile, buried treasure would make anyone smile. But what if he didn't get it, didn't properly understand? As she took out the Things his face would get tired from smiling, as if it was Christmas and he was politely receiving gifts he didn't really want. He'd nod, and ask all the right questions, and everything magical would drift away from the Things like the eddying fumes of cars and be gone, and by the time she had taken them all out of the chest she would see them through his eyes: the cheap childish trinkets of a little girl, and once she'd seen them that way, they'd never hold any power again.

She took a deep breath. All right, so she couldn't show him the Things. There was still the little matter of a haunting to share.

★ ★ ★

Ben watched Holly's face as she started to talk. He told himself that this experience was amazing. She'd created a world of her own out here. It was the kind of thing people talked about doing, but never did, not for real. Certainly he would never have managed it. And she had invited him into this world; she had trusted him with it. On top of that to be sitting, hidden, inches from cars passing at a hundred miles an hour was pretty amazing, too. The smell of the fumes was everywhere, like glue, or paint. If they stayed out here long enough they'd probably get high – maybe that was why she came...

The trouble was that none of these amazing things were registering with him. He wanted to take pleasure in them, to be surprised and delighted by them, but he'd forgotten how. None of it touched him. He'd been trying: had been saying what he hoped were the right words. But it was as if he was in a game where he made up what he should say and how he should act, while all the time feeling more and more numb. He concentrated, knowing he had to stay focused. She'd started telling him the craziest story he'd ever heard and he had to react, had to show her he was listening and impressed and interested, though the more he tried the more scary he found it that he wasn't feeling any of those things at all. Should he take her hands? Maybe that's what a normal person would do. It would probably just be creepy, though, if he did it. She told him all this stuff about Yvonne then paused and he knew he had to respond.

"So... that's crazy," he said.

Holly shrugged. "I know. And I thought maybe I was crazy, right? Hallucinating, brain injury, whatever."

He gripped his hands. Stupid, he told himself, to use that word, of course that was the meaning she'd take. "Holly, I didn't..." he started but she interrupted, putting her hand on his arm. He looked at it, feeling the pressure of it but nothing else.

"No, but listen, all right?" she said. She started telling him about some guy called Will Sadler who had a ghost too, and about Douggie turning up and a freaky tall guy who'd known about the whole thing, and all the time he was staring at her hand, for much too long, he knew. So he looked up and smiled and shifted forwards to show that this mattered to him, because what she was saying was extraordinary and of course it did matter, it really did.

He'd moved so close that he had to look at different parts of her face, each eye in turn, or her mouth, because otherwise her face didn't make sense, and he kept looking around her face trying to make sense of it when he realised she'd stopped talking and was looking into his eyes. Suddenly he saw what was going to happen, and knew he couldn't let her do it, but before he had a chance to move she leaned forward and he felt the flutter of breath against his face and they were kissing. For a second he did nothing, then he felt both their lips open and their teeth touch and her tongue and suddenly that sick feeling surged inside him again, and this time he knew there was nothing he could do; this time he was swept away by it, and it raced over him, and he was drowning.

★ ★ ★

120

Holly thought it had been visible in his face the moment she pulled away. When they'd kissed she'd felt as if blood was radiating through her, not trickling along veins. His mouth and lips had been hot and vital and alive and the furthest thing from kissing Danny she could imagine. But when she opened her eyes she saw his face twisted and full of sourness. She wanted to tell him that she hadn't meant to do it, but he rocked back onto his heels and away from her.

"Ben?" she said, puzzled. He didn't reply, just shook his head. It was so immediate: he was looking sick. As if she disgusted him. She could still feel the blood moving through her flesh, but coldly now, and her skin was prickly and painful. "Ben," she said again, and he stood up. He was so revolted by her that he was going to leave without a word. If he'd been different she might just have felt sad and stupid, but this was Ben: this was a person who would never do something so horrible, who must know how he was making her feel and didn't care, because something about her was so awful that he was prepared to do it. That made her furious, and she stood up too. They were in full view of the traffic, and the cars hissed past, full of astonished faces turned their way.

"Don't just go," she called over the noise, which was louder now they could see the road, but he was already walking away. She went after him and tried to turn him round, but he was a lot bigger than she was. She didn't let go of his arm, though.

"Holly... I've got to go," he said, still not looking at her.

Holly registered the thought only a second before she started saying it, feeling a sensation of helpless disaster. "Why? Got to find Julia and tell her all about this?" Inside she shrivelled up to hear herself say it, but she stood her ground.

"What?" he said.

"Well it's like you can't spend ten minutes apart, right? Like you're married."

She knew how stupid she was being but she wasn't prepared for his expression: he was looking at her with contempt, almost hatred.

"Just fuck off, Holly," he said. "All right?" Then he climbed over the barrier and waited on the edge of the road as if he was crossing a high street not a motorway. Before she could decide whether or not to follow him he saw a gap and ran across the road in a few easy strides.

Holly watched him climb the embankment and then looked around at the cars, realising how exposed she was, and sank quickly down to her knees. She carefully shuffled around so her legs were in front of her and lay down on her back. The grass fringed her vision and all she could see between it was the white sky. She lay there with one hand on her stomach, feeling stupid and tearful and angry, waiting for Yvonne. It didn't take long.

23

Holly thought that what had happened with Ben at the Reservation was probably one of the worst things in the world, and she'd have been quite happy to defend that against anyone who said that the deaths of a sister and a father were perhaps worse, but she found out when she got back to the house that actually it was the second-worst thing in the world, because the worst thing was what he'd done afterwards. She walked in to find them all in the kitchen, apart from Ben, and from the way they all looked up together when she entered she knew it was bad. Sal and Julia left quickly, Julia looking at her with open fascination, and Malcolm was the one who said what she already knew: Ben had told them about Yvonne's ghost. Ironically Yvonne drifted in exactly as her name was mentioned, not that she or anyone else would notice. Holly stared at him from the doorway for a moment, feeling trapped and panicked, vaguely aware of Belinda smoking and Eva watching her beadily. Then she fixed her eyes on the ground instead, but that wasn't much better. She could sense Eva's hungry gaze even without looking.

Afterwards Holly went to her room, Yvonne on her heels as ever, and imagined killing her whole family. This wasn't like fantasising about Yvonne's death; that had been about being alone, and now she knew she'd never be properly alone, not even after she was dead. This was different: this was about the act of violence. She mostly imagined killing Eva, though she knew that was just cowardice. It wasn't brave or special to want to kill Eva, there must have been hundreds of people who shared that desire. Really she must have wanted to kill Ben, even if she couldn't admit it to herself. How could he have done this?

She knew that one of the adults would insist on talking to her, so it was no surprise when there was a knock on the door and Malcolm appeared. He left the door open and sat on the end of her bed.

"Look, Holl," he said, "I can't imagine you're going to enjoy this, but you know I have to ask about what Ben's told us."

She nodded, sitting on the bed with her legs drawn up, wondering how much Ben had said and how much she'd have to lie. He asked about Yvonne, which was easy: she just gave him an edited version of what she'd said to the psychologist. She said how alone she felt and how it seemed like Yvonne was with her all the time. While she spoke she didn't look at Malcolm; instead she stared into the distance as far as he was concerned and in fact into Yvonne's pale impassive face and felt a vicious sense of triumph at fooling him, at fooling everyone. Then he asked her, as she'd feared, about Douggie and the truck. So Ben had told them everything, then. This time it was much harder, because what she'd seen and what it might mean was racing around her mind and she desperately wanted to tell Malcolm, but only if he would believe it, and she knew he wouldn't. He'd lump it together with what he obviously thought about Yvonne and tell her some rubbish about how it was a traumatic time and it was natural to think there were reasons for bad things to happen but that didn't mean anyone was doing this on purpose and blah blah blah. So she just shrugged and said how upset she was to find out that Douggie was working for MAFF, and that she had been asking Ben how he could go around killing animals when he looked after them too, that was all. She could tell Malcolm wasn't really satisfied, but he didn't seem to think she was dangerously crazily. After a while he nodded.

"There's one last thing," he said. "Ben is… this isn't the first time Ben has got like this, ok? So I don't want you to think it has anything to do with you, or being here, or anything like that. We're all under pressure, and Ben… well. He's reacted like this before."

Holly shrugged again, feeling that she was behaving like the perfect teenager as if she had instructions on a card, and he went away. She did believe him about Ben; Malcolm had seemed genuinely concerned, and besides, she didn't think he'd make something like that up. But he didn't know that the change had nothing to do with pressure, and everything to do with her.

Over the next few days she began to see the completeness of the transformation. The Ben she thought she knew had gone. Now he was blank and cold and wouldn't look at her. It was as if his living, breathing person had been replaced by an inert waxen imposter, not properly alive. He wasn't nasty to her; he just wasn't anything to her, which was even crueller. She wanted to shout at him but the thought of him absorbing her rage, bland and indifferent, was unbearable. So mostly she tried not to think about him, and not to look at him, even during their lessons, so that she didn't have to be reminded of his expression after they'd kissed; didn't have to wonder what it was about her that had repelled him with such violence and such finality.

It was almost as bad with everyone else. They'd all started to treat her differently, apart from Belinda, who was rough and kind and absent as always. Eva, Julia and Sal all had an avid new-found interest in her, though each of them showed it in different ways. Eva said less to her, but kept eyeing her from a distance like a hungry magpie. Sal looked at her more and more too, and that eye contact almost burned. Sometimes Sal even started conversations, though she was usually so opaque that Holly had no idea what to say in response. Julia was the worst, she was always touching Holly compassionately now that she'd found out there was something wrong with her, putting her heavy hand on her arm, just like she used to touch Ben (that had stopped since he'd changed).

Even Malcolm, who Holly had thought would be the one person along with Belinda not to make her feel awkward, was different around her: she often caught him looking at her with a deep, thoughtful expression that he tried to alter as soon as she looked up, but too late. And in the middle of it all was the new Ben. Being in the same room as him was like being that bird in the jar in the picture when they were sucking out the air. He was draining all the life in the house. She started to spend a lot of time outside. Yvonne was disappearing every day now, for at least an hour, and she walked by herself. Once she went to the Reservation, thinking that the Skull could help her, but she hadn't even dug out the box; it felt wrong, as if Ben had really broken something.

Three days later it was what had been their birthday and was now just her birthday. Holly had been expecting it to be mostly hideous but at least low-key. That was before she counted on Eva, who tried to persuade Belinda that Holly should have a party.

"I know it won't be easy, darling, in the circumstances," she said sweetly when Belinda looked at her incredulously. "I'm just saying that at a time like this perhaps it's important for all of us.

You know, to show we are carrying on with life. Surely her friends from school would like to support her, wouldn't they?"

The last bit was said in an undertone that Holly nevertheless heard perfectly clearly. She'd been eavesdropping while making herself look busy by watching Julia, who was in turn watching Ben with a pathetically pleading expression. He was silently playing one of the very few computer games Holly and Yvonne had owned, which he'd been doing more or less non-stop since the Reservation, on the rare occasions he wasn't asleep in his room. For a horrible second Holly thought that Belinda, who was hardly speaking any more, would simply let it happen on the grounds of least resistance. She imagined Nathan Osgood and Tom Weaver and all of Yvonne's other friends being driven through the disinfectant trough that had been installed at the end of the drive, past the box that Vic had made for the postman, who would no longer enter, and up to a house that was full of the anticipation of death, on a day when everyone would be feeling only the shadow cast by Yvonne's absence. She imagined the terrible silence as they ate too-soft cake and drank coke (unless Malcolm gave them all cider, which wasn't impossible) and listened to music that Holly didn't like while no-one danced. If Ben hadn't become what he'd become it might have worked: the old Ben would have been surrounded by crowds of boys and would have suggested games and it might have been fun. The new Ben probably wouldn't even come, just stay in his room and hate her remotely from there.

Luckily Malcolm came in from the garden while Eva was speaking, in time to tell her that the idea was spectacularly ill-judged and insensitive even for her, and although that started an argument that lingered in the corners of the house all afternoon, it did get Holly off the hook. It was decided they would have a birthday lunch instead. Malcolm announced a school holiday in honour of the occasion, though Holly suspected this was mostly so that he could stay up drinking the night before and avoid Julia's eager questions in the morning, which she'd started asking to make up for Ben's protracted silence in class. Belinda was out in the fields again, where she went more and more often even though there was less to do, so Holly spent the morning of her birthday in the yard trying to get answers from Vic.

It didn't go well. He had been even less talkative than usual since the movement restrictions had come in. When she found him in the yard he was staring down the hill and over the Motorway.

"They're starting, then," he said heavily. She followed his gaze. Across the Motorway, on the floor of the valley, she saw heavy smoke as if they were burning stubble but much thicker. Beneath it was a line of glowing light.

"That's..." she started, and he nodded.

"Burning the carcasses," he said. "They soak them in paraffin. That's why they go up like that."

For a moment Holly wondered if the fire was on Will's land but then she realised it must be further off and felt relieved. She didn't know why: all his animals were dead, after all, what did it matter where they were burnt? They watched the fire in silence for a while, Holly feeling rage and doubt and the desire to know all surging inside her. She had to learn more, to find out what was really happening and why. Vic was greasing the big Case tractor and she started helping, wondering how she could begin without sounding crazy. Eventually, trying to seem casual and off-hand but feeling cringingly awkward and obvious, she asked if Vic knew where Douggie had worked before he came to the farm. Vic didn't, just said she'd have to ask her Mum, which wasn't much good as Holly didn't know how to find her nor how to talk to her right now even if she did. Vic didn't have answers to any of her other questions, either, about where Douggie lived or what he did with his spare time, just grunting in response. The one useful

128

thing he did tell her was when she asked about friends: "He's one of that whole lot," he said.

"Which lot?" she asked quickly.

He lowered himself to the ground with a groan, ready to reach under the engine. "Those lads from the army base, other side of the Downs," he said. "There's always been a few who make a pain in the arse of themselves when they've had too many. Fights, smashing stuff up, silly stuff."

Army lads, Holly thought. Maybe that's why Douggie joined up with the slaughtermen – to work with the army. The tall man, the one who knew: if he was in the army, if he'd known Douggie from before, then he might have recruited him deliberately. She asked if Vic could describe any of the people Douggie hung out with but either he couldn't or he'd just had enough of speaking. He disappeared under the tractor for a minute and when he levered himself out he said it was time for lunch, so they went in and Holly discovered that there was still room for surprises: because although no guests had been invited, someone had asked Douggie, and she was suddenly confronted with the man himself who muttered, "Happy Birthday," and thrust a card into her hands before she could draw herself up and ask why he was persecuting Will Sadler, and whether – it couldn't be true but she couldn't help thinking it – whether he was deliberately spreading death and destruction wherever he went.

24

Lunch was bad, very bad. Ben and Belinda were in their own worlds, as usual. Holly found herself in an unlikely coalition with Julia, because she'd hated Douggie ever since she'd found out he was a slaughterman. The moment she saw him Julia said indignantly, "What's he doing here?"

Douggie flushed but Malcolm took him aside and Eva gave Julia what she clearly hoped was an inaudible lecture on manners that the whole room had to endure. Sal seemed to feel the same as them, so far as it was possible to tell, and they all sat in a sullen line glaring at Douggie. Holly noticed that he was particularly uneasy under her gaze, and never took her eyes off him – partly because she enjoyed that discomfort, but mostly because she wanted to see what he did about Yvonne. If the tall man could see ghosts, and this was all somehow related, then maybe Douggie could, too. However, if so, he was a good actor: he showed no awareness of Yvonne at all.

Given that Sal and Julia seemed too angry to speak, Ben and Belinda were non-starters, and neither Vic nor Douggie exactly conversationalists at the best of times, the burden of talking should have fallen on Malcolm and Eva. Normally in these circumstances they did talk a lot, carrying on a coded public argument by swapping waspish statements. Today, though, they both seemed odd to Holly. Eva was distracted, and spent a lot of time focused only on her knife and fork. This meant Malcolm didn't have an opponent, which ought to have given him the chance to run wild, but he wasn't like he'd been when he first came to the farm, full of stories and jollity. He made occasional jokes, but was sardonic at their reception. He was also determined that everyone should drink a lot of wine, but Douggie was his only taker.

"You and me, I think, Douggie," he said, getting another bottle. "If anyone deserves a breather from their work, it's you." Douggie seemed to flush again, though given the amount he'd drunk it wasn't surprising.

After the main course there was cake and a horrible rendition of Happy Birthday. Holly looked at Belinda while she made her wish to make it clear that she was wishing for the farm to survive, though she added private requests for liberation from Yvonne and answers respectively. Ben asked in a monotone whether they knew it was illegal to sing Happy Birthday on television because it was still in copyright and Eva tried to fill the silence that followed that remark with an encouraging noise of feigned interest and Holly realised he had become a boy, he really had, that was all that was left of Ben.

"Right, Holly," Malcolm said as the cake was cut, pronouncing his words carefully. "Birthday means games. And yes, let me forestall you, no-one is in the mood for games, but if I learnt one thing as a teacher it is that moods can be acquired when necessary, and I think the necessity is plain." He wasn't slurring but when he said 'necessity' Holly could see him frowning with the effort.

The game involved pens and paper and guessing famous people in pairs. Belinda said she had to go while they did this and she'd be back for tea. As she left she put her hand on Holly's shoulder and Holly wondered if she'd been able not to think about Yvonne even for a second all day. She wished Belinda could see Yvonne, just once – she was standing by the window now, watching the table; but then again Holly would only have wanted Belinda to see that Yvonne was happy, and since it was impossible to know what Yvonne was feeling, perhaps it wouldn't have been any comfort. Vic excused himself too and Eva said that someone had better clear up so Holly was left with the seats emptying between her and Douggie and a horrible fear that he was going to have to be her teammate. In the end though Malcolm said he should pair up with Douggie so that they could treat it as a drinking game and Ben and Sal were together, obviously, which left her with Julia.

Julia whispered that if they had to guess famous people all the ones they put into the hat should be murderers like Douggie, but she couldn't think of very many after Hitler and Jack the Ripper. Ben and Sal started whispering too, probably coming up with obscure philosophers that no-one else would be able to guess, and Malcolm was fixing the rules about when he and Douggie had to drink, the answer to which seemed to be nearly always. Everyone's absorption in their teams meant Holly had to find things to say to Julia. For a wild second she considered discussing Yvonne's ghost and Will Sadler and the whole story. Julia knew, after all, they all did now, even though no-one was talking to her about it. Watching Julia carefully completing her name cards, though, in loopy handwriting with circles above the 'i's, Holly realised she was unlikely to be much help all-in-all.

Despite how everyone was feeling the game was almost fun. One person in each pair had to give clues and the other person had to guess as many of the names as possible. Malcolm and Douggie were hopeless, mostly because either one or both of them would be drinking instead of talking. Also, Douggie didn't know anything, Holly realised. He was bad on film stars, bad on politicians, bad on actors and really anyone at all. Ben and Sal were too slow, because Sal refused to speak any faster than her usual dreamy pace even though there was a 60-second limit, and all this meant that she and Julia won by miles. The only odd thing was that Malcolm was quite scornful of them for some reason, or at least of Julia, and said twice that her knowledge of minor celebrities was to someone's credit, he supposed, but not his. She didn't seem to mind though and by the end Holly found herself laughing with Julia at the margin of their victory. Even Ben smiled once or twice.

"Right, the ladies wiped the floor with us, what's next," Malcolm said, pouring himself another large glass. Douggie shook his head and got unsteadily to his feet.

"Got to be back at work," he said. Immediately Holly felt the feeble glow of pleasure fade from the room. She looked at him in dismay. Work? He could hardly stand up. Was he going to go and butcher more animals in this state?

Malcolm said owlishly, "Douggie, if you don't mind me saying, I think that's a very bad idea," but Douggie shook his head.

"Meeting. Find out which... I mean where... where we're going next."

Sal muttered something about scientific precision but Douggie didn't seem to hear, just nodded to the table and made for the door. Halfway there he turned. "Holly," he said. She froze, aware of everyone watching her. "Holly, I just wanted to say I'm really, really sorry. About... about everything."

Holly stared at him. Why? What everything? What did he mean? She could hardly ask in front of everyone, and anyway Douggie turned away immediately and stumbled out. Holly flexed her fingers, which were suddenly tight. What had he been trying to tell her? Was that a kind of confession?

As the door closed Malcolm stood up clumsily too. "Party's not over," he said abruptly, seeming huge now he was on his feet and scarily drunk. Holly hadn't seen him like this, though it was only the way he was most days after lunch, just without the smile. "Dancing," he said. "Sal... bad idea. Julia, you wouldn't want to. Holly?"

He held out his hand to her. She didn't know how to say no without provoking him, but before she could speak Sal said, "God, look at it," and pointed to the window.

They all followed her gaze. Outside the smoke from the fire in the valley had risen. It was a thick unswaying column, a black line unevenly bisecting the white sky. Ben said he was going to look, and went to the door. Sal followed and Julia looked at Holly, and they both looked at Malcolm, and then they got up and followed too.

"Very well," Holly heard him say as they left. "I shall dance alone."

25

Outside the air smelt acrid and sour. Julia lifted her collar and breathed through it. The smoke wasn't black, Holly realised, now she could see it more clearly, but a kind of greasy grey-brown. Ben was in the middle of the yard, watching the solid pillar rise higher and higher. The others went through the garden towards him. Holly hesitated; she wasn't sure she was prepared to stand next to him, to endure his indifference. As she paused she realised Douggie hadn't gone yet, he was still fumbling with his car door. She had a sudden spiteful wish that he would crash, which seemed fairly likely since he could barely stand up, but then she felt ashamed. She didn't know, not yet, what he had to do with this. So ask, she thought. Ask him. The idea of accusing him made her feel hollow with fear – if he did know what she was talking about, who knew what he might say or do; but as she watched he dropped his keys and stood looking for them, blinking. If he was ever going to be harmless surely it was now?

She walked slowly towards him, and stopped far enough away to run. "Douggie," she said.

He looked up quickly. "Holly!" he said. "Oh shit. Holly." He bent down and clumsily took hold of the keys.

"Douggie," she said again, then took a deep breath. "What's going on?"

He leaned against the door of his car. "What?" he said.

"It's… the slaughtering," she said. "The killing…"

She trailed off. She had no idea how to put this. It's something to do with ghosts, Douggie. Tell me. She glanced at Yvonne, and he followed her gaze without any reaction. Surely he was too drunk to be acting? Unless the drunkenness was itself an act. "Why are you doing it?" she said eventually.

He pushed himself upright, and pointed at her with one finger. She took a half-step back, but he just sighted along his finger, and said, "Bang." Then he smiled. It was a horrible smile; it reminded her of the humourless grin on the tall man's face. "That's all it is," he said. "Bang. Bang. Bang. Good money at the end of the week. See?"

She shook her head. "But… you just said you were sorry," she said. He stared. "Inside. You told me you were sorry?"

"Oh. Yeah," he said. "For your sister. Obviously. Why else would I be sorry?"

He frowned at her, his eyes watery and vacuous. She could smell the thick reek of wine on his breath, even from where she stood. He couldn't be lying, she thought, it was impossible. But that only meant Douggie didn't know what was going on. It wasn't that surprising: if there was some plan, some conspiracy, they would hardly tell everyone. Douggie clearly wasn't an insider, but he might still be able to tell her something useful.

"One of the men," Holly said slowly. "At Will Sadler's. He was tall – the driver. You know?"

Douggie nodded heavily. "Liam. Liam Purvis. Yeah. He's all right. Listen, Holl, what is this? Why are you asking all this stuff?"

She shrugged, staring at the ground, trying to give nothing away. "I just wanted to know… why he's doing it," she said. "Why…"

"Why, why, why," he broke in. "Always bloody *why*. Look, Holly, I know it's bad, right? What's going on. Horrible. Shit. I know. But trust me, there is no why. Horrible shit happens all the time.

Liam's in the army, right? Sees terrible things every day. Like he says, at least this time, right, the fuckers aren't shooting back at him. Eh?"

He laughed. Holly felt sick. If she was wrong and there was no plan, somehow that would make it even worse, she thought. If it was all just people like Douggie spreading death and misery round the country for nothing more than good money at the end of the week and a *laugh*... how could anyone live like that? But she remembered Liam's eyes as he looked at Yvonne. There was more to this than Douggie knew.

She didn't have anything else to say to him and maybe what she was thinking was obvious on her face, because after waiting for her to laugh too, he scowled.

"Look, Holly, I was just trying to be nice, ok? But if you want to have a go at me for putting a few bullets in a few dozy fucking cows you can piss off, all right? Fucking kids. Everything's easy when you're a fucking kid."

He turned away, fumbled the keys into the car and got inside. She stepped back as he pulled the car round, screeching. Talking to him had made her feel weak and shivery, but she had at least learned something: she had a name. Liam Purvis. It was a start.

As his car disappeared down the drive Holly looked around for the others. They hadn't moved from the yard. She still felt reluctant, but she told herself to go over and join them. Whatever Ben might say or do to her, she wouldn't let herself live in fear of him. When she reached them Sal looked across at her.

"Like the Bible," she said. "Sodom and Gomorrah."

Holly nodded, looking at Ben. His face was set and he hadn't seemed to notice her. She followed his gaze. The column had

thickened since they got outside and tendrils were coiling out
from it. They had a clear view down across the valley, and she saw
that close to the ground the smoke was spreading across the land
like fog, parting now and then to reveal a line of choked red fire.
The smoke was in the sky above them, too. The light was fading
towards evening anyway, but as well as that there was something
murkier about the air, as if it was stained. The sight of the fire
was hypnotic, and Holly could see how they'd all just stood here
and watched. *Liam Purvis*, she thought. He had done this, or if he
hadn't done this he had used it. She had to find out why.

She was brought out of her absorption by Ben saying, "Oh
fucking hell. *Dad.*"

They all turned and saw where he was looking. It was dim
enough now for the windows of the house to be showing brightly,
and Malcolm and Eva's bedroom was clearly lit. Malcolm was
jumping up and down and it took Holly a minute to realise he
must be dancing because she was distracted by the fact that he was,
again, naked. She felt a terrible compulsion to watch. From this
distance and because he was turning round and round the detail
was hard to make out, but she registered with awful fascination
the flopping thing – no, things – between his legs as he threw his
hands and head around.

"He's such a loser," Ben said bitterly.

"At least he's different," Sal said equably. "Anyway, you don't
have to watch him." She turned away as she said it. Holly looked
down guiltily though she realised Julia was still watching and she
felt her eyes being drawn inexorably back to the window, too.

"Yeah but he doesn't have to stand in front of the whole fucking
world, does he," Ben said. "Why can't he just be… I don't know.
Normal." His eyes met Holly's as he said it and for the first time
in ages she didn't flinch: he hadn't showed the usual spasm of
disgust. Julia was still watching, even though Malcolm had moved

138

away and was only sometimes visible now, but she started suddenly and made a little exclamation.

"What's that?" she said, pointing. Holly looked, but Julia was only indicating a patch of dirt on the ground a few yards away.

"What's what?" she said.

"That. It just fell," Julia said. "From the sky."

Sal stirred. "I saw it too. Maybe a bird dropped it?"

They all walked over to the thing on the ground. In the gloom it was hard to make out, but Holly felt a sense of unease. It wasn't dirt: it was solid, a dark flat thing an inch or two across. She hunched down and was about to touch it when she realised what it was.

"Oh God," she said. "We should go inside."

"What?" Ben said. "What is it?"

Holly looked at him. "Skin."

"Skin? What do you mean, like…"

"Animal skin," she said.

"What?" Julia said, her voice high.

Holly felt tired and sad and sick. "From the fire," she said. "On the wind. It's pretty burnt."

"So… that's a piece of diseased cow?" Julia said, her face screwing up in horror.

"Let's go in," Sal said, but as she did there was a soft noise and ahead of them another patch dropped from the sky. They looked up fearfully. The smoke had spread and was reaching out over them like a second layer of clouds, and against the last of the light in the sky they could see scraps in the air, tumbling and blowing. For a long second Holly tried to tell herself they were bats but they were moving slowly in the air and sinking. Suddenly the soft noise again – and again. Julia screamed and Ben said, "Fuck this, we need cover."

He hurried to Third Barn and pulled at the heavy sliding door.

Julia was first but as soon as the gap opened she stopped, which meant Holly ran into her.

"Go on," Holly started to say, then trailed off, looking over Julia's shoulder. Eva was sitting on the floor on the other side of the barn, sobbing. Really sobbing: her red mouth was open in a soundless wail, and spit was running from it. Holly stared. Eva's skirt was rucked up showing the top of her tights and her thick make-up was dissolving. Her face was *haggard*, Holly thought. She didn't know how old Eva was but she looked ancient. Eva had heard the door open and had her hands up as if to protect herself from their view but she didn't stop crying, it didn't look as though she could. Holly felt a hot flush on her face, but despite that she was cold and unmoving and didn't know what to do. Next to her she could feel that Ben was frozen at the sight too. Holly didn't know how long they would all just have stood and watched if Sal hadn't for once dropped her distant act and taken charge.

"I'll take care of her," she said quietly, stepping inside the door. "Go back to the house. It's ok."

She smiled faintly at them, then pulled the sliding door closed. Holly looked at the others but their faces were blank, like hers felt. They all looked up at the sky then Ben shrugged and started to run through the skin and filth in the air and Holly put her head down and ran after him, with Julia next to her, not thinking about what was falling around them but even more than that not thinking about Eva's face and mouth and how broken she had seemed.

26

Holly wondered what she would have said, a month ago, if she'd been told this was her future: to be sharing a car with Eva and Yvonne's ghost, on the way to an appointment with a medium. She thought of her life before all this happened: going to school, being with Yvonne nearly every second of every day, an Yvonne who laughed and chatted and was often spiteful and had a conscious will of her own rather than the pathetic shadowy spectre sitting in the back seat of the car. It was starting to feel as if all that had happened to a different person, as if it had been a different life, but she refused to let herself think that way. Life had changed and Yvonne had changed but she hadn't, she was the same. Still trapped, she thought, looking in the rear-view mirror. Still not free.

It had taken a long time for Sal to come back to the house and she'd been alone. She'd shaken her head when Holly and the others had looked at her. Sometime after that they'd heard the door but Eva had gone straight upstairs. There'd been no noise from Eva and Malcolm's room and Ben had said scornfully he'd have passed out anyway, so she might have had time alone to fix herself up. When she'd come downstairs she'd looked like Eva again but there was something different. Holly didn't know if it was the memory of what she'd seen or if Eva just couldn't hide it, but her other face, her haggard crying face, had been somehow visible: as if her smile and her repaired make-up might dissolve in a second like jelly and reveal what lay beneath. Ben had been watching Eva too and afterwards had caught Holly's eye with a flicker of their old complicity.

Since then Eva had walked around the house like a hollowed-out version of the person she'd been, teetering on the edge of the children, jumping every time a door opened, and generally seeming like a nervous wreck. She had come into Holly's room one evening and sat on the bed and started to cry again, though not like in the barn, this time just a few tears, pressing a handkerchief against her face so that her make-up would remain intact. Holly wrapped her arms around her knees, her usual strategy now that her room was so often invaded, and sat in silence, her face hot and shiny, feeling stupid and naive not to be able to help. Eventually Eva stopped crying and said she was sorry, sounding angry with herself, and brought out a folded poster of the medium: Marian de la Mare, Seer of Souls and Psychic Channel to the World of the Dead.

"She's in Ledborough. I saw it in the health food shop on the High Street. I know it's probably awfully silly, darling, but might it be worth trying?"

Holly looked at it and then up at Eva and took the plunge. "So... you believe me?" she said. "Have you ever..."

Eva shook her head. "No, I haven't," she said. "But there are all sorts of things we can't explain. And twins, you know, have always had that strange connection. Well of course you know that better than me."

Holly ducked her head, deciding not to disabuse her, and read the poster again. It didn't really fill her with confidence that Marian was a genuine medium: it was purple and yellow and full of large words in italics and pictures of audiences weeping with joy and testimonials that were clearly made-up. Looking at it, though, and at Eva, who seemed much less hard-edged than she had before,

142

and instead anxious and woolly and as if she actually wanted to help – Holly couldn't see a good enough reason why not.

On the way there Holly stared out of the car window. There was something odd about the fields they passed, and she wondered if she was somehow sensing the atmosphere of dread that had settled on the whole countryside, but after a couple of miles she realised it wasn't that, it was the simplest thing in the world: the fields were empty. Usually at this time of year there were sheep everywhere, the hills were dotted with them. Not any more. The blankness of the green slopes was frightening.

As they reached the outskirts of Ledborough Eva said casually, waiting to turn right, "Holly, darling, I wanted to ask you about Ben." Holly gripped the edges of her seat. Not now, she thought, not now, he seems to be getting a bit better, please don't make me go through this… "Of course you know he hasn't been – himself."

Holly nodded tightly, then realised Eva wasn't looking at her, and said, "Yes," in a clipped, abrupt voice.

"I just wanted to ask – and please don't think I'm spying on him – but I just wanted to ask if he'd talked to you about it."

Holly breathed out slowly. Surely that meant Eva didn't know why he'd changed, so at least she wasn't facing accusations. "No," she said. "He hasn't said anything. Literally. Nothing." It came out with more bitterness than Holly had intended, and Eva looked at her.

"I'm sorry darling, I know you and he.."

"What?" Holly asked much too sharply.

"Well, you obviously enjoyed his company. It must have been a shock when he… It was to us, the first time."

Holly looked down at her knees. "What happened?" she said.

"Oh, it was something at school." Eva suddenly sounded near to tears again and Holly felt another lurch of sympathy. "Malcolm won't talk about it and of course the idiot headmaster doesn't know anything. Ben just came home one day like… that. For about a month. I thought that was it, that was him becoming a teenager at last, and it was so… well. Sad. Gradually it got better. Then he was like it again when Malcolm had the whole discipline business. I expect the children've told you all about that."

Holly tried to make an ambivalent noise that didn't commit her either way. It came out sounding very odd but Eva didn't seem to notice.

"When we came here Ben was properly his old self again. Then suddenly, no warning, the shutters come down." She flashed Holly another quick glance. "He really hasn't talked to you? I wouldn't tell him, it's just… I wish I knew. It was so out of the blue this time."

Holly sunk lower in her seat. In some ways she felt comforted, more than when Malcolm had spoken of it. If this was a regular occurrence then maybe she was less guilty for ruining the person he was. In other ways, though, it wasn't much help. Kissing her was the equivalent of Malcolm losing his job. That was great.

It took Eva nearly twenty minutes to find the address. It was somewhere in the estate of new houses at the back of Ledborough, and all the roads looked the same.

"We don't want the wrong door for something like this, do we?" she said, and Holly smiled, almost liking her. Eventually after going back up a road they'd already been along twice they saw the right numbered house. Holly looked at it warily. It was a blank face of red brick and too-small windows and a door with frosted glass. There was no sign of anything mystical. Holly had hoped Eva would wait in the car but she got out too and they rang the bell, standing together on the doorstep. A huge shape loomed behind the frosted glass and Holly assumed it must be some kind of shadow, but when the door opened she realised that was just how big Marian de la Mare was. She was wearing a long blue dress and lots of scarves around her neck and she was enormous, overflowing in all directions like something rising in an oven. She wore perfume even stronger than Eva's, which was saying something, but apart from that they were opposites. Marian had short faded blonde hair and was wearing a pair of glasses with a string leading back round her neck, and although she did have a lot of make-up it was very randomly applied, unlike Eva's carefully constructed face. She beamed when she saw them, really beamed, and Holly couldn't help the wide smile on her own face in response.

"Come in, dears, come in," she said, ushering them forwards. Holly suddenly realised she'd done nothing to prepare in case this woman could actually see Yvonne – hadn't thought at all about what she might say in front of Eva. However, Marian showed no sign of awareness whatsoever. They went in, not to a darkened room like a larger version of Sal's den, which Holly had expected, but to a kitchen overlooking a tiny patch of lawn bounded on all sides by a high wooden fence. Marian offered about thirty different types of tea. As she made it she asked which of them she would be speaking to with a smile and a glance over the top of her glasses like the most perfect of doctors. Holly felt an instinct to trust her, and told herself to stay sceptical: that was all part of the deal, that was how people like Marian operated.

"Just me," she said quietly but with conviction, and Eva tried not to look disappointed. Marian gave Eva the tea and waved her to some magazines, releasing fresh draughts of perfume, and told Holly to come with her.

Holly thought it might at least be worth asking some general questions, even if Marian was a complete fraud. After all people in her situation must have come to see Marian before – she might have heard something useful. They went into a little room that fitted the bill much more closely. The walls were a rich dark green with pictures showing symbols of eyes and the sun and lines of runes. There was an old cherrywood bureau with lots of cubbyholes overflowing with bits of paper, and a piece of silk on the writing surface, and some small cast-iron ornaments and a pack of tarot cards.

Marian lowered herself carefully onto a low sofa, covered with throws, invited Holly to sit at the other end, and without any preamble said, "So it's your sister I take it?"

Holly looked at her cautiously. "Um…" she started, but Marian simply indicated Yvonne with a nod of her head.

"I'd ask her to make herself comfortable too, but they can't hear us, more's the pity, because it would be so lovely if we could speak to them, now wouldn't it?" She twinkled and Holly tried to speak and instead burst into tears.

27

Holly didn't know how long she spent with her head against Marian's huge arm, her hair being stroked and feeling that she had never been this warm in her life before. It was as if she'd fallen asleep: when she finally shook her head and straightened up, wiping her eyes with one of the tissues that Marian wordlessly produced, she thought she might have been there half-an-hour already.

"Now I expect you have some questions, dear," Marian said as Holly moved away at last. "I'm afraid I probably won't have nearly as many answers as you'd like, but I'll do my best."

Holly tried to pull together her mind, which felt dazed and fragmented. What came first? "How... have you always been able to see them?"

Marian shook her head. "Not always. Someone very dear to me passed, and that's when it started. Same as for you, I should think."

Holly looked around the small room. "But I haven't seen... anyone?"

"No," Marian said quietly. "No, I'm afraid I lost him."

"Forever?" Holly could hear the edge in her voice, but she couldn't help it. "He went away... for good?"

Marian looked at her hands. "Yes," she said, simply. Holly could tell that she found this a painful subject and part of her knew she should be sympathetic, but she had a gnawing hunger in her and she had to know. Until Yvonne had started disappearing she'd been sure she would be stuck with her forever, but now, each time she went, Holly had to cope with a surge of hope and then the answering disappointment, and the cycle was wearing her out. The idea that ghosts might eventually leave their victims in peace – that Will may have had his ghost for a lifetime but that others became free – that idea, suddenly presented to her, was over-whelming. Please, she thought, please…

"So… they leave? Eventually? They leave?" she whispered.

Marian smiled sadly. "Not usually, as far as I know," she said. "I'm afraid I'm something of oddity."

Holly hadn't known how strong the surge of hope had been this time until she felt it ebb away again.

"Not… usually?" she said.

"No. Well. I don't think anyone knows. But for most people – and we aren't talking very many, of course, that I've ever come across – I think for most people they tend to stay with you. If that's a comfort?"

Holly gazed at her beseechingly. A comfort. "But…" she said. "She's already started… Sometimes she disappears. For an hour, sometimes more. Surely that means…"

Marian patted her leg. "I honestly don't think anyone knows. You'll have to see what comes."

Holly looked at Yvonne flatly, the certainty of her fate coiling itself back around her. As ever, Yvonne exuded a sense of indif-ference but persistence. Even alive she had been stubborn. Dead, why would she ever depart?

Holly found it hard, at first, to ask anything else. Marian said she would give some general pointers, if that would be help-

148

ful, and Holly nodded. Marian said it was rare, having a spirit, though not as rare as people would think: she must have met a dozen people who had been accompanied by the dead over the course of her career. Because you only saw them if you saw them, it was hard to explain the idea of spirits, and most people didn't bother. Not after the first couple of times of being pitied or laughed at, anyway, Marian said. No-one had ever managed to communicate, that was the hard part: being so close to a loved one but not knowing how they felt "in the spirit realm", whether or not they were happy. She'd known people who tried everything, Marian said, Ouija boards and coded messages and sign language and "you name it, really, dear, but no joy. And that of course is the great sadness, but people mostly just come to take comfort in their presence. Knowing they are being looked after."

By this time Holly had got used to the dull ache of disappointed hope in her stomach and she heard Belinda's voice saying that no-one else would pull her finger out for her, which was one of her mother's favourite sayings, so she sat up and told herself she had to make the most of this opportunity. All right then: most ghosts stayed. Marian's hadn't. There might be something about Marian's experience that she could use.

"Do you mind talking about your…spirit?" she asked, feeling mean because she knew already that Marian did. "About what happened?"

Marian folded her hands on her lap. "I don't usually, dear," she said. "That's… private to me."

Holly nodded. "I don't want to know… anything personal or anything like that. Just… what happened when he left." She saw Marian blink several times and hurried on, "But please don't, if you don't want to," meaning it a little, but feeling like a horrible fraud anyway.

149

Marian compressed her lips, looked at Holly and smiled. "I'm sorry, dear, it's all rather difficult. I had some other… personal problems at the time, you see, and was very occupied with those, and at the end of that whole process… well. I almost didn't notice him go, but suddenly there I was. All alone again."

She gave a little laugh and looked away and Holly knew she couldn't press it any further: Marian either wouldn't or couldn't tell her anything. There must be something else, she thought urgently. Something…

"You said it was rare," she said slowly. "But is there anyone else you know of? Who lost their spirit?"

Marian nodded. "Just one," she said. "A little while ago. Poor boy. He lost his brother, and it was particularly awful for him, I think. Afterwards he took so much comfort from having the spirit near him. His guardian angel, he called it. I thought it was a lovely way of putting it." Holly flicked her eyes to Yvonne. She thought the phrase would appeal to her, too. "Then, of course, to be abandoned by the spirit, to lose that angel," Marian went on, "it's… well, it's a second bereavement, you know. I did my best to help, but…"

Holly leaned forward avidly. "And this was near here? I mean he lives near here?"

"I think so," Marian said. "Of course he joined the army, and you're so often away, but…"

She went on speaking but Holly's mind had stuck and she wasn't hearing anything. "The army?" she said faintly, not knowing if she was interrupting.

Marian looked at her curiously. "Yes, that's right, dear. I don't know if he's still in it. It's been some…"

"What's his name?" Holly asked, but knowing already what the answer was before Marian said, "Liam Purvis. A nice boy, though it was so very hard for him."

Holly was finding it difficult to breathe. The mirthless grin, the terrible sense of oppression – a nice boy, Marian said... Somehow, despite the shock of it, she was almost unsurprised. Since she'd first seen him and the other men with guns at Will Sadler's, she'd sensed so strongly that all of it was connected to what was happening to her. Liam had lost his ghost and now he and who knew how many others were roaming the countryside with bolt-guns and rifles spreading death and misery wherever they went. Even if there were no others, and he was acting alone, there was nothing to stop him exploiting this disease: bringing it first to Will and next – wherever he chose. One report here, one contaminated sample there...

And if, Holly suddenly thought, feeling the chill of it – if the loss of his ghost, his guardian angel, had hurt him so badly, then maybe he had a grudge against anyone who still had one. Maybe, and she almost wanted to laugh despairingly, maybe he wanted to punish all those lucky enough still to be haunted. For a long moment she imagined that punishment: the destruction he could so easily bring to all of their lives, motivated by nothing but jealousy and malice and stupidity. Then she thought of Douggie doing it for pay and for fun, and didn't know which was worse.

She realised belatedly that Marian had asked if she knew Liam. She struggled to the surface and said faintly that he was involved in foot-and-mouth.

Marian nodded compassionately. "Oh dear, I imagine all you farming lot are involved in that, aren't you, poor love. Has your family been affected?"

"Oh..." Holly said. "Yes – I mean. Sort of." There was no point in talking about it: in trying to explain what it was like to sit and wait and fear the worst. She knew from school that no-one outside the country understood what it was like, and no-one in the country wanted to speak about it. Marian seemed to sense there

151

was no point pushing. Holly knew she had to ask about Liam and why he might be doing this but she had no idea how to put it into words.

"You haven't… heard anything about what's happening, have you?" she asked eventually. "About foot-and-mouth and, I guess, spirits?" Marian looked baffled and Holly rushed on. "I… I just had this idea that maybe because that man, Liam was involved… that it had something to do with spirits. And just, if you knew him, then you might…" she tailed off. Marian's expression hadn't changed, or if it had, it had grown warier and was reminding Holly of Dr Gould. "But you haven't seen him in a while, you said?" she finished desperately.

Marian shook her head. "I'm afraid we didn't part on the best of terms. I often see people at very turbulent times, of course."

Holly nodded, and smiled to suggest that was all she'd really been asking, and then because she couldn't think of anything else to do she shuffled over and leaned into Marian again and felt her arms go around her, but even in the warmth of that embrace she saw nothing when she closed her eyes but Liam walking up the drive, a gun cradled tenderly in his arms, his mind full of hate and revenge.

28

When they got home from Marian's Holly realised something was wrong. The door was ajar as ever but the house was silent. Eva walked around calling out and went upstairs but no-one was in.

"I don't know where they can have got to," Eva said, but Holly knew. The only place everyone would have gone was Top Yard where the dairy was, and the shed, and the pens. If everyone had gone, there must have been a reason and that meant only one thing, didn't it?

"Come on," she said urgently to Eva and hurried through the house. Eva took ages to follow on her stupid shoes and Holly was far ahead of her and all she could think was that there hadn't been any gunshots, not yet; but her face was screwed up in anticipation of that first flat echo of the gun.

She ran to the driveway that curled up to the yard and cut right and scrambled up the bank and at the top let out a long shuddering breath. She'd been expecting vehicles and lights and guns and there was none of that, just Malcolm and the children and Belinda and Vic standing by a pen at the edge of the cow-shed. It could still be bad, one of the cows could be sick and Holly thought how ironic it would be if they got some horrible disease that wasn't foot-and-mouth and they all died anyway, but when she got there she realised it wasn't that at all. Quaint was in the pen and next to her was a new-born calf.

Vic saw her first and said, "Hey up," and Holly knew she should look cool and professional but she couldn't help smiling. It was hard not to help it. Julia looked like she was in heaven.

For a while they all stood and watched as Vic examined Quaint and the calf. Then Eva finally arrived and every bit of liking for her Holly had developed on their trip disappeared. On the way home Eva had been even nicer, not asking anything despite her obvious curiosity, but as soon as she joined the group she started cooing over the calf with pure saccharine and talking about the miracle of life and other bogus nonsense. Holly knew perfectly well what the miracle of life was, it was as often as not twenty minutes with an arm shoulder-deep inside a cow and it was slime and placenta and the smell of iodine from the disinfectant spray and it was beautiful, yes, but it was also hard work and difficulty. She smiled privately at that thought and felt glad, as she did quite often, that she was Belinda's daughter.

In the end Vic wiped his hands on a cloth and said everything looked fine to him but they could get Micky Newton out. Belinda snorted because everyone knew Micky had other things keeping him busy. Malcolm said it was time for a drink and Holly let them all walk down to the farm without her because she wanted to be on her own and think, but when she looked up she realised they hadn't all gone. Ben stood on the other side of the pen watching her coolly.

She felt herself blush and looked away from him, scrutinising the calf in minute detail. For what felt like ages but was probably only a minute he didn't say anything. Then he said, "Why were they worried? Why did they talk about the vet?"

She looked up. It was the first direct comment he had addressed to her since the Reservation and he wanted to know about calving.

"Um… it's early," she said. "When they come early it sometimes means they're sick. They can get infections and… stuff. Especially in the winter."

"How did they know it was early?" he said.

Holly swallowed. Was this how they were going to talk from now on – like an interrogation? But at least it was talk, so she told him about calving patterns and how the cows were mated at set times to balance milk production.

"Most calves are born in the spring and the autumn," she said. "You have to feed the mothers a lot in the autumn though. To get them producing enough milk."

"Right," he said. "Mated?" She explained that, too, how most cows were artificially inseminated but Belinda sometimes borrowed a bull from Colin Thomas. Ben nodded, and asked what would happen to the calf. It was a bull calf so Holly said it would normally be sold either to be raised for beef or for veal, though Belinda didn't like her animals going for veal. She wondered how long this abrupt question and answer session would continue but after a long pause he nodded again and finally he smiled. His face was so open and so like Ben's, suddenly.

"So… I guess what I mean is I'm sorry," he said. She held his gaze. It wasn't like she was going to forgive him just like that, but seeing his face full of warmth and life again it was very hard to resist. "Come on," he said, stepping forward and taking her hand.

She pulled away, but not very hard. "Where are we going?" she asked.

"You're going to introduce me to every single cow on this farm," Ben said. "And I'm going to try and explain why I was so mean to you. And when we've met them all you can decide if you're going to forgive me."

Holly nodded slowly, only to say she was prepared to do it, but he probably knew as well as she did that the answer was already halfway to yes.

For the first part of the tour he didn't say anything and Holly didn't introduce him to any of the cows. Instead they just wandered slowly around the pens. The air up here was different from any-where else on the farm, full of the sweet smell of dung and milk and wet concrete, and Holly breathed it deeply, trying to con-trol the unsteady beating of her heart. Finally Ben leaned against the top rail of an enclosure, watching Stella who was enormous with what looked like twin calves, and asked which piece of crazy whacko news she wanted. Holly didn't trust herself to answer so said nothing. He leaned out and patted Stella.

"It's a choice between mentalism and sexual initiation, basically. Well, a combination. But we could start with one or the other."

"Right," Holly said, not sure she knew how to ask about either of those.

He turned and smiled at her. "It's all right," he said. "Because… well, it isn't, really. But nothing matters in the end, does it. So…?"

Holly thought about it for a little while and realised that if she said the words 'sexual initiation' to him she might actually die from embarrassment, so she went for mentalism, though as it turned out neither story took long. The first time he'd felt… down, Ben said delicately, had been over a year ago. It hadn't been nearly as bad, that first time, as it became. However, it was enough for him to go to the school counsellor, who said that he of course wasn't qualified to judge, but that didn't stop him talk-ing about mood swings and ADHD and hypomania and how you had to be careful with this kind of thing because it could lead to full-blown bipolar disorder and he should have consultations with qualified people.

"By which he meant people to feed me drugs," Ben said. "I looked it up on the internet. It's simple, right? When you feel like shit they pump you full of antidepressants, and when you cheer up they pump you full of stabilisers instead. It's great. You get to eat lots of pills every day before breakfast and nothing ever hurts again."

Or maybe you never hurt other people again, Holly thought. She didn't say it, but because this was the old Ben it was as if he knew. He said the only reason to do it, unless you started feeling that you really couldn't cope with the downswings, was to make life better for other people; but once you'd had the drugs maybe you could never get back to your former self, which was a scary thought. Holly looked at him as he scratched Stella's ear. Even the cow seemed grateful to be near him and Holly thought if Ben had some sense of his own power, his capability, then the idea of losing it must be terrifying.

"How does it feel?" she said. "When... you know. You start feeling bad." He looked suddenly bleak. "You don't have to tell me," she added hastily.

"It's all right," he said. "It... it's like you don't recognise anything. You don't recognise people. You look at them and you know who they are but you feel nothing and it kind of makes you... it makes you want to get away from them. Because it's horrible. Seeing their faces and feeling so indifferent... it's like hating them, somehow. And... I don't know. Everything tastes of rust."

He smiled self-deprecatingly. She met his eye and wondered what he'd seen when he looked at her after they kissed. Was it just that? She thought it was probably much worse. He turned away and exhaled and said that just left the sex bit, and that he had a fairly majorly embarrassing confession, which was that he was almost a virgin.

"Oh," Holly said, feeling herself blushing again and praying he wasn't going to ask how experienced she was, because admitting that she'd kissed only one other person who was now dead didn't feel like a conversation she wanted to start. Also she didn't know how you could be almost a virgin and didn't want to ask that either. After a moment, though, he carried on. He told her that there had been opportunities, but it had always felt wrong, so at parties he'd got used to being the guy whose shoulder girls slept on instead of being the guy they had sex with.

"Anyway," he said, as they walked through into the main cattle shed, "I was good with that. But then, recently, I had this thing. With this girl. Woman. Er.. teacher."

Holly nodded, her face to the ground, knowing she was still blushing. She didn't know how much he was going to tell her. Part of her hoped nothing. Part of her hoped everything.

"I'm not going to give you the awful details," he said, again as if reading her mind. "I liked her a lot, you know? She's… well. Everyone at school fancies her, and she came onto me, and I thought, fine, let's do this. But then we were in bed at her house and she has cats and the whole place smelt like… and then close-up, she… I don't know. It wasn't good, anyway. Really not good. I didn't… Whatever. But she seemed to think it was great. And afterwards she was lying there with this little smile and she said, was that all right for me? And suddenly I just thought of eating in a restaurant when the waiter comes over and says is everything all right for you? And I thought how she's basically a friend of Dad's. And suddenly I felt… just worse than I know how to say, really. I couldn't breathe, and I was shaking, and I wanted to kill her. Or myself. Or both. Like I really couldn't see a reason, suddenly, not to do it."

He looked up at the roof of the shed above them. His face was drawn for a moment and he looked old; there was something of how Eva had been in the barn in his expression. Then he looked back at her and smiled, but Holly could see the effort in it. "Anyway. That was the worst time. I felt, you know. Awful. It went on for weeks, and I guess it was obvious because Mum and Dad got really worried about me and ever since they've been on the psycho bandwagon. Go to the doctor, darling, take the pills darling, blah blah. And… yeah. Since then I haven't been near anyone, a girl, I mean… until. You know."

"Ok," Holly said, though she felt a long way from ok, but he turned to her quickly.

"Don't say that," he said. "Please. It really isn't ok. I know you must be thinking that I kissed you and all I could think about was that woman, and it isn't like that. I… it was a surprise, but it was good. Really good. Kissing you. And I didn't want… I didn't think…" He broke off with exasperation. "Look, I don't want to say it isn't you, because I know how that sounds. But it really isn't you."

Holly looked back to the birthing pens. "It's all right," she said flatly. "I do get it." She didn't mean her voice to sound so harsh because she knew how bad Ben – this Ben, her Ben – must feel about this. She also knew that she should be sympathetic because whether or not the counsellor was right, he clearly had a condition of some kind and it wasn't his fault. But where she tried to find pity for him she only found self-pity instead. She was ashamed of it but she couldn't help it. Self-pity for how he'd treated her. Self-pity that now he was back, and she could feel the warmth of him on her skin like sunlight, he was so soon snatching away the possibility of anything between them. But when she turned around there was an unreadable expression on his face.

"You don't get it," he said, and reached out and pulled her to him. He held her against him, her whole body against him, and she could feel the heat of his hands either side of her waist. "I'm saying I can't promise anything," he said quietly against her ear. "Not that I don't want to try."

Holly told herself to think about that as he held her. About how even this version of Ben could promise her nothing, let alone the Ben left behind after his mood changed; and about how anything they did, any intimacy, any kiss, might be the cause of that change; and about how crazy it all was – but even as these thoughts ran through her head she felt herself relax into him and couldn't make herself care, because whatever happened, she'd have had this moment. For the rest of her life, at the very least, she'd have a memory of the way she felt right now.

29

The day after Holly got Ben back the army came.

She and Ben were the first ones to see them. They were walking round the yard talking and talking. They hadn't really got anywhere but Holly still felt as if she was plugged in to an electric current. As they walked their hands brushed against each other sometimes, and the shock of it shortened her breath. His fingers curled against hers as it happened and he half-smiled and that meant, she thought, that surely meant he felt it too. Even the smell from the fire, which was burning low, didn't seem so bad, though she worried that was because the smell was soaking in, had permeated her clothes and skin and hair until she didn't even notice it any more.

Holly told him about Douggie and her visit to Marian and he agreed that the only way forward was to get to Liam Purvis: Ben said that maybe he was responsible for what was happening or maybe he was just taking advantage of it, but either way something was going on, and Holly nodded gratefully because his certainty made her feel less mad. She was wondering how to talk about his condition, or whatever it was, and seem mature and understanding and not like his Mum and Dad, when she saw an army van turn into the drive.

"Ben," she said quickly, her voice tight. His hand closed around hers for a second then released it. He said they should go and find Belinda. Holly didn't want to move, though, in case the van went straight up to Top Yard and they tried to start the killing there and then. So they stood together and watched. There were two more vehicles following the army van, both white and unmarked. Micky Newton got out of one of them and a soldier who didn't seem much older than Ben got out of the army van, carrying a thick sheaf of papers. Then more soldiers climbed down from the back of the van, but remained in a group, talking to each other. There was no sign of Liam Purvis. Not yet.

"Holly," Micky said, with what seemed to her like smugness, and the soldier asked if their mum and dad were home. Holly felt an odd tingle at the idea she and Ben could be brother and sister but before they could get into a conversation Vic was there, wiping his hands on a cloth, and his slowness and calm were somehow reassuring. He said tersely that the boss lady would be back soon and he didn't want to hear anything until then, and he asked Holly if she and Ben wanted to go inside. Since she didn't, she said nothing, and he didn't ask again.

After what felt like an hour but was probably a few minutes Belinda came up the drive in the pick-up. Holly saw her face: she was looking grimly at the army vans but at least she didn't seem vacant and detached. A reflection of grey sky slid across the windscreen as she turned and parked and Holly couldn't see her any more. For a moment she didn't get out and Holly felt really afraid because whatever else was true about Belinda, this was what she was made for. Their whole lives might hang on what was about to happen, and if Belinda couldn't do what she did, Holly thought, that would be it: everything would be finished. Then the door opened and from that moment on, it was her mother as Holly knew her. She walked up briskly and silenced Micky with a nod and asked the soldier what he was doing, in a voice that made him seem even more like a child. He said it was bad news, which Holly thought was hardly a shock in the circumstances. He said that as they all knew livestock had been culled on Lower Marsh Farm and the Ministry had declared that livestock on adjacent farms had to be culled as a precautionary measure. Holly could tell he didn't like this, every time he said the word 'cull' his face twisted a little, though Micky didn't seem to mind very much and was watching avidly.

Belinda nodded several times. Holly had seen her do this before. The most brilliant part of it was that she listened closely and was never rude, and yet people ended up doing the opposite of what they intended, without ever getting angry – though if anyone did lose their temper Belinda was able to be much, much angrier back. She said she understood that perfectly well, and the soldier's face relaxed a little bit, and then she asked what the test results on Will Sadler's livestock had shown. They all looked at Micky Newton.

"Er… I don't have that information," he said. Belinda told the soldier it was entirely possible that none of Will's cattle had been diseased when they were slaughtered, which meant they were next door to healthy animals not sick ones.

For the first time Holly thought they had a chance when the soldier asked Micky why he didn't have the results. He shrugged. "Up to MAFF," he said. "Might be three or four days yet."

The soldier sighed and looked at his papers and said he couldn't wait, they had to authorise the cull now. Malcolm had come out of the house and Holly thought he might just wade in and ruin everything given how he'd been lately, but Belinda stopped him with a look. Not for the first time Holly felt a surge of pride: like this Belinda was amazing. She asked the soldier evenly what he could see at the bottom of the hill. They all turned to look at the Motorway. He put a hand to his forehead. Belinda asked whether he'd known that the Motorway divided the two farms, and did he think that cattle might have ambled across it to spread the disease? Holly caught Ben's eye, feeling herself blushing. The soldier shuffled through his papers again.

"I don't..." he started to say, then stopped. Malcolm stirred and Holly saw Belinda give him permission to speak.

"It is illegal, you know, to slaughter healthy animals without proof of infection," he said. "Or even any proof of infection nearby. That's pretty clear in the directive, wouldn't you say, Mr Newton?"

Everyone turned to Micky again. He wasn't looking smug any more, he was looking truculent. "Look, no-one's going to pretend any of this is easy," he said. "But it is necessary."

Holly felt herself shudder. Was that it, for him, just doing what was necessary? Or was he involved with Liam somehow? He hadn't seemed to notice Yvonne, but maybe he was just being careful. He was certainly avoiding Holly's eye through all this.

Malcolm shrugged. "I guess it's in your hands," he said. "These guys are just doing their jobs. You're the one who'll be liable."

The soldiers at the back of the army truck had been listening for a while so Micky had quite a big audience and nothing much, it seemed, to say. Eventually the soldier in charge said tiredly that they'd need to talk to someone about this and that he was sorry, but the way he saw it his superiors would probably tell him to come straight back, and Belinda said in her even voice, "That's fine, we'll be waiting for you." Holly could tell that he didn't know whether to be worried by that comment or not. And that was it. He and Micky turned away and the white vans were reversing and they'd won. Had they? Holly watched the last of the soldiers climb up into the truck, his rough uniform tucked into huge boots, and she thought about them coming back with their guns lowered and just marching stolidly past, and not even Belinda could stop that, surely.

It soon became apparent that she was going to try. She said everyone needed to meet in the kitchen. They found Julia in the sitting room and called upstairs for Sal, who came down with Eva. Ben told them what had happened. Julia said fiercely how unfair it was. Sal said nothing, just looked thoughtful and Eva sat in a chair theatrically and said, "Oh God," a lot.

By this time Belinda and Vic and Malcolm had sketched out a map on the back of a yellowed and crinkly envelope. Everyone apart from Eva gathered round the table as if they were in a war film. Holly craned her head to see the map. It showed Top Yard and the cattle shed and the roadways.

"Short of coming through a hedge, and they won't, there's two access points and that's it," Belinda said, and Vic nodded. Eva asked what was going on and Malcolm said what did it look like, if the army came back they weren't getting on to the farm. Eva stood up this time, still theatrically.

"What are you all *talking* about," she said. "We can't… it's the army. For God's sake, this is ridiculous. They'll have guns and the police will be there and we… we can't, we just can't."

"It's a question of delaying them, right?" Malcolm asked Belinda.

She nodded. "I very much doubt it was on Lower Marsh," she said. "He's no sheep, and it wouldn't have gone to the cattle. Stupid bloody thing to have killed them all in the first place."

"So all we have to do is delay until the results come through," Malcolm said. "A couple of days. They'll show no infection, which means we can't be infected here."

"And that's it," Vic said. They all looked at him. Holly didn't think she'd ever heard him talk in front of such a large group. "That only leaves Colin Thomas, and his animals are on the lower part of his land, which is classified as separate. Everyone else that touches us is arable. If Will Sadler's lot are negative, we're clear."

Holly thought even Eva must be able to feel the hope and determination stirring in the room, but she said that it just wasn't sensible. Malcolm tensed his hands and Sal said, "Daddy, don't," but he started a long speech anyway. He said that what the government was doing was criminal and immoral and if Eva thought that trying to save Belinda's livelihood wasn't *sensible* she was even more of a stupid fucking bitch than she seemed.

Holly sat completely still, her ears ringing with the force of it; she'd never been in the middle of a fight like this, only listening from above. Eva said shrilly, "Thank you Malcolm. It's very obvious why you care so much about it."

He took a step towards her. Holly felt half-frightened, half-delighted with horror. She didn't know what Eva meant: why should Malcolm care especially? Because he liked to fight, that was what had got him fired? Belinda said this was ridiculous and she was having a cigarette and Eva said, "Well I think you'll agree that if you're stupid enough to do this I should take the children to Guildford."

For a moment Holly's brain did not compute, then she realised what Eva was saying. *Guildford?* Ben said, "Mum!" and Belinda said from the door that if MAFF believed the farm was Category A then Eva wouldn't be able to leave anyway. Eva wheeled round to her and Holly didn't know what would happen if they started fighting. She thought it wouldn't end well for Eva; but then she had her own kind of weapons. Before they could get started, though, Sal spoke.

"Mummy, we're staying. And helping," she said.

Holly didn't know if it was because she spoke so rarely, or because of the quiet finality in her voice, but she knew that was it. Julia nodded vigorously and Eva looked at the room then turned and walked jerkily out. Holly watched her go thinking that it must be pretty lonely to be Eva, but that it was hard not to believe she deserved it. Ben smiled at Holly and even the presence of Yvonne didn't seem to matter quite so much now. They were in this together.

30

If they were going to stop the army they had two entrances to block: the main driveway, and another gate up on the high lane above the farm. Vic and Belinda decided to use one of the heavy rollers and the cultivator. As they went out to the barn Belinda asked Holly to move the Massey Ferguson. Holly started the engine in front of everyone telling herself it was ridiculous to feel so proud, driving a tractor was hardly difficult, but still she felt wise and powerful reversing it out of the shed and to one side while the others coupled up the machines.

The whole thing took longer than everyone thought. Pretty soon it was getting dark and they had a conference. Belinda and Vic and Malcolm agreed that they should finish the job now they'd started. Vic went to get the little generator so that they'd have light out at the gateways. The children could help till ten, Malcolm said, and Ben said they were helping till the job was done, whenever, and Malcolm grinned at him and Holly felt a surge of pride and love and she couldn't tell which one of them it was for.

Before setting out again they all went in for a tea break and to get warm. Holly went upstairs to get another layer beneath her coat; she was freezing already and it was only getting colder. The door to Malcolm and Eva's room was open and she paused outside it. Eva was sitting on the bed, her back to the door. It didn't look like she was crying but Holly twisted her mouth at the sight of her sitting facing the wall while everyone else was downstairs together. She remembered how much she'd liked Eva on their trip to see Marian – well, not liked exactly, but not hated either – and took a step into the room.

"Are you all right?" she said tentatively. Eva turned, but didn't stand up and start smoothing her clothes and saying she was fine, which was what Holly had been hoping for. Instead she stayed sitting down and said she didn't think she was, really. Holly didn't answer and there was an awkward pause. Then Eva said she had something to tell her. Reluctantly Holly left the sanctuary of the doorway and sat next to Eva on the bed, looking anxiously over her shoulder at the door.

"I know you don't have long," Eva said. "It's all right. It won't take long."

"It's just… the army could come back any time," Holly said. "If we're doing it we have to do it now."

"I know," Eva said. "I know." She took a deep breath. "Listen, Holly. I haven't told anyone yet, apart from Salome. But I wanted you to tell you especially, because I want you to understand the reasons."

Holly looked up at her. Eva's make-up wasn't as good as usual. Her face was lined this close-up, and the skin of her neck was mottled. She looked as old as Gran.

"What I want to tell you is that I'm leaving," Eva said. "I would have done anyway, even if this hadn't happened. I know I might not be able to go for a while but as soon as this is over I will. Not forever… but for a bit."

Holly lowered her head and felt Eva's hand against her hair, stroking it, but hard. "Don't worry," she said, with an edge in her voice. "The children will stay, and Malcolm. Obviously."

Holly started to protest that wasn't why she'd looked away though she knew it must have been obvious. Eva smiled, brittle, more like herself.

"It doesn't matter," she said. "The important thing is that you know why." She dropped her hand from Holly's hair. "It's... well. It's rather awkward talking about it, but you've probably always known about Malcolm and your mother, haven't you. You were old enough when it started. I shouldn't feel so ashamed."

Eva was looking at Holly as she said it, so Holly couldn't react, but inside she was thinking *hold on, hold on, hold on*, as if her mind was stuck. Malcolm and her mother? Malcolm and *Belinda*? As well as Eva and Daddy? Suddenly it seemed that the whole world was in flux.

"Paul and I... I mean your father and I... I don't want you to think we were silly about it. Of course your father wouldn't have been, and I was perfectly prepared to be civilised," Eva went on. She seemed to have no idea of the turmoil Holly was in. Paul and I. *Paul and I.* Not the sinners, but the sinned against. Paul and I were civilised about it... which meant Malcolm and Belinda were the ones who... *Belinda.*

"Anyway. What you saw the other day... I don't want you to think I won't be all right. I will. Perfectly all right. And it's important that you know that, with everything that's happened to you. That's all."

Holly thought her head was full but when Eva mentioned the other day she realised there was room for a disorienting flash memory of Eva's face in the barn, of that expression, that open misery. She realised she was nodding and Eva was saying, "You never let it show, do you. You know so much and your face doesn't let any of it out."

And then Eva was kissing her and telling her not to let on, not yet, not till things were easier, and Holly found herself walking out of the room. And before she could even begin to process what this meant there was a shout from downstairs and they were all heading back outside and she descended slowly to the hall to find

Ben waiting for her. She followed him mechanically out into the dark. *Malcolm and Belinda*.

It was a busy night and for a while Holly didn't have a chance to think at all. The way it worked out was that Malcolm and Belinda – *Malcolm and Belinda* – and Ben stayed out by the gateways building the barricades. Vic drove the low trailer back and forth with logs and barrels and anything else moveable to plug the gaps around the roller and the cultivator at each gate, and Holly rode on it with Julia and Sal, helping with the loading and unloading. Each time they dropped off Ben smiled at her. He smiled at everyone else too but not the same way: when he saw her his whole face seemed to gladden the way she knew hers did. She wondered what he would say about this when she told him.

After each delivery Holly sat with Sal and Julia on the back of the trailer as they drove away, their legs dangling in the cold air. Malcolm and Belinda and Ben were lit up in a brilliant circle of light from the generator. Holly could see the light glimmering between the branches of trees even after they turned the corner back towards the farm, and she watched it, thinking of the three of them out there, surrounded by darkness. Unloaded the trailer was light and bounced over every rut; sometimes they had to grab each other to stay on and Julia and Sal were laughing. Julia especially had embraced her rustic destiny and was sweaty and smiling and happy. While she chattered to Sal – who was almost chattering back, which was something – Holly tilted her head to the sky. It was mostly clear and there was a half-moon spreading a milky light across it, through which the stars shone icily. She watched them, feeling the metal of the trailer freezing even through gloves, and tried to put her thoughts in order.

Malcolm and Belinda. Her first response was that it felt almost obvious but then again it didn't. Belinda wasn't... she didn't... Holly couldn't find the words to express how this just didn't fit with her entire conception of her mother. Malcolm and Belinda meant lying, and she'd never thought Belinda lied, not really, her world seemed too straight and clean and simple for that. And it wasn't just lying, Malcolm and Belinda meant sex. Dark rooms and whispered endearments and all the stuff that Yvonne had been so keen on telling Holly about; and now she was supposed to apply it to Belinda? Her mind couldn't do that. Let alone imagine Daddy and what this must have meant for him – but she refused even to start down that road, it was too much, her mind went blank when she thought of him as if someone had pressed mute on a television.

Holly thought instead of Eva coming to the house and knowing all the time what had happened between Malcolm and Belinda. She suddenly pictured Eva picking her way up to the farm in heels and sneering at everything and imagined feeling frightened and lonely and putting that feeling into Eva's head. Holly felt bad that she'd never done that before, never even tried to understand, but she couldn't feel bad for long, because the thought of Eva, all thoughts, in fact almost everything in her head including Yvonne, were being pushed aside by another idea. An insistent drumming idea pulsing in the centre of her brain. Holly turned and twisted away from it because she knew how wrong it was, but nothing she did would silence it. *Malcolm was staying and Eva was leaving*. That meant – and now in a rush she let herself think it – that meant that maybe Malcolm and Sal and Julia and oh god Ben would be staying forever. That she wouldn't just get bursts of feeling part of the Family, but would have that sense of inclusion all the time. She would become Family herself. She looked back at the circle of light, almost completely gone now, and felt a rushing sensation through her whole body. It was the same feeling as when the soldier thought Ben was her brother; it left her almost shaky. When they pulled up back at the farm Julia helped her down off the trailer and Holly suddenly smiled widely at her, her heart surging. My *Family*, she thought.

By midnight they were done. Each gateway was blocked by the machines in the centre and half the junk from the back of the old sheds piled unevenly around them, right up to the hedges. There was no way through, not even on foot.

"That's it, unless they bring tanks," Malcolm said. Holly knew he was joking but they all looked at him nervously. It was decided that they needed four people to keep watch: one on each gate for an hour, then switching with the other two so that the first watchers could get warm and sleep. It was also decided, despite Holly and Julia's vociferous protests, that the four would be Vic, Malcolm, Belinda and Ben and Sal, who counted as one because they had to stay together. Holly said it wasn't fair then felt her cheeks redden because that sounded like a little girl. She wouldn't sleep anyway and surely this one night, of all nights, she should be staying up. Belinda was adamant, though, and after they'd stood a moment, all looking at the finished work, their breath clouding in the chilly air, she said it was time to get the girls inside. Holly saw her face twitch when she said it and everyone looked at the ground awkwardly, all thinking of Yvonne at the same moment, though Yvonne herself, standing next to Malcolm, didn't react at all, obviously.

When they got home Holly went to her room and got into her cold bed still wearing all her clothes, feeling that she was being somehow cheated. It wasn't that she thought she'd be needed to help fight off MAFF – everyone had agreed that the army was hardly likely to sneak out in the middle of the night, and that keeping watch was just a formality. It was the idea of sharing the mission with the others. With Ben. She could see so clearly what that would be like: out there in the dark, surrounded by the shadows of the land and the stir of grass, shuffling in their clothes to keep warm, their eyes keenly searching the horizon, always searching, perfectly in harmony, Yvonne reduced to an irrelevance in the face of this common purpose. She could sense that the night they kept watch for the army would have been one of the most important nights of her life; a night that would have shaped her future, that she'd have looked back on forever. And now it felt like that whole future had been taken from her. She looked at Yvonne, standing at the foot of her bed. This is what I got instead, she thought.

Holly felt her eyes closing despite herself, and, yawning, set her alarm for six, thinking that at least she would be the first one up to see how the night had gone. She slept, dreaming of facing down the army by herself, and being cheered, and the phone ringing again and again with people wanting to congratulate her and it seemed to take a very long time to realise that the phone really was ringing, and that Ben and Sal and Malcolm were calling out to each other, and that they had been wrong about the army waiting till morning after all. She scrambled out of bed, suddenly completely awake, her heart racing. It was five o'clock and still pitch dark. They were back.

31

It was over almost before Holly got there. Malcolm protested when she came downstairs but there was no time to protest very much and he just told her to keep out of harm's way, and that went for Ben and Sal too, he said. They nodded but Holly could see the determination on their faces and hoped she looked that way as well. Malcolm was fumbling for keys to his car as they hurried outside but Vic was driving along in the pick-up from the main gate where he'd been keeping watch and they all jumped in the back. Vic drove fast, and Holly clung on to the side of the pick-up to stop it banging against her arms as they slid over the bumps of the track, thinking of Belinda alone against whatever forces the army had brought.

When they lurched to a halt by the gate it was still dark, but the scene was lit up by the headlights of army trucks and more white vans, like searchlights. For a moment Holly couldn't see Belinda, and then she realised she was off to one side talking to the same soldier as before. Then she looked at who they had brought and her throat closed because back-lit by the headlights and too tall, Liam Purvis was standing darkly on the other side of the blockade. He was here for the slaughter.

Malcolm strode over to Belinda and Vic went to the barricade, but neither the slaughtermen nor the army were trying to get through it, they just stood on the other side with frightening calmness. There were so many of them and their presence was so official that it seemed hopeless. If anyone could stand against them, it was Belinda; Holly knew this was the moment when she could prove her magic once and for all; but as she watched Belinda and Malcolm and the soldier she had a chill feeling in her stomach. Belinda was different, not tall and fierce and capable but staring down at the ground, and Malcolm put his hand on her arm. Then the soldier said something and they all looked over. Holly had the uneasy feeling they weren't looking at the blockade, but at her. In fact the soldier was indicating her, wasn't he, the way he was nodding his head? She had a sudden terrible fear that this really was all her fault: that the whole operation was about ghosts and they had come because of her and Yvonne... but surely that couldn't be true, and surely the soldier wouldn't be admitting it, even if it was? Then Belinda abruptly shook her head and walked away. She came towards the barrier and Ben started to say something, but stopped, because they could all see her face was running with tears. Vic listened to her and nodded and it was all gone, the fight they had prepared for had disappeared in smoke and the army patiently started to dismantle the barriers and Holly wanted to kick and punch and scream at the injustice of it.

Ben and Sal surrounded Malcolm and even Sal was furious. Malcolm started explaining: the soldier, who was the officer in charge of the squad, had said his superiors had told him to clear the farm whatever the circumstances, and if they tried to protest the animals would be killed anyway but they'd get no compensation and lose everything, the farm, the house, everything. Ben objected but Malcolm raised a tired hand and said that wasn't what had changed Belinda's mind. The officer had said that if she allowed it to happen now he would stay and see that the job was done properly, but if he had to go back to the base his commander would come and the cattle would be bulldozed, literally bull-dozed, crushed against the wall of the shed using lorries, smashed to pieces, calves and all. Holly was standing apart from the other two watching Belinda, who had her back to everything and was looking out into the darkness, but she heard the rough edge in Malcolm's voice and knew he had tears in his eyes. Ben and Sal were silent and Malcolm said that the officer had seen cows that had been shot over and over again but weren't dead being beaten to death with crowbars, and men chasing cows on quad bikes and breaking their legs to stop them running, and men standing next to dying cattle who were giving birth despite their injuries hold-ing shovels ready to beat the calves to death and Sal said, "Daddy, don't, please don't," and he finally relented.

Nobody said anything for a moment, then Ben said quietly that he couldn't imagine how Belinda must feel. Holly knew that she couldn't, either, but that she might be closer to it than anyone else in the world, so she started walking to her, not knowing what she was going to say. Before she reached Belinda, though, she found her way blocked by the first gang of men in white overalls, with guns on their shoulders. She realised with a shudder one of them was Liam Purvis.

The others continued but he stopped. Holly felt the nausea and headache rising, though because she was ready for it now it didn't feel so bad. What was it? Was it the loss of his ghost that she could sense, that made her feel sick? Marian hadn't had this effect though. He grinned at her and she thought maybe it was the dizzying force of hate he radiated.

"They tell you?" he asked, craning towards her as if he was inspecting a specimen. She took a step away.

"What?" she said roughly, trying to sound tough and uncaring but hearing the smallness of her voice.

"This is all down to you," he said.

Holly stepped away again, shaking her head, panic in her throat. She was right, then, she thought, looking around at the men, they were all here to punish her... She looked wildly at Yvonne, standing pale in the lights of the vehicles.

"Because of her?" she whispered. "That's really why..."

Liam looked at Yvonne, then back at Holly, his eyes dancing with amusement. "What, that thing?" he said. "Believe me, no-one cares about that, and it sure as Christ doesn't care about you. We aren't here because of her. Like I said. It's you that's brought us."

Holly shook her head. He was lying, he had to be lying.

"Think about it," he said. "About how we established contact between here and Lower Marsh. Cattle can't cross motorways, but little girls can." Holly felt a terrible sensation in her hands and feet, a sudden hollow ache. "Confirmed contact with an infected farm," he said. "Plenty of witnesses. Job done, right? Job done."

He walked away and Holly squatted down where she stood, suddenly feeling as if the air were leaden and pressing her into the ground. She had brought this here. It was all down to her. Not Yvonne. By going to see Will Sadler, she could have brought back the disease; she hadn't thought of that possibility, it hadn't even occurred to her. And because of that, everything they had prepared for, the whole night of planning and determination and fight, had been ruined. It was her fault. With a huge effort she straightened painfully and walked to Belinda, feeling as if she couldn't breathe. She looked up at her and she couldn't help saying, "Mummy?" For a moment Belinda didn't react and Holly thought she might never look at her again, but then with an effort that Holly knew must have been exactly like the way she got up, Belinda's head turned and she registered Holly's expression and she said, "Oh love, it isn't you," and her arm came down over Holly's neck. Holly tried to say, "I'm sorry," but her voice gave out.

32

Belinda had thought she'd walked most of the dark paths of life in one way or another. She didn't mean to be self-pitying but burying a husband and a daughter had given her a sense of the shit of the world, that was all. Yet this was new. This was different. The little berk from the army had looked so pathetically relieved when she gave in. You'll have your compensation, then, he said, as if that meant anything. You can start again. Start again... Half the animals they were about to slaughter for no good reason she'd known from birth. Six, seven years, older some of them. And some time after they'd been reduced to a mass of staring eyes and stiff legs and stink and rot a lump of money would arrive in the bank, and she could start again. Dad had spent his life building that herd, and she'd spent half of hers getting it right, and she'd still been maybe ten years off a really settled group of animals. It would take twenty, thirty years to get back to where she was now. Could she face it? The endless rounds of auctions and buying animals that turned out to be sick and others that didn't mix in properly and produced too little and would never be any good, knowing that by the time it was starting to come together she might be dead herself... It was like setting out to walk across Africa and spending years of your life getting halfway and then being picked up by a giant hand and put right back at the beginning. Start again, Mrs Jones. Start again.

Holly had stopped shuddering against her side now. Belinda

would have liked to know what idiot told her she was responsible. Who would do that to a child? No matter what she said part of Holly would always believe it, of course she would, Belinda would have done herself. She'd had no idea Holly was crossing the motorway or had even met Will Sadler, and if she'd known what was she supposed to do about it – apart from tell her to be careful? Which she undoubtedly was, being Holly. Part of her was curious to know why Holly had gone but most of her was too tired. And like she'd said it didn't matter; it made no difference. The army were coming anyway, Holly's contact with Lower Marsh had been grist to the mill, that was all. The decision had been taken and all that was left was to make sure they did it right as Lieutenant Henton had promised.

So when they were all back in the house she said quietly that she was going to the yard and no-one else was to come. Vic had gone home, couldn't bear to stay, and she didn't blame him. That meant only Malcolm raised an objection: he took her to one side and said forcefully that it was bloody stupid to go, it wouldn't do any good, but if she insisted then he was coming with her. She told him that if he thought he was leaving Holly and his children to sit inside the house listening to gunshots for 14 hours with only Eva for company he had another think coming, and she could see him give up. He flashed that wry smile, the smile he always had, and said all right, then; but if she stayed too long he'd fetch her in on his back if he had to, and she couldn't help feeling a little less bleak despite herself.

Then she went out and watched them prepare to kill her animals. Seeing the slaughtermen surrounding the herd with their guns propped casually against the wall almost made her buckle; but she allowed her mind to go a little darker, and although it meant she was a little further away from the world and a little deeper inside the black emptiness in her head, she was at least in control. They started setting up a killing pen near the shed. The cattle were already uneasy as if they could smell what was coming. She told them to move the pen to the other end of the yard beyond the feed bins. "It'll take all fucking day if we do it there," one of them grumbled and she said she didn't care if it took all fucking week, they weren't killing the animals that close to the main herd. Henton came along and told them to do it as she wanted it done. She could see what they thought of him, the slaughtermen, from the sneering way they obeyed - but at least they did it.

And then far too suddenly it was ready and they took the first of them, Ginger. Ginger wasn't having any of it, she dug in her heels and they had to shove her all the way to the crush, slapping her back and flanks with their sticks. Belinda knew she was just unhappy at the change and had no idea what was coming but it looked so bloody much like courage and she suddenly thought Malcolm was right, she couldn't bear this. She turned her back when they put the bolt to the cow's head. The crack of it came sooner than she had thought and she felt it; not in her guts but on her skin. They were already lining up the next of them and leading them forward and the killing machine had started and she knew that nothing would stop it now.

★ ★ ★

Holly sat with her back to the wall for nearly an hour, listening to the shots echo. They were all in Ben's room. Malcolm put his head in sometimes but the rest of the time he was with Eva. Holly could hear shouting but no-one seemed to have the energy to listen properly. Julia was crying and Sal's face was white as it went on and on and on. Yvonne stood near Holly, but turned to the window. Perhaps even she could hear this, or sense it, from her

181

remote distance. Then although nothing changed it just reached a point where Holly couldn't stand it. She quietly got up and went out.

Ben followed her. "Holly?" he asked warningly. She said she was going to see Belinda and he should stay inside, but he didn't. She thought someone would stop them on the way to Top Yard but no-one did. They cut the corner up the bank and suddenly there it all was in front of them. Over on the left a mass of cows were heaped on their sides and Ben said in a sick hollow voice, "They're still moving."

Holly could see them twitching but she knew those animals, she knew their names and she couldn't look too closely. Ben registered her silence and said quickly that it was just reflexes, he was sure it was. She turned away and looked down the yard. There were men everywhere: leading the cattle forward and going in to the herd to separate them off one by one and leaning against the sides of the pen in case any of them tried to push their way out and it was as if they were workmen by a hole in the road, the way they stood and gossiped and laughed. At last Holly saw Belinda, standing by a post, her arms folded, and from the way the soldiers lowered their heads when they passed Holly knew that they understood how much courage this took and she felt another surge of pride.

Because she was watching Belinda, Ben saw it first and touched her arm. The cattle were agitated in the main pen, tucking themselves close together, their heads lowered, then starting and running first one way then another, and a knot of them in one corner had got into a panic. Two suddenly bucked up, their front legs sliding over the backs of the others in front, the white showing around their eyes. That set the whole group off and they surged towards the fence. The slaughtermen weren't looking. Holly heard the others shout but before the men could react and brace the posts the fence was down. The cattle pushed forwards and through the flailing arms of the two slaughtermen and started scrambling up the bank to the field.

Liam Purvis and two others were closest and Holly saw Liam say something to the others and then casually they lifted their rifles to their shoulders. "No, no," Holly murmured under her breath but even as she watched they fired into the mass of animals, all three shots almost simultaneous. Two of the cows staggered; from this distance she couldn't see which ones they were. One of them slipped, then kept going. The other went down on one front knee and tried to rise but blood was spurting from her neck and her muscles weren't working. Holly could see her eye staring and underneath was a jagged hole where the bullet must have come out and part of her face was missing.

The officer called out but ahead of him Belinda was walking woodenly towards the three men and Holly suddenly knew, for certain, what she would do: she would take the gun away from one of the men and shoot him, and then the other two would shoot her. It was so clear and vivid a premonition that for a dizzying moment she thought it had happened already. That was it: her whole potential family was gone in an instant and instead she would spend the rest of her life in Guildford calling Eva Mummy. Liam was still sighting along his rifle and he fired again but the other two had noticed Belinda's approach. They lowered their guns and held them foolishly at waist height, like children with toys. Holly knew what it was like to face the cold rage and fury that Belinda was capable of giving off, and she knew they wouldn't stop her. The officer had sprinted forwards and he got there almost at the same time as Belinda. She reached out for a gun and pulled. The man resisted for a second, no longer, and released. Belinda held the gun in one hand. Liam seemed only just to have noticed and he started to turn, and all he had to do

183

was pull the trigger. Here, in Top Yard, with the men all suddenly silent and the cattle slipping and lurching up the hill and fanning out into the distance and a tarpaulin flapping in the wind and the rich reek of slurry in the air, Holly knew there was nothing to stop her mother dying.

And then the long slow moment as Liam turned passed, and everything speeded up. The officer got in between all of them, his hands raised, and Belinda set off after the animals. He called to her but she kept going. Liam was watching and his gun was pointing that way but the army man pulled him round and started shouting at him and suddenly all the guns were lowered, their snouts meekly to the ground, and Holly realised Belinda was not going to die today. She walked up the slope to the cow still on its knees, its head sideways against the ground, and she put her hand against its flank then stood a few paces away and holding the gun at waist height she fired, and the cow jolted and its back end fell to the ground. Then she just stood looking down at it with the gun held loosely in her hands until a soldier came and took it from her. Belinda turned and walked back towards the yard. Holly saw her expression, and she had to get away.

Ben was still watching, his face slack. Holly slipped past him towards the house then left and through the gate. She kept going at a steady walk over the End and down the slope towards the Motorway, Yvonne keeping pace alongside her. She slipped through the fence, over the lip of the embankment and down to the tarmac, waiting calmly for a gap in the traffic. When it came she jogged across the road. Once she reached the Clearing she began to dig. Yvonne watched silently as she uncovered the surface of the chest, sweeping away the earth and lifting the lid. She sat in front of it and took out the Things one by one and arranged them around her. She placed them carefully and methodically: the Skull in front of her, the Lantern behind her back and the Eye to her left, the Cogs and the Lens and the Clock, all of them spaced out evenly in a circle. When she was done she sat for a moment quite still, though it felt as if her whole body was trembling. Then she picked up the Skull and put her boot on it. She pressed down against the soft earth and for a long time just held it there, sensing the resistance, ready to smash it into the ground and pick up all the Things and hit them again and again against the barrier till they cracked and broke and her hands bled.

After a long moment, though, Holly lifted her foot. The Skull was pushed into the earth and sticking up at an angle. She shifted position, and curled up against the cold bare ground. She didn't know if she slept or not, but the day gradually faded around her and it was properly dark by the time she heard voices through the sound of the traffic. She propped herself up painfully, her hands chilled, white and purple. She heard the slither of footsteps through the long grass and then there was Malcolm, with Ben and Sal behind him, Ben looking at her pleadingly. Holly sat mutely among all the Things that were hers, looking up at them. Malcolm squatted next to her and brushed his hand against her hair. Then without saying anything he picked her up and she clung to him as he carried her away. He struggled with her over the barrier and she could see the clearing with things lying in it like litter, and then he was hurrying with her across the road and it was gone.

33

Two days later Holly stood at the bottom of the drive, shivering in thin, persistent drizzle, waiting for Marian de la Mare. The last of the diggers that had dumped all the bodies of the cattle in trucks had gone. The farm was full of men disinfecting everything and the house was busy because Eva was at last actually leaving and everyone was arguing about that, so no-one even noticed Holly slipping down the drive. She had dutifully changed her clothes and disinfected her shoes though it seemed fairly pointless because there were no animals left to infect in this whole part of the country now. She tilted her face to the rain, feeling it striking her skin, seeking resolve from it. She knew she would need it. Marian had agreed to take her to the army headquarters to find Liam Purvis. If Marian ever turned up – and if Liam was there – it was Holly's last chance.

She had woken up after the cull not knowing how she was going to feel. In the night, after Malcolm had brought her back from the Reservation, she'd felt only a deep black destruction of everything and a kind of hollow pleasure from it, almost, that she remembered on the worst days with Yvonne at school: a spiteful vicious glee that everything was smashed and ruined and beyond repair. When she opened her eyes she felt nervous in case that feeling was still with her, because if it was, she knew she'd be powerless to fight it. In fact she had felt empty, clean, blank. Holly realised that for a long time she had been sustained, somehow, by the half-disbelieving fear that foot-and-mouth and the slaughter and everything that went with it was connected to Yvonne, and to ghosts, and to being haunted. Now she knew she'd been wrong. Liam hadn't been playing with her, she was sure he hadn't – the indifference and contempt with which he'd looked at Yvonne had made that clear. And the worst part of being wrong was that nobody was interested in Yvonne; nobody was coming because of her. Nothing at all would happen about Yvonne's ghost unless Holly made it happen. She swung her legs mechanically to the floor, certain of one thing: she was getting rid of her sister. Marian didn't know, or wouldn't say, how she'd lost her ghost. Maybe Liam would.

The absolute surety she felt must have worked on the phone to Marian, because although she'd initially sounded dubious, she'd given in pretty quickly. She had promised to be at the farm by 12 and to take her to the army base to see if Liam was there. "But that's it, Holly, dear. We're not going to chase the boy all over the country. We'll just do what we can, all right?" Holly had said that was fine although privately she thought her job was to be as much like Belinda as she could, whatever Marian said.

It was nearly quarter to one when Marian finally arrived. Holly hadn't been able to picture her in a car at all. It turned out she drove a little box-like thing that she more than half-filled.

"Sorry, dear, it's terribly confusing when you get out of town this way," she said as Holly got in. "And you were out there in the rain! Why didn't I get you both from the house? It would have been nice to see your mother again."

Holly felt a jolt of surprise at the casual reference to Yvonne, who had drifted in to the back seats, and also at the mention of her mother until she realised Marian meant Eva. She imagined

187

taking Marian up the drive and pushing her gently into the mass of shouting people. She'd probably have settled most of them in minutes, apart from Belinda. Maybe even Belinda.

"It's fine," Holly said, hunching down in her seat, grateful that Marian was one of those people who turned the heating in the car to maximum. They set off and Holly quickly discovered that Marian talked a lot when she drove, and was unable to concentrate on both that and the road, which meant she was by the far the worst driver Holly had ever known. When she was animated, talking about how hard the whole thing must have been for Holly's family, she sped up and they screeched round blind corners. When she was sympathetically telling Holly that it was going to be all right and looking at her more often than at the road she slowed down until they almost stopped. Then she'd remember and accelerate and the gears would grumble but she wouldn't change them, just wait patiently until eventually the car was hurtling along again. At least gripping the seat in terror was a distraction.

It didn't take long to get there. Holly could feel her pulse quicken as they pulled in to the entrance. Marian had said there might be barriers and Holly should know they might have to turn straight round again, but there was nothing, not even an inspection point. The site was chaotic, crammed with soldiers and military vehicles and vans and people with clipboards and men clearly from London with mud on expensive shoes, and they parked behind the main warehouse with no problems.

"Let's have a wander," Marian said, after she had prised herself from the car. She set off without a trace of anxiety, and Holly hurried behind feeling far less scared than she'd expected thanks to Marian's coolness.

Everywhere they went people seemed far too busy to be curious about them, even though one of them was enormous and dressed in turquoise and smelt like a whole shop of perfume and the other one was a child. Holly kept her head down thinking they'd be challenged at any moment, but they were even allowed inside offices without question. Maybe it was Marian's sense of entitlement: she walked into rooms as if she belonged there so the staff, who were probably all temporary, must simply have assumed that she did. Eventually Holly saw a door that said 'Mess Room and Non-Military Personnel' and touched Marian's arm.

"Good idea, love," Marian said. She marched across and went straight in and Holly followed to find herself in a room full of soldiers and slaughtermen, including Douggie, and Liam Purvis in the centre of it.

They all looked up, they could hardly have done otherwise with the entrance Marian made, and the room fell silent. Douggie blushed, which Holly thought was odd. There was a tiny pause and then Liam stood abruptly and walked straight towards them. Holly didn't feel sick though, perhaps because he was focusing on Marian. He said nothing, just pushed past them and walked out. Holly glanced at Marian, who shrugged, and they both turned and followed.

He was waiting for them in the courtyard. As soon as they came out he said, "What are you doing here?" seeming suddenly younger and much less sure of himself than Holly remembered.

Marian frowned a little, then shook herself and said, "Liam, I've brought this young lady to have a bit of a talk with you. And to see you for myself."

Holly watched, amazed. He was behaving like a man, like a young man. Like Douggie. That was all.

"Get away from here," he said. "I don't want to be seen with you."

Marian seemed to think it was going to be all right. She smiled and said, "Now come on, Liam, there's no need for that." She was so bland but at the same time unmoveable and Holly started to think they might actually be able to make him talk. "We used to be quite friendly, didn't we?"

"That was then," he said.

"Well, I think I helped you a little, you said as much yourself," Marian said comfortably. "And now this young lady needs some help and I think you'd like to give her that help, wouldn't you."

It wasn't a question, Holly could see that, and Liam looked around at the offices and the people standing in groups, some of them looking over with interest, and he snarled, really like an animal, then said, "Come on," and led them to another door. Inside it was like a school lunch room, lots of plastic tables and a smell of old sandwiches. He let them go in then stooped under the door and stood by it.

"Well?" he said.

34

Holly wanted to come straight out with her questions – no, her demands – but her throat suddenly felt thick. Before she could speak, anyway, he looked at her full in the face and she felt a touch of the old pressure against her forehead.

"I know why you're here," he said. "Douggie Small told me all about it." He turned to Marian. "Your little friend wants to know why all this is happening," he said. "Do you want me to tell her?"

Marian shook her head. "Why do you have to be like this?" she said. "You never used…"

Liam cut in. "I'll take that as a yes," he said. "But she won't like it."

He stepped closer to Holly, his head almost brushing the ceiling, his eyes bright. She wanted to stop him, tell him she couldn't care less about why, that there was only one thing she wanted from him, but his advance silenced her.

"People have been saying there's a conspiracy," he said. "I know, I've heard the talk. This was all part of some grand plan, animals were being moved round the country in secret, spreading the disease. And you know what? It's almost true, that's the sad part of it. Animals, maybe sick animals, were transported everywhere. And why? Because of greedy crooked little farmers like you and your family. You get government money for each animal, right? So you tell the government you've got a hundred sheep when it's only fifty. Before the inspector arrives to pay the money, you move in fifty more sheep. He signs the form, the sheep move ahead of him to the next farm, and on and on. That's the secret. That's your whole fucking mystery. Money. Cheap little crooks bringing it on yourselves, that's all you are, the lot of you."

His eyes gleamed, and Holly knew he thought he was hurting her, but none of this made her feel anything. Not afraid, not angry, nothing.

"I don't care," she said quietly. "I don't care about what you say and whether it's true and I don't care if you're so angry you want to kill everything you see. I don't care about you."

Something about her stillness and her quietness seemed to disturb him and he looked down at her uneasily. Marian started to speak but Holly raised a hand, feeling really like Belinda, and she fell silent. "All I care about is why you don't have a ghost," Holly said. "I know you did and now you don't and I want you to tell me how it happened and then I'll go away. And that's all."

"Oh Holly," Marian said with pain, but after a long pause Liam nodded. If anything he looked sourly amused.

"All right," he said. "I'm surprised she didn't tell you – " he indicated Marian with a dismissive wave of his hand – "but if that's what you want you're welcome to it."

He turned towards Marian. She held her ground, but he loomed over her. "All you need to know," he said, not looking at Holly, "is that everything this woman says is a lie. She tell you about spirits, right? About comfort? About guardian fucking angels?"

"Liam…" Marian said, but he just grinned down at her, lips tight over his teeth.

"You heard," he said. "A lie. You told me that Jamie cared for me, I'd been blessed that he stayed with me, it was a gift. Well that was fucking bullshit, it was, proper bullshit." He turned to Holly again. "I tell you what happened. I worked in a warehouse and one day there was an accident and these two guys were killed, right? So I went over to them and Jamie saw it and bang, like that, he was gone. And I knew what had happened well enough. He'd seen how it was supposed to be. You die, you go, that's it, goodbye. He hung around me because he was a coward and he couldn't face it, that's all. Like that thing hanging round you. A fucking coward."

Holly was listening avidly, her eyes wide, fixed on him. Marian said, with infinite pity, "You must be in such pain all the time," and Liam sneered.

"Yeah? How about you?" He grinned at Holly now and Holly could see in that wild empty grin that Marian was right, he was saturated with anger and pain to the point that nothing else was left. "You want to know how I'm sure? About Jamie?" he said. "The same thing happened to her. Her dead husband trails around after her for years, then her best friend ups and kills herself, she finds the body, fucking bingo. He gets it. Job done. No problem. Gone."

Holly looked at him unsteadily. Marian was staring at the ground and Holly knew that what he'd said about her was true. And his own story, too, that must surely have been the truth, she thought; he had nothing to gain from lying. So where did that leave her? Needing to show Yvonne death. That was hardly something she could just fix up. She'd already seen three dead bodies in thirteen years, which by any standard was more than her share. Now she was supposed to find another one?

Liam walked to the door but just before it he turned. "You want my advice?" he said. He jerked his hand at Yvonne. "You show that thing what I see every day: hundreds, thousands of animals being shot and torched. Take it to a pyre and stand there and watch them burn and you'd better pray it gets the message and finds some courage and is gone. Otherwise..." he paused, and grinned again, or snarled, Holly couldn't tell. "Otherwise you'll be stuck with it for life, and the only one showing it how to die will be you."

Marian drove Holly home, talking all the time. She told Holly that she was sorry and that Liam had become a very confused and hurt man and Holly didn't need to listen to anything he said, but Holly let the flow of talk wash over her. Instead she gazed through her window at the smoke rising, thinking about what Liam had said. If ghosts really needed to face death, then what better sign of it all around the country than these choking fires, this blood, this slaughter? She remembered Yvonne facing the window as their own herd had been shot. Was that her sensing the killing, trying to comprehend its meaning? Every time she disappeared, perhaps she was drifting out to watch the smoke heavy in the sky, feeling some instinct drawing her forward. The more Holly thought about it the more convincing the idea became. She had a sudden vision, not just of Yvonne, but of ghosts all over the country standing formless and irresolute in empty fields, watching the great columns of smoke rise all around them. Perhaps there were centuries' worth of them to be called: tattered fragments of children and men and women, the great horde of the dead, tugged from churchyards and overgrown ruins and old houses, gliding down country lanes and across the windswept open fields, feeling themselves impelled inexorably to the conflagration. And perhaps if Holly joined that silent procession, if she stood with Yvonne and the rest of the dead gazing mutely into the flames, feeling the heat on her skin and the grease and the rankness all around her, perhaps then, she thought, Yvonne would at last understand, and she would at last be free.

35

When Holly got home she half thought she should leave for a pyre there and then, but she didn't know the way and it was wet and cold and getting late; and more than that it was her only hope, so delaying the moment when she found out whether or not it worked was no bad thing either. Also she had to see Ben. Even the fragile promise he'd given her felt strong enough that she couldn't imagine not sharing this with him; not sharing everything with him, for as long as they would have together. When she got to his room, though, she found Sal and Julia there as well.

"We didn't know where you were," Ben said, and Julia said, "Mummy's gone."

"I know," Holly said awkwardly, and went in and sat down with them. They started talking about Eva leaving and what it meant. Holly caught a significant look from Ben which she understood to mean he hadn't told them anything. Except Holly now knew that what he had to tell them wasn't true. As, she presumed, did Sal, given that Eva had talked to her so much before she left – though Sal was unsurprisingly giving nothing away. That left Julia as the only one who knew nothing at all, and she was the one talking most. Poor Julia, Holly thought, and found herself really meaning it.

After a while Holly asked where everyone else was. Malcolm was in his room drinking alone, which wasn't unheard of, Ben said, but still a bad sign. Belinda had walked off in the middle of the argument about Eva leaving and hadn't been seen since. Holly nodded as if to say, of course, that's exactly what she would do, I knew that. She wondered if she should try to find her. Since the cull they had only seen each other about four times. Once Holly had put her arm round her and Belinda had leaned against her for a while, but then she'd gone to be by herself. And that, Holly knew, was what she would always do. However bad it was, she would always deal with it in her own private way.

Then Ben asked again where Holly had been. Sal and Julia were silent and Holly realised it was a bigger deal than she thought.

"It's just that no-one knew where you were," Sal said quietly. "They thought…" She broke off. What, Holly wondered? What did people think?

"Belinda said you'd be fine," Ben said hastily. "But, you know. What gives?"

For a moment Holly tried to think of a convincing lie but it felt very tiring and she suddenly wondered if she could just tell all of them the truth. Sal and Julia knew most of it, anyway, thanks to Ben. She hadn't imagined telling anyone apart from him, but he had betrayed this confidence first. And more than that she remembered the preparations before the army came, and all of them being together, and how good it had felt. If they were to be a Family – she told herself not to think it, but it was already too late – then shouldn't she be able to talk to Sal and Julia about this?

It had been quite a long pause now and no better idea had occurred to Holly so she took a deep breath and told them. She told them everything apart from the advice Liam had given her about the pyre; that she didn't want to risk by speaking openly about it to them all. When she stopped talking no-one spoke for a moment, and Holly wondered if Sal and Julia would think she was mad and be too embarrassed to say anything; but then she realised that Julia was literally open-mouthed, she had never seen anyone do that for real before, and even Sal looked almost out of her depth, and suddenly questions poured out of them.

"So… Yvonne's here right now?" Julia asked eventually after Holly had told them again about Douggie and Marian and Liam. Holly nodded and glanced involuntarily at her.

"Right there?" Sal said, watching, and Holly said, "Yes," faintly. Sal said she wanted to stand on the same spot to see if she felt anything and Holly directed her, feeling dazed, and then Ben stood there and even Julia, who shrieked immediately and ran away and they were all talking animatedly about it and Holly realised that it might always have been like this if she'd told them right from the beginning, and the thought brought a sudden lump to her throat.

By suppertime Belinda still wasn't back and Malcolm was still in his room, so they went down to make sandwiches and Ben asked about the plan. Holly had been thinking that there was one thing she could do before going to the pyre: she could go and see Will again. That would put her hope to a smaller test than the all or nothing of the fire. If they found Will; if Will's ghost had been disappearing, too, given everything that was happening – or, Holly thought, *had even left already…* so she suggested it diffidently. Ben said it was a brilliant idea but Julia immediately looked worried. Before she could express her disquiet though Sal pre-empted her and said she'd come along, if Holly didn't mind, and that decided it. Ben said they could take food and it would be an adventure and more than anything else it would get them off the farm for the first time in weeks, so Julia shakily nodded her head and they were going, it was that simple.

As Ben talked enthusiastically about it Holly watched Sal. Whenever she'd thought about the Family she hadn't really included

Sal, partly because she guessed she'd be leaving for university soon, but mostly because of her remote indifference. Since Eva had left, though, or even maybe before that, since they'd found Eva in the barn, Sal had seemed more like her old self: cool and aloof, yes, but graciously taking part, which made everyone feel as cool as she was. Maybe seeing Eva like that had cut into Sal's hermetically sealed world, Holly thought; had been enough to haul her back to reality, or at least closer to reality. In which case, that was another good thing to have come out of Eva's departure, she thought guiltily. It was true, though – having Sal with them made the whole trip seem less daunting. Holly joined in with the planning, answering Ben and Julia's questions as best she could until suddenly they fell silent and she turned and saw that Malcolm had come downstairs.

He stood in the doorway. He wasn't swaying but his eyes were glassy and they bulged. "We few, we happy few," he said, and now he was slurring his words.

Julia was looking at the table and Holly remembered his odd scorn the last time he'd been drunk and felt a fierce stab of hope that he wouldn't be unkind to her again. She was helplessly growing feelings for Julia and she wondered if this was what happened to normal people with Families even when they didn't really like them. Malcolm came and sat heavily at the table. Sal asked if he wanted food and he only waved a hand but she cut him bread and made him a sandwich and he started eating it clumsily.

"Here we are, then, surviving," he mumbled through a mouthful. After a while they heard the door and Belinda came in. She dropped her hand on Holly's shoulder as usual as she passed, then sat at the other end of the table with a glass of wine. Holly couldn't remember the last time she'd seen Belinda eat anything. Steeling herself Holly asked if she was all right. Belinda smiled vaguely at her.

"We'll get there," she said. Looking up and down the table Holly thought it was hardly the ideal Family yet, but maybe Belinda was right. Then she looked at Yvonne, standing mournfully on the other side of the room. As long as this worked.

The next morning felt good. Ben was grinning and even Sal half-smiled when she met Holly's eye. They had shared purpose, they had made a plan, they were doing something. Ben said he'd do the talking if anyone asked where they were going, but Malcolm was yawning hugely and saying he was going back to bed and Belinda said nothing as usual. They pulled on boots in the back porch and then they were out and walking round the house four abreast. Like this Holly felt ready for anything, she felt...

She stopped walking. Four abreast. Not five. The others stopped too and looked at her quizzically. Holly turned fast and scanned the garden and the stand of trees and the sheds and then she saw her: Yvonne, on the far side of the trees, drifting off towards Back Field. It was the first time Holly had seen her leaving. This was her chance to follow, to see if Yvonne was really being drawn away.

Ben asked her what was wrong. "She's going," Holly said simply. They all followed her gaze. She took a few quick paces after Yvonne then looked back at the others. "We have to follow. I mean... does anyone mind if we... on the way..."

Ben grinned. "Mind?" he said. "Lead on, Macduff." Holly smiled at him gratefully, then started off on Yvonne's trail. Come on, she thought. *Come on.*

36

Ben fell into step alongside Holly, taking care not to be too close, not to crowd. She kept looking up, presumably at Yvonne. It was so weird seeing her focus on something that wasn't there, watching her eyes track across an empty field. Holly was walking really fast, almost running, and flexing her fingers as she walked.

"What is it?" he said. "She's left before, so…"

She flashed a quick look at him. "Yeah, it's just… something Liam said. I think each time this happens she's kind of… being drawn away."

He nodded slowly, knowing there was something she wasn't telling him, and that it was because of what he'd done to her: that he'd really hurt her. Not for the first time he felt self-loathing surge up in his throat but before it could really crawl out and into his mind he pushed it firmly down. It worked, though it was still squirming and he didn't know how much longer he'd be able to control it. He told himself, had told himself a hundred times, that whatever he started to feel wouldn't be real, and that what was real was what he felt for Holly right now. But he'd tried leaving messages for himself before, and once the emptiness overtook him they'd seemed as meaningless as everything else.

Holly led them past the yard and the cattle shed, which were still taped off after the disinfecting, through a gate and along a hedgerow on one side of a field, heading uphill. It was windy, more so as they left the shelter of the farm buildings. The grass rippled and shook in the wind and the shadows of clouds ran quickly across the hillside. He looked over his shoulder as they climbed. Sal was right behind them and Julia was lagging at the back but he knew she wouldn't complain. She'd been so much more… accepting, maybe, was the word. Ever since the army, if not before. Since they'd come here. Sal too, actually, despite all the circumstances.

Ahead of them and to the right the land swelled up to a high mounded hill. He'd climbed it when they first came to the farm, just to get to the highest point. He'd sat looking down at the house and the barns and the motorway beyond, shivering in the cold, but feeling serene. Just… calm. At the time it had felt like it would last forever, it always did; but it had only been a brief window before the energy had started to build and build again, until he felt like he did now, nerves all firing signals all the time, starting to buzz. Restless and hollow and wanting something that was always just out of reach.

When they got to the end of the field, Holly turned away from the hill, towards the last hedge before the bare slopes of downland. She stopped and looked ahead, shielding her eyes with her hand.

"What?" Ben said, following her gaze, hoping for a glimpse of something ghostly but as ever seeing nothing.

"I can't see her," Holly said. "She went to the far corner but…"

She broke off and started really running this time, stumbling over the uneven grass. In the corner of the field the hedgerow thickened into a clump of bramble and thorn and Holly ran right up to it. He came up behind her and she held out her arm to stop him. He looked over her shoulder, hands on his hips, enjoying breathing hard, feeling like he wanted to keep running and running. There was an opening in the bramble ahead of them like a pathway and inside it was dark, but he could see bare earth and the sinuous narrow trunks of the thorn bushes.

"Where does this lead?" he said.

"Nowhere," Holly said, catching her breath too. "It's not a path. Must just have been the cows. Using it for shelter."

She was peering intently into the thicket and he said, "She's in there, right?" Holly nodded. "What's she doing?"

"I don't know," Holly said. "Just standing."

She stepped forward, ducking her head under the low jagged branches. He looked back along the field. Sal was coming over the slope of the hill, walking not running, and he waved to show where they were going. She nodded and looked behind for Julia, and he went into the thicket after Holly. He had to bend right down at first but inside he could stand almost straight. The air was cold and still and the earth underfoot was dry. Over their heads the thorn bushes made a complete roof, their trunks supporting it like twisted, writhing pillars, and all around they were enclosed by deep banks of weed and bramble. He glimpsed the grey grass of the downs beyond.

"It's like a cave," he said, whispering for some reason. Holly nodded absently. She put her hands in the pockets of her coat, and her face was grim. "No leaving going on, I guess?" Ben said.

She shook her head. "Nope. Nothing," she said. "Same as ever."

Ben nodded. He couldn't think of anything to say, so he put his arm round her and she leaned into him. Behind them footsteps approached and Sal came in, crouching but still catching her hair in the sharp branches, and Julia behind her.

"This place is amazing," Julia said, breathing heavily.

Holly moved away from Ben. "Yeah, well. Nothing's happening though," she said.

"But… this is where she comes?" Ben said. "When she leaves you?" Holly shrugged and he said, "So there must be a reason."

Sal nodded. "Maybe this is Yvonne's place. Like you and the motorway," she said.

Ben saw Holly flinch and said quickly, "Yeah, but it's nothing like that, is it?"

"She did come here, though," Julia said. "Look."

Ben turned. She was on the other side of the clearing pointing to the branches. There were faded red ribbons twisted round them. The ribbon was wet and mouldy but it had definitely been put there on purpose. Holly wandered slowly forwards as if she was in a trance and reached up to the ribbon. Ben followed. It had things tied in it, a rusted key and a sprig of some kind of plant and for some reason a plastic set square.

"You had no idea?" he said quietly to Holly and she shook her head.

"There's stuff too," Julia said. In among the roots of the brambles there was a square of blue tarpaulin and something underneath it.

"Shall we?" Ben asked. Holly looked at him searchingly.

"It's Yvonne's private things," Sal said, but in her usual way so it was impossible to tell what she meant by that.

"I think it should be up to Holly," Julia said. Holly looked at her and then at him and nodded slowly. He squatted down by the tarpaulin. It was wrapped around a wooden chest, discoloured and bulging with damp. He remembered Holly sitting by that metal box on the reservation surrounded by her stuff, the skull and the lantern and the cat's eyes and the rusting pieces of engine. How weird would it be if this box contained exactly the same things, item for item. What would Holly do? Pass out, probably.

He turned to find Holly right behind him. She'd seen the box and she was swaying already.

"You're sure?" he asked, and she nodded again. He had to wrestle to get the box out from the bramble but the last stalk finally tore away and there it was. Holly looked over her shoulder at wherever Yvonne was standing. "Nothing?" he asked.

203

She shook her head. Their eyes met for a moment, then he got his fingers under the lid and pulled. It wasn't locked but the wood was warped and for a moment wouldn't give; then it yielded with a screech and the box was open. Inside it was full of stuff, wrapped neatly in clear plastic bags. He started handing them up to Holly. The first one had three rosettes in it, their tails carefully folded up. The next one contained butterfly wings, glittering and iridescent even through the dull plastic, then the third shells, some still crusted with dark sand. There were more and more, dozens of them: he saw bags with yellow stars that must have been glow-in-the-dark and another with a tin moon and more with cast-iron miniatures of dragons holding crystals. Sticking up at the back he saw a plastic-wrapped folder and drew it out then looked up at Holly. Her eyes were full of tears.

"All her things," Julia said. She was crying too. Holly tried to say something but couldn't. Ben opened the folder. It was full of Christmas cards and birthday cards and at the back were some photos, sticky with damp. The first one showed Holly on her own against a sunlit wall. He unpeeled it carefully. The next one was Holly too. He started to feel a terrible presentiment. The next one was Holly as well. And the next. He opened the card. It was addressed to Holly, with love, from Grandma. That was all it said. There were dozens of cards there. Sal was next to him and he showed her. She frowned, not understanding.

"Holly…" Ben started to say, but she shook her head, wiping at the tears with the back of her hand.

"I know," she said. "And the stuff."

Julia looked at them all in the gloom under the bushes. "What is it?" she asked.

"This," Ben said. "All of it. It isn't Yvonne's. It's Holly's."

37

Holly didn't say much going down the hill to the motorway. Julia had tried: Yvonne must really have loved Holly, then, she'd said, looking from Ben to Sal for support. No-one had answered, and Julia hadn't pushed it. They all knew, Holly thought, even Julia must have known really. Whatever Yvonne had been doing, it wasn't love. At least not as Holly would understand it, though what with Yvonne on one side and Belinda on the other and Ben wherever he was in this picture, she couldn't claim to be an authority on the subject.

She tried to fit this into her mind. All of the stuff had been things she wouldn't really miss: the shells she'd collected on holiday and then forgotten about, bits and pieces she'd won at school and put in a drawer somewhere, the rosettes for their brief and abortive attempt to enter riding competitions, which even Yvonne had asked to stop going to after they'd seen how Pony Club people looked at Belinda and at the cars they drove and at the state of their tough little pony's coat. They were things that one day she might have liked to find, but would never actively have sought out. And Yvonne had taken them and stored them all. The pictures, too.

"It's probably like voodoo," Holly had said, as Ben started stacking the little bags away again, and half-laughed. The others had met her eye and looked away without smiling in return and Holly had realised they either thought she was serious, or that she was right, and found either difficult to deal with.

"It's... fascination, maybe," Sal had said, as Ben pushed back the box, and he had been bravest: "It's creepy, whatever it is," he'd said.

Really, though, all Holly knew for sure was that Yvonne was troubled by her: inexpressibly made uneasy, in the same way that she was by Yvonne. There was no revelation to it, exactly – given how horrible Yvonne had often been at school, it was obvious that there was a problem. But Holly had never understood so clearly a kind of kinship with Yvonne. It was as if they'd both been orbiting, unknown to each other, one central fact: the mistake of their duality. Was it confusion, she thought, looking at Yvonne's ghost, simply that: the sense of aberration that kept her here? And if so – because everything for Holly was reduced only to this context now – how more or less likely did that make the chance of Yvonne leaving? The only certainty was that Yvonne hadn't felt any pull to leave so far; had in fact being going to a place that was all about Holly. For a moment Holly felt a gulf of disappointment opening up in her, but she turned away from that darkness. This could be a good thing. It could mean that Yvonne hadn't yet looked beyond her, and twinship, and being alive, so the first sight of the fire might shock her into departure. It was possible, she told herself. She had Ben now, and the next best thing to sisters. Many things were possible.

They headed straight across country for the tunnel. When Holly had told the others about it the night before Julia had asked why they couldn't just run across the road in a gap in the traffic. Holly hadn't been able to explain, exactly. She felt that she had lost the reservation for good, but her instincts still shied away from that action, from breaking the barrier that the reservation represented – it retained that vestige of its former power. In the end she'd just shrugged and not answered and Julia had accepted the silence with her new-found good grace.

This time, with all of them together, Holly felt almost immune to the horror of the tunnel. Julia hung back a little but Ben led the way in. There was no sign of the dead badger and Holly wondered briefly what might have taken it but she had unpleasant visions of rats and decided it was best not to speculate and then suddenly they were through, a hundred times more easily than before.

"Which way, then?" Ben said, and Holly said she didn't know. The others looked at her and suddenly Sal laughed and they were all laughing now that they were out in the broad expanse of the valley, and the darkness of the tunnel and the thicket were behind them. Holly explained that she hadn't made it as far as the house last time, but there was a lane up on the right that must lead to it, so they should try that way.

The lane took them in a long loop off to the north. One side was mostly open, with low hedges and fences, but on the other was a high bank that sheltered them from the wind and it was quieter. Ben started kicking along a stone with real concentration, stopping and getting it out of the grass if it skewed off to either side. Holly watched him. Every now and then he gave her a quick smile but mostly his head was down. She knew he was slipping. He had the same odd energy and restlessness that she remembered from the reservation, not that she liked to think about it much. She felt a fear, not far off panic, at the thought of his mood turning, at the extent of the change that could be coming. So soon, she thought, so soon... she'd told herself she would be ready, the next time, but she knew she wasn't. She didn't begin to know how to prepare for this.

After nearly twenty minutes there had been no sign of a turning or an entrance. What with the detour up the hill they'd been walking for nearly two hours, and Julia in particular seemed exhausted.

Up ahead there was a wooden fence and on the other side a pool fringed with trees. Julia asked if they could all stop for a bit. Holly saw a quick spasm of irritation cross Ben's face, but Sal nodded. She and Julia climbed the fence and sat on the grass looking across the water. Ben sat on the top bar of the fence, drumming his heels, staring into the distance.

Holly leaned next to him. "Are you all right?" she asked, as casually as she could.

"We should tell them," he said abruptly.

She looked up at him. "Tell them what?"

"Mum," he said. "And your Dad. They ought to know."

Holly must have looked like she felt, because he said quickly that she should have heard them, yesterday, before she'd come back. Julia had been talking and talking about why Eva might have left and what had gone wrong and Sal clearly hadn't known because she'd been getting more and more annoyed the whole time. "And I just thought they should know," he said. "Not knowing isn't fair."

He looked down at her from his perch. The wind caught his hair and blew it in front of his face and his eyes were dark behind it. Now that she'd seen this happen once before Holly noticed all the little changes with a sad kind of detachment. She could tell that he wasn't feeling the darkness descending yet, but he certainly wasn't himself any more either. In some way that was impossible to define he was losing his warmth. His face had curled up almost in disgust when he'd spoken of Eva.

"Only if you don't mind," he said, watching her. "Everyone knowing about your Dad, I mean."

Julia overheard that and turned towards them from where she was sitting. "What about her Dad?" she said.

Ben said, "Holly?" and she opened and closed her mouth. It was happening so fast, and she didn't have time to think. She couldn't let him tell the others what she knew to be a lie; but did that mean she was telling everyone about Malcolm and Belinda right here? That seemed impossible too so in the end she did nothing. She let it happen. Ben jumped down from the fence.

"We've got something to tell you," he said.

They reacted pretty much as Holly expected. Julia protested, almost tearful, until Ben overrode her, speaking fast and forcefully. Sal leaned against a post looking into the distance and not revealing if – as Holly suspected – she knew the true version; though she had a faint half-smile, typical Sal, that suggested neither this nor anything else came as a surprise to her. Holly just looked at the ground as Ben was talking, feeling hot sharp pulses of guilt that she was doing nothing to stop him. She told herself there were good reasons to keep silent. Eva had told her the truth in confidence, for one thing. And for another Ben's state was clearly fragile, and it wouldn't be fair to contradict him in front of the others.

She knew, though, that neither of these reasons were really stopping her. A dark part of her mind wanted them to believe it: to believe the lie. If this was what they all thought, that Eva had been the one to betray both marriages; if they blamed Eva; then when – if, she corrected herself, if – Malcolm and Belinda got together, they'd be more likely to accept it. What kept her silent was the idea of what she herself stood to gain. As she admitted that, she saw again Eva's face as it had been in the barn, and felt a physical shudder of pity run through her. The dark part of her mind retreated, but she knew that she had let it win, and the shame stayed on her skin like grease.

After Ben finished talking Sal walked off and stood looking out over the pool. Ben joined her and Holly watched them, knowing

Julia was watching too. They didn't talk, Sal and Ben, just stood by the water's edge. For the first time in what seemed like ages, perhaps because Sal was spending time with them again, or because Ben was changing, Holly was aware of how like each other they were, and how unlike everyone else. The dark hair and skin, the black eyes, the gap between them and the world. She wondered if Julia felt the same sense of separation, had always felt it, and if there was a loneliness in that. Maybe it would be different if they were all together, Holly thought, and Julia wasn't the odd one out. Maybe it would really work.

Watching Ben and Sal, and seeing how much more like her he became when his mood was shifting, Holly realised: the Ben who stood on the edge of the pool now, and the Ben who would be left behind once the coldness had overtaken him… they were as much the real Ben as the one she knew. They weren't aberrations from his true self: they were his different true selves. She couldn't just wait for the one she preferred to return, time after time. If what she felt was real, then when he left for whatever darkness it was that his mood brought on him, she'd have to follow. If she could. She didn't know where she'd find the strength she'd need to do it, but she had to try. Somewhere, in her mind, her stomach, her bones, she knew there was no alternative. Holly held on to the rough wooden fence, feeling the blustery air cold on her skin, and watched Ben starting to close himself off; watched him leaving her. *I love you*, she thought.

38

When they decided to move on they went round the pond and across the next field, instead of following the lane any further. Holly walked with Sal in silence and Julia and Ben were ahead. Holly looked up as they reached the end of the field and stiffened. Ben and Julia had stopped and something looked wrong. Julia suddenly turned and put her arms round Ben. He must get hugged all the time, Holly thought, remembering the thicket. She and Sal hurried forwards.

"What is it?" Sal said but Holly knew the smell and was expecting it, so even as Ben said, "Don't look," she leaned over the hedge. There was a dead bull on the other side, lying against the long grass and thistle at the edge of the field. Looking at its head there was only a neat round hole that indicated anything was wrong, though there were flies and movement around the sweep of its shoulders and belly and she could see the bubbled edges of rotting flesh down there out of the corner of her eye. Behind her Holly could hear someone being sick and she realised with slight surprise that it was Sal. Then she looked back at the head and thought she could see something dark and shiny moving inside the hole and even she was suddenly unsteady. She pulled away, and looked around for Yvonne. Was she watching this, absorbing this, learning from it? But she was standing a little way off, looking apparently into the distance.

Ben stepped towards Sal who was wiping her face, but she

shook him off and said, "Let's just go." They walked along the hedgerow to a gap in the corner.

"How could they just leave it?" Ben said, but Holly raised her hand to silence him. The next field was a huge square of pasture, almost perfectly flat, and it was littered with bodies.

"They left all of them," Holly said.

The field looked like the high downland where there were stones everywhere rising from the earth, but the outcrops here were flesh. Holly had thought the smell was strong for just one animal. The wind was blowing away from them so it wasn't suffocating, but there was no mistaking the sweet stink of corruption. Apart from the wind ruffling hair, the flanks of the cattle were eerily solid: still and inert.

"There are *hundreds*," Ben said, and Holly guessed he was right, there were nearly two hundred maybe, bigger than their own herd. From the look of it the slaughtermen had done what they started to do at home: stood and shot the cattle as they were. Maybe Will left the cattle out anyway, or maybe he'd opened the gates, thinking he might give them a chance. And Will had had to watch it all; and then, which was ten times worse, had been left to live amongst it. It had been weeks ago, Holly thought, remembering standing next to him when the slaughtermen arrived. He'd been living amongst this for weeks. She felt the pity of it, but couldn't help feeling hope, too, that it had been enough: that this experience had taught his ghost, and that perhaps it had already left him. Yvonne again wasn't looking, exactly. But how could she be immune to this?

The others were staring bleakly at the littered field. "Maybe they left them all on purpose," Ben said. "Like a punishment."

Sal shook her head. "I read about this," she said. Despite having just been sick she now seemed as poised and calm as ever. "In the paper. It's happened other places too."

"But they took the cows from our farm," Julia said, and despite herself Holly almost smiled to hear her say 'our farm'. Then she looked out across the field and she did smile, a tight stretch of her lips, because otherwise she might have been sick too.

Sal said it was pretty common for them to be left, though: sometimes they meant to build a new pyre and didn't collect the bodies until it was ready and sometimes they just forgot. Either way, she said, it could hardly be healthy around all of this, so they should get to the house and then get out of here. The farm buildings started just beyond the open field but they didn't have to walk through the dead cattle, Ben said, pointing out a long curve of land that would lead them up and around the back of the house. He and Sal and Julia started walking, wanting to get out of sight of the field, but Holly just stood looking at it.

"Wait," she said. She was imagining what might have happened to Will. To have lived so long surrounded by the bodies left to rot; maybe to have lost his ghost – she had been so focused on the relief she would feel that she'd forgotten what it might have done to him. Maybe he would have felt Marian's grief, or Liam's anger... she thought about the gun. And the dogs.

She tried to explain this to the others. She could see Julia's face screwing up and didn't blame her, even she suddenly thought they should go back, but Ben didn't let them discuss it. He looked at Holly and must have seen the decision forming on her face because he shook his head and said, "But you need to know. Right?"

She gripped her hands together. "Yeah, but..."

"So he's mad," Ben cut in. "So we'll be careful. We'll keep out of sight and when we get to the house I throw stones at it or something and if anyone sticks a gun out of the window we run away."

Julia said they couldn't, it was too dangerous, but Ben said if they did find Will on his own waving guns around then apart from anything else he needed help, and they could call the police and the ambulance and get it for him. Besides which, he said, he would go on by himself if they didn't want to come with him, and at that Holly knew she at least had no choice.

"All right," she said. "Let's go."

The last half-mile took forever. They walked up to the back of the farm but the gate leading into the yard was surrounded by buildings and in full view of the house. There was no sign of life but dust and straw skittered across the concrete, and somewhere corrugated iron was banging, and even Ben said it wasn't safe. They went back and found a gap in the hedge and squeezed through. They were in another long narrow field and on the other side was a lane. Even though it wasn't that close to the house they all ran across the strip of field ducking. When they got into the cover of the hedge on the far side Holly realised she'd started to feel an odd kind of exultation. She was near laughter, and sensed that if she did laugh she might never stop, but as long as she kept it under control it gave her power, as if she could run faster than she ever had before and get away from anything, even bullets.

Sal's face was blank and Holly couldn't tell if she was getting the same rush. Julia definitely wasn't, though, she was shaking. When they pushed through the hedgerow and stepped down into a dry grassy ditch and up onto the verge of the lane she shook her head. "I don't want to do this," she said, but the energy was crackling through Ben now and he said they could all wait here if they wanted but he was getting to that house. Out on the lane and shut in by hedgerows on either side it felt worse, somehow, like a trap. Holly looked at the other two. Sal shrugged and Julia turned away. Ben was already walking down the lane, bent low beneath the line of the hedge, looking at the house as it came into view. Holly had a sudden vision of him jerking and falling from a bullet's impact like the cattle and she knew she couldn't stand here and watch that happen to him.

"I'm going," she said, and ran along the lane up to Ben, who was by the entrance to Will's drive. The house was close to the road behind an unkempt patch of garden. He looked around as Holly approached.

"Cars must pass along here, right?" he whispered. "He's hardly going to shoot us on a public highway, or whatever."

He wanted to stand up but Holly pulled him back. "Ben," she said. "You have to think about this." She didn't know if she would dare say it but then it came out in a rush. "You know what's happening to you, don't you? Right now. You must do."

Again his face showed a flicker of something dark, close to anger, but she watched him fight it down. "Holly... I know," he said. "All right? But this is how I am now. And right now we're finding this guy."

He looked at her, defiant, and Holly took a deep breath and kissed him hard on the mouth. For a moment he didn't respond then he pushed back hungrily. She didn't know if Julia and Sal could see and she didn't care. He pulled away after a moment and gave her a long considering look, and she knew he understood what that kiss meant: that she accepted whatever was coming. Suddenly he smiled.

"Here's to not getting shot," he said, and sprinted forwards across the gateway. Holly shut her eyes but then made herself open them and look not at him but at the house. There was no movement. The ground-floor windows were netted and the upper-floor ones were blank. The whole place seemed deserted.

Ben got into cover on the other side of the gateway then looked back at Holly and saluted. Again she felt the strange humourless

215

laughter almost erupt. She looked at Yvonne next to her and was about to whisper *do it and come what may*, but she remembered what happened the last time she said that, and instead, very clearly and precisely, said, "Fuck it." She pushed herself up and ran through the gate, across the overgrown lawn to an old apple tree in the corner, half-buried in ivy. Next to it was a huge rusted garden roller that hadn't moved in years and she skidded behind it, her heart beating so hard she could feel her arms shaking. Yvonne was slowly following across the grass. Ben came sprinting round the corner and threw himself down next to her.

"You're fucking crazy," he said, and Holly said, "Like you can talk, schizo," and this time they both did laugh out loud.

After a minute Holly had her breath back, and before she could think about what a bad idea it was she stood and ran straight up to the house and pressed her back against it. She saw Ben shake his head, and then he ran out from the cover of the roller and across the garden after her, but instead of stopping he went past her and on round the side of the house. She followed slowly, creeping alongside the wall. Around the corner there was an uncurtained window, and Ben was peering cautiously through it. She slid along the wall and joined him. On the other side of the glass hung long sticky coils of flypaper, black with flies, and it took her a moment to make out what she was seeing beyond them. A kitchen, full of dark cabinets and a table covered with dirty plates. Two chairs were overturned on the floor and next to them, arranged in neat lines, were the bodies of three dogs. Each one had been shot cleanly in the head. A rifle was propped against the wall by the last of the bodies.

"Jesus," Ben whispered, and Holly nodded slowly. "That's his gun, right?" he said.

She shrugged. "One of them."

They exchanged a glance and half-laughed again. "So... he

must have done this," Ben said. "The slaughtermen would never have killed the dogs. He did."

Holly nodded. Next to them she could feel Yvonne drift close. *Look*, she thought intently. *You want death? It's here again.*

"What now?" Ben said. "If he killed the dogs then..." he trailed off. Holly looked at him and knew they were having the same thought. Then maybe he'd killed himself. Or maybe he was waiting in the house, ready to kill anything or anyone who came near. She sensed movement behind her and turned, her heart racing, but it was Sal.

"Did you see the note?" she said. They shook their heads. "On the door. Come on."

They followed her back round the house. There was no sign of Julia and Holly guessed Sal had just left her in the lane. The door had glass panels and the note was stuck behind one of them, almost invisible against the netting. On it was a single word in thin biro: 'GONE'.

"I guess that's it," Ben said. "He's gone away."

Holly was only half listening, though. She stared at the note. Gone. *Gone*. She remembered coming here before. *Not dead, not dying, not going.* Suddenly she found it hard to breathe. Gone. Dead and gone. Was it Will who'd left, or, she thought, her heart racing, was it Will who'd been left – after all these years, had he been left in peace?

39

If the door had been locked the decision would have been harder, because they'd have needed to break in. But when Holly reached out and the door opened at her touch she knew she had to go inside. Had to look for him. Because either he was gone, in which case she'd be safe, or there was a good chance he was dead too. Why else would he have shot his dogs and carefully arranged their bodies? Maybe his ghost had left him alone at last, and alone he'd thought there was some point to dying and none to living, and had said his farewell to the last of his animals then found some quiet room and pulled the trigger. If he had, Holly had to find him; had to look, no matter what horrible damage the gun had done to him; had to show Yvonne and if need be fall to her knees and beg her to follow him.

The others tried to stop her. Even Ben shook his head and asked if she was sure. Sal was urgent in telling her she was stupid and Julia, who had finally joined them from the lane, said they all had to get away, go home, immediately.

Holly shrugged. "I don't mind doing it alone," she said. She did mean it, but she also knew Ben would stiffen at that, after all his talk about solo heroism. He looked at her almost accusingly but she smiled at him and she saw him realise what she was doing. He didn't smile back but he nodded gravely and said, "I'm with you," which was about all she needed. Sal said she supposed someone had to look after them, and Julia said she wasn't being left by herself, so in the end Holly had all of them behind her as she stepped gingerly into the darkened hallway.

The house was dank and still and smelt strongly of death, like out in the fields but a hundred times more so. The cold unmoving air that entered Holly's mouth and nose reeked of it. It was also silent, properly silent, and after they had all paused in the hall for a few minutes she was almost sure that nothing was living inside the house. It didn't stop every door feeling like it had a gun behind it, though. Julia hung at the back clinging onto Sal, who let her, which Holly thought was interesting, and either she or Ben at the front would push open each door then pull back, horrified by the sudden din of squeaking hinges, ready all the time to run.

There were a lot of little rooms downstairs and each one was the same: filthy, with grimy dirt on the walls and even the ceiling, and dark patterned carpets crusted with mud and hair and muck. Most of them were wallpapered with the same pattern of little pink flowers, and in many places the paper was brown and discoloured and bulging away from the wall. Apart from that it wasn't so much like the house of a mad person. He hadn't collected bones or stored his own excrement in foil packages or scrawled crazy writing over the walls, all of which Holly had seen on TV. It was even fairly tidy. High-backed armchairs stood on their own away from the walls and there were low tables with piles of papers and letters on them and china figures on all the flat surfaces, yellowed and crackled with age and dirt. All his mother's stuff, Holly guessed. It was as if Will had lived in this house without touching or changing anything, as if it had all just existed around him as shelter and he'd had no interest or even awareness of it.

The kitchen was down a dark corridor and when they got there the smell was very strong: the dogs must have been left a long time. They knew what was in there so didn't look. Then there was a large cupboard full of ancient tins and some mouldy dog food and that was the downstairs. Which meant they had to go upstairs now.

"We can do this," Ben whispered, though Holly heard his voice rise a little into a question and realised even he wasn't sure. That gave her the confidence to repeat, "We can do this."

Julia wouldn't come and she pulled so hard at Sal that she shrugged and stayed behind too, so only Ben and Holly went upstairs, taking them slowly, one at a time. By now they had been in the house too long, surely, for Will still to be lying in wait but Holly imagined, every step, what would happen if he did suddenly leap out. The first thought in her mind was that Ben mustn't die, which meant she had to be in front of him; but the second thought was that she couldn't die and leave him, and she didn't think she'd ever had a thought quite like that before. Each step they climbed, each hard beat of her heart, she realised more and more what feeling like this about another person really meant.

By the time they reached the top she had locked her hand around his and that was how they explored. One by one they pushed open doors. Holly was so sure what they would see, could picture so clearly Will Sadler hanging, his heavy boots turning in the draught from the door opening, that she saw a flash of it every time an empty room appeared in front of them. Again there was almost no sign of Will having left a mark on the house. Most of the bedrooms were hung with tattered cobwebs and rotting curtains, the beds made neatly with mouldering covers, as though they had been untouched for years, and Holly guessed that was true. How long had Will said? Forty years? Was that how long he'd spent in this house, using nothing but what he needed, leaving the rest as the domain of his mother's ghost?

His room was obvious: there were piles of filthy clothes and the bed was a mass of sheets so dirty they'd gone beyond grey in places to a kind of greeny-brown. There was a bad moment when she walked around the bed and saw a body in what was only a pile of clothes. She jumped and called out and Ben came quickly to her, his arm around her waist, before they both saw it was nothing. Then he looked down and pulled her to him and standing in Will Sadler's bedroom, in a house so desolate that Holly wondered how she'd ever found her own home cold, she properly found out about kissing. It went on and on and her whole self seemed to contract to the heat of his mouth and the curl of his hair where she held the back of his neck and the blood that raced through her chest and through his, pressed against it, and their breath mingling. After what might have been ten minutes they broke away and she looked at him, seeing on his skin the flush of embarrassment and desire she felt on her own. Then Holly looked at Yvonne and remembered her endless accounts of snogging. Had she experienced, each time, what Holly was feeling now? If so Holly could almost forgive her those triumphant stories. A feeling like this – how could it not burst out of her?

Ben was looking into her eyes searchingly. "Holly...." he said quietly. "How I'm feeling... this doesn't change it."

"I know," she said simply.

He nodded, looking very serious. "But... you do know, at least I want you to know, that if... that when everything turns to shit, then if anything survives, it'll be this. You do know that?"

Holly looked up into his eyes. She did know, she thought. That was just it. She didn't worry, she didn't wonder whether or not it was real. Maybe that would change in the days ahead, when he was telling her to leave him alone and looking at her with that freezing coldness and pain in his face; maybe then she would feel doubt, but not now. Right now she felt more certainty than she ever had in her life.

They looked everywhere, in the grimy bathroom and the cold airing cupboard and even in the loft, which Ben climbed up to. "That's it, then," he called down. "He's not here."

His voice sounded loud after so long creeping around in silence. After they'd heard it and knew it was safe Sal and Julia started talking too, and somehow that was the first time that Holly felt they were intruding. Before Ben came down from the loft she asked if there was anywhere up there his body might be lying hidden, anywhere at all. She could feel Julia looking at her with sick fascination but she had to know. If he was here she had to see it. When Ben shook his head Holly knew she only had one thing left to do.

"I'm going to the kitchen," she said quietly. "Before we leave."

Ben looked at her a moment then said, "All right," and they went downstairs and left her to it. When Holly pushed open the door the stink was thick like a wall, but she calmly went in and squatted by the dogs and looked them up and down, and then at Yvonne, feeling almost patient at last. It was as if the certainty Ben gave her was filling all of her life – she just knew that this was what she had to do. Yvonne showed no sign of awareness but for several long minutes Holly made her stand near those animals. Tomorrow they would go together to the fire, she thought. Tomorrow this would all be done.

40

That night Holly slept badly. It had seemed simple enough coming back from Will Sadler's. The others had said they were sorry she hadn't seen him, hadn't known either way about his ghost – though it was clearly good news for Will himself, Ben said, with a faint smile. Holly had shaken her head silently. She'd been sure. Will had gone for one reason: because his ghost had gone before him, and left him free.

Now, though, half-asleep in the dark, that confidence was already fading, and in its place were doubt and dreams. In the dreams again and again she saw Will, dead after all in a dozen terrible ways, and his dogs dead with him. In between these recurrent visions Holly lay awake in the dark, looking at Yvonne, wondering how it was that she didn't understand. They lived on a farm and saw animals die, not all the time, but often enough. Daddy had died. After all that, how could Yvonne have been ignorant of what death meant? Suddenly Holly felt a surge of misgiving. If she got to the fire and it didn't work, was she really coming home with Yvonne? Was that the price she had to pay for life with the Family; and if it was, could she pay it?

That anxiety woke her properly and she pushed back the covers. It was just after four o'clock. She got up and pulled on her cardigan, thinking vaguely that if she went downstairs for a glass of water her body might decide it was tired enough to let her sleep after all, but when she stepped quietly out onto the landing she saw a line of light underneath Malcolm's door. For a moment she hesitated, then she went towards it. When they'd got back from Will's last night he'd been drunk again, but not in the way he'd been recently, thick and muddle-headed and mumbling. He was lively and laughing and just a bit too loud. He asked where they'd gone all day and straightaway Sal said calmly that they'd been on the downs. He nodded and rambled on for a while about orienteering and German sensibilities and the wisdom of physical education then said they should start up the school again, which was the surest sign he was drinking less. And now he was awake, evidently. And maybe sitting up in bed reading and if Holly went in he might look at her over his glasses and smile and she knew only Daddy had worn glasses but still, she thought, still, he could tell her it was all going to work out; he could give her back a sense of assurance and make her feel up to this task.

As she put her hand to the door Holly felt a stab of disquiet but it didn't stop her quietly opening it. Afterwards she wondered why she didn't knock. Obviously she should have knocked, that's what people did. Maybe it was because no-one had knocked on doors much at the farm since Daddy died, not counting Belinda's pre-entrance crashing, or maybe it was because in that moment of doubt she'd already sensed something was wrong and knew what was coming. Either way she just opened the door and realised she wasn't the first person to come to Malcolm's room tonight because Sal was sitting on the edge of the bed. The light was dim and it took Holly a moment to process what she was seeing. Malcolm was flat on his back asleep, snoring, and he was naked, his legs splayed wide. Sal was stroking his hair with one hand and she had the other flat against his chest and was looking down at him, at his naked body, and it was something about the way she looked, the little smile, and then the way she looked up at Holly and didn't change her expression at all that made Holly back away in silence, her mind suddenly full of things breaking one by one.

Holly was dressed by the time Sal came to find her, sitting on the edge of her bed, ready to go. Sal stood at the door a moment. "Can I sit down?" she said.

Holly didn't reply and Sal came and sat next to her on the bed. "It's not what you think," she said. Holly shook her head. She didn't think anything, so she didn't know how Sal could be so sure. She just knew that something was corrupt and wrong, and that it couldn't be made right. Sal looked at her calmly. "It wouldn't matter, anyway," she said. "Even if it was. He's not my father."

Holly shrugged. "I know," she said. Nor mine, she thought. Nor mine.

"Good." There was a silence. "Anyway," Sal said, "that won't happen. I thought it might have done, once. But it won't."

Holly looked at her hands in her lap, and remembered Sal's hand, flat against his chest, her fingers soft against him.

"Listen," Sal said, sounding faintly annoyed, as if Holly was forcing this out of her, "I just want what makes him happy. For a while he seemed to think that was me, which is why... Anyway. But that wasn't right. Now it seems like it's Belinda, and that's fine with me."

Holly looked up at that. Sal was staring at her with calculation, maybe, or challenge, but no sense of apology. "You..." Holly started, but didn't know how to finish. How could she fit what Sal was into words?

"It's good," Sal said. "Don't you see? We both want the same thing. Daddy too, and that's what matters."

"And Eva?" Holly said.

225

Sal smiled as if she had been waiting for that question. "Mummy isn't right for him," she said. "It's obvious, isn't it? She can't do him any good. She saw that in the end."

In the end, Holly thought. So all the time Sal had been talking to Eva, all those quiet careful conversations, this was what she'd been working towards? Holly suddenly remembered the barn, and Sal's expression as she'd pulled the door closed, and how Eva had been ever since: how nervous and unsure she'd seemed... Eva was her *mother*. Holly thought of Sal's distance, her remoteness. Maybe that wouldn't matter to her. Maybe nothing did.

Sal stood up. "You won't tell anyone," she said, her eyes dark and her hair low on her forehead, looking more like Ben than ever. "Not that there's anything to tell. But you won't." She wasn't asking, Holly knew, and she wasn't instructing. Just observing. As Eva had done. And now Holly really was the person that Eva thought she was: the girl with secrets who wouldn't talk.

Sal paused at the door. She seemed to notice for the first time that Holly was dressed. "Going out?" she said.

Holly nodded. Going away, actually, but it wasn't worth saying.

"Take care," Sal said, then after another moment she smiled. "One day you might understand this. Or you might not. It doesn't really matter, does it?"

Holly shook her head. No, she thought, looking at Yvonne. Maybe it really didn't.

After Sal left Holly went downstairs, lifted the keys to the pick-up off their hook, and walked outside. The night was overcast and pitch dark. She knew her way to the pick-up though and when she found it she opened the door and slid onto the cold vinyl seat and then sat, looking through the windscreen, her breath clouding inside the cab. Malcolm's light was still on, and she looked at his window a long time. Sal was… whatever Sal was, but Malcolm – how could he have let her? How could he allow it? He must have known the wrongness of it as much as she had. Holly thought of Belinda in Malcolm's bed. She thought of Julia and all her painful efforts to show her closeness to Ben, and now thought she understood. It must have been lonely enough being separate from Sal and Ben, being excluded from their bond. To have watched Sal and Malcolm together and sensed another bond there, another way in which she was an outsider – it wasn't surprising she'd got as close to Ben as he would allow her. And Eva… there was no-one for Eva to have turned to. Her own child, Holly thought. How was that possible?

And finally she thought of herself: how safe and happy Malcolm had made her feel, and how obvious that must have been to everyone, no matter how much she tried to hide it. Obvious to him, too. He must have thought it entirely natural: another person revolving around him like a planet around a star. What will the world bring me next? Whose turn is it to show me adoration, and of what kind? Not that it seemed to matter to him what kind of love he got, nor who from. She had wanted him to be as much as a father, and he was only a child – more of a child than she was. She thought of him wandering naked around that house in Guildford, lounging there naked, and saw how monstrous it was.

She wondered what she'd wanted from the Family. Ben, yes, but not as a brother. And the others? Had she really expected them to fill the hole in her life left by Daddy, and by a sister who had never been a sister at all? Had she thought that she'd get rid of Yvonne and come home to Belinda happy in Malcolm's arms ("Call me Mummy, Holly, now we're all together again") and to her cousin-sisters and uncle-father, all in perfect harmony? And to have Ben with her always, a cousin-boyfriend who struggled valiantly with an illness that of course he would beat, for her sake, it would be the very least he could do – was that where she'd thought she'd end up?

Holly put the key in the ignition and after a sluggish couple of turns the cold engine started. She hunched round awkwardly in her seat and started reversing. She wasn't a very good driver, not in cars, but it didn't matter. She didn't have far to go.

41

Just as it had been with the army, getting in was easy. Holly had never driven on roads before but there had been no traffic, no-one to see her leaning forward peering over the edge of the wheel. She'd navigated by the smoke in the air, which had been dimly visible in the first pre-dawn light. Once she got close it took a while to find the right turnings but eventually she found a track that led past two deserted sheds and up to the pyre itself. Nearby there was a portacabin and a booth for a guard but both seemed to be empty. She drove into the site, the pick-up bouncing and lurching across hard ground rutted with tracks, and pulled onto a strip of grass. For a moment a shudder of disgust stopped her getting out, but then she pushed the door open convulsively and stepped out into the heat.

The fire was set in a long line about fifty yards ahead of her, stretching from edge to edge of a wide field. As the smoke billowed from that line she could see another beyond it, the same, and then a third, with a few yards separating each one. It was still quite dark and the only real light was a sour glow emitted here and there beneath the thick smoke, though most of the fire was grey with dust and ash. The heat of it wasn't like bonfire night, when the dry crackle of logs made her skin stretch and tighten. This heat was rank, almost moist. There was no wind and the smoke rose in heavy, lazy curls. The embers at the base of the fire growled and spat. Holly lifted her scarf to her mouth and stepped a few paces towards the line of fire then just stood and looked at it. Blackened stumps of legs were raised out of the ash like fists, and the air reeked with the smell of burning skin and hair.

She turned her head to one side. Yvonne was standing by her shoulder, a little behind her. Holly stared at her face but as ever she couldn't tell where Yvonne was looking, what she was seeing. If she was seeing anything. Then she looked along the edge of the fire. What had she been hoping for? An orderly line of ghosts queuing patiently? She didn't know exactly, but some presence… some sense of departing. And here there was nothing.

She steeled herself. *Watch them burn*, she thought. She felt like she had seen enough death to last her a lifetime but if she had to show Yvonne more she would. She walked forwards again. Making progress into the heat and the smell and the smog was almost more than she could force herself to do. Her eyes stung and even through the scarf the hot greasy air was acrid in her mouth and throat but she walked, not looking ahead, keeping her eyes on the ground until the heat was burning the skin of her forehead and she looked up. She was still ten yards or more from where the great ashen heap began but now she was surrounded by the vicious eddying heat of the fire and another step, even one more, was beyond her. She tried to stand upright and watch like Liam had said but each breath was coming shallower and shallower and her eyes were streaming so she ducked down, gasping for air. She made herself look, though, through the tears. Now she was this close she saw that the shifting grey ash was a crust and that red-gold masses of flame writhed underneath it, the heavy air shimmering where lines in the crust broke apart. She was almost kneeling now and looked up at Yvonne willing her desperately forwards, or away, or up, or gone, but Yvonne stood still, air made stone.

Holly looked beyond her, deep into the smoke, hoping desperately to see shapes dissolving into it, but she saw nothing. She felt dizzy and not far off falling and if she fell she knew she might not be able to get up again. She had to go back, to retreat, but she couldn't move. Her mind was unravelling and her heaving chest felt like it belonged to someone else, and she wondered vaguely if this was how it started: a long slow drift away from clarity and thought, and into the troubled dream of death. She looked up one more time into the heart of the fire – and suddenly, beyond it, between the two great lines of burning animals, she saw a figure. It too was looking into the fire. It was solid, as if it was a real person, but no-one could be standing in the middle of that heat.

It was enough to make her act. She pushed herself upright and stumbled backwards, away from the flames to find air that she could breathe, never taking her eyes off the figure. If it was here to depart; if she could see it happen; if Yvonne could see it... Her legs seemed to have no strength and she fell backwards but she kept kicking and dragging herself away. Yvonne was drifting after her and it may have been her imagination but was she turning? Was she watching the flame? Or even the figure? The air was clearing now and Holly felt less frighteningly disconnected from herself. She gasped in air, a deep dull ache throbbing in her chest. The smoke swirled but the figure remained visible, a dark shape in the heart of the fire. It merged for a moment with the thick grey mound of ash and then drifted closer still and she realised it was not walking into the flames, but through the flames, and towards her and Yvonne. Every movement now brought it into clearer air and Holly lay on her back before it, propped on her elbows, her face smeared in filth and dirt and her eyes running and every second she was more and more sure, and then it was standing at her feet and looking down at her and she knew. Her throat was full of ash and dust but she forced her voice to work. "Daddy?" she said.

42

Holly had to crawl some of the way to the pick-up but she made it and pulled herself inside. It was almost no relief: the air in the cab was full of the same damp heat. Exhaustedly she started the engine and drove out and away. The pyre was on the edge of Dewhurst, a tiny village or not even that, with a few houses and farms and an old church and an even older ruined chapel in the churchyard. She stopped on the verge outside the church and switched off the engine and opened the door and breathed deeply the clearer air. Then she looked across the seats. Part of her wanted to laugh, a crazed laugh. Instead of getting rid of her ghost now she had two. And the worst of it was that she knew why. Even as she had dragged herself along the ground to the pick-up and pulled herself into it, even while she had thrummed with the shock of seeing Daddy's face again, she had understood what this meant, and she had been protesting against it.

Now, away from the flames, that understanding remained unshaken. Liam Purvis was wrong and Marian was wrong and Holly knew why she was haunted but it wasn't fair, it didn't make sense. As Daddy had approached her, even before she recognised him, she had known that he was not moving of his own will. She was drawing him forwards. She'd felt it in her chest as surely as if it had been a winch winding. She had stood in the smoke of death, and tasted it on her tongue, and in the moment of that distress she had summoned him, and he had come. And it wasn't fair, it wasn't: because if Daddy had come to answer her call then that meant, and she saw it as sure and clear as the stone spire that rose before her – that meant Yvonne had answered her call as well. She wasn't refusing to leave. Holly was refusing to let her go.

Holly leaned back against the headrest, her eyes closed. Even though she didn't want to accept it, she knew it was true. That sensation as she had drawn Daddy to her had been the same feeling she'd had driving home with Belinda after the accident. That must have been the moment when she tugged Yvonne from the world of the dead, and bound the two of them so tightly together. Why, she thought, why? All this time she had been longing to be free... how could she have been the one clinging on?

And there was something more. Marian and Liam had lost their ghosts after they'd witnessed death, but Holly realised now it wasn't the ghosts who'd needed to understand: it was themselves. They had seen the death of others, and it had finally allowed them to accept their own loss. She rocked her head slowly from side to side. That made sense, but not for her. She had seen death over and over. Daddy himself wasting into the dead thing he became, Yvonne, Danny, the loss of the herd, the massacres that had scoured the countryside: she had faced them all. What more could have been asked of her, she thought; what more could she possibly have done?

She climbed out of the pick-up and leaned against the church wall. The long grass between the graves was covered with dew and glittered black-green in the first light. The dead: buried, gone, departed. But not her dead. They stood either side of her, silent jailors. Except if all this was true then she was the jailor, and they were her captives. She felt a sudden surge of anger. So all she had to do, then, was release them. Allow them to depart. Command it.

Holly turned first to Yvonne. She'd looked into that distant face so often, trying to work out what Yvonne wanted, why she wouldn't leave. Now she had to work out what she herself had been wanting all that time. She thought of Yvonne's wooden chest, hidden in the thicket, full of her own things. Had Yvonne understood this in a way that she couldn't? This desire to hold on to the other person – even more than that, to own them? If she had, Yvonne's face gave no clues. Looking at her in the still damp morning, with the smoke of the fire silently rising beyond the church, Holly had no insight, no thought. Nothing.

"Go," she said aloud. "Go on! Go!" The sound of her voice was harsh in the stillness and she realised she was turning into Will Sadler. Yvonne rippled, but remained. Holly breathed deeply. No good. So turn, then, she told herself. Look at Daddy. Look there for understanding.

Somehow, though, she couldn't do it. Couldn't move. *Turn, Holly, turn.* The thought was so strong it was as if she was saying it aloud. But nothing happened. Holly felt her heart beating dully, her whole body rebellious and inert. In the end she had to reach out to the wall and grip the stone with her hand, almost to drive herself round, to make herself face him at last. Daddy stood in front of her, unfocused like Yvonne, his hands by his sides with their strong veins and the soft dark hair on their backs, and it was looking at his hands, not up at his face, that made something move in her mind. Daddy, back but not back, here but silent, forever out of her reach. Suddenly she shook with longing. Her skin was tight with it, like wind filling out a sail, her whole being suffused by it.

"Come back, Daddy," she whispered. "Please come back."

Holly sat at the base of the wall in the last darkness of night. She looked across the graves at the mound of the ruined chapel, surrounded by a huddle of trees. She imagined the years that had raced along since it was built, the shrinking of stone into earth, the passing of a thousand summers, the ebb and flow of light from dawn to dusk, time and time again. Now the building was only a little worn hillock, wearing down to nothing. Becoming forgotten.

Dawn was lightening the sky and the grass uncurled towards it. A bird had begun to sing in the copse, and in the houses beyond the chapel, dark oblongs against the east, people were waking up and radios were spilling out voices; and all of it was ignorant and forgetful, and it was so unfair. She wanted to summon all the ghosts who had known this place, the Romans and Picts and Saxons, until everything she saw was wreathed with the remembered dead, and she was haunted by them all.

And it was that desire, that need to keep them from their graves and have them remembered, that made Holly finally understand. She had seen death all right. She had lived with it, she had tasted it in the air, but she had not accepted it. Accepting it, she realised, had nothing to do with death, but with life. The life from which the dead had departed. If she was to continue forwards, she had to leave the Holly who'd known Daddy further and further behind. That was what she hadn't been able to accept: not that Daddy had left her, but that she had to leave too. Had to look back at the little girl who'd stood with Yvonne by his graveside, and know herself to be someone different.

Holly remembered Yvonne's funeral, and folding away the too-small dress she'd bought when Daddy died, swearing not to forget the person who'd worn it. Now she knew she had to break that promise. She had to accept that year by year she would leave her old selves behind; that one day this Holly, sitting by this wall, in this moment, would only be a memory held by someone else. A woman with her name, taller and heavier and busier, who would look back down the long vista of years like a tunnel and wonder if she had really seen the ghosts of her father and sister, people she remembered only from photographs. Who might see a photograph of Holly as she was now, and smile without remembering, and close the album and turn away to a life beyond.

Holly looked wryly up at Yvonne, and silently asked her forgiveness. Daddy was the reason she had held on to her so tightly: because the Holly who'd known Daddy had been half of Holly-and-Yvonne, and she had not been prepared to let that Holly go. All this time she had thought she wanted to be alone, but now she knew she'd only wanted to remain the same – to be the girl who longed for freedom, not the girl who had it. She didn't know how to live alone. Only the Holly who was ahead of her knew that.

Then she looked at Daddy, looked him full in the face this time, understanding what Marian had meant about abandonment. She had only just got him back and the idea of losing him again was unbearable. For a moment she thought about refusing to release him: holding him and Yvonne in a vice-like grip and remaining forever as she was right now. But even if she could, for a while at least, she knew that it wouldn't be fair. They only lingered on sufferance for her. That was why the dead couldn't speak, because if they could speak they would ask, all of them, the same favour: to be allowed to dissolve like smoke into the rich damp air and the deep green stillness and the high vault of clouds. To be left in peace.

Holly rose stiffly and climbed back into the pick-up, her ghosts alongside her. She drove home and parked in the yard. It was still only seven o'clock and the house was quiet. Somewhere up in the hills that rose behind it, Belinda was probably walking through empty fields: a Belinda full of desires and hope and lies, whom

236

Holly had never known existed. A Belinda who had shut herself in a world stripped of the living and the dead so that neither could torment her. Somehow the Holly who lay ahead of her had to find a way into that world, because Belinda was what she needed. Not the Family, just her family. She and her mother, the ones who'd been left. Together they would make something new out of all this destruction. They would create a future, and the person she was now would vanish into it. Holly thought of Ben asleep, time sweeping over him, hustling him down a road towards darkness. Perhaps the Holly she'd become would be strong enough to follow him, or perhaps not, but either way the task was hers.

She climbed out of the cab and turned away from the house, towards the road that had always bounded her horizon. She'd looked down on it her whole life, and she'd been under it, but she'd never crossed it. She knew what she would do when she got there. For as long as she could bear it she would stay in the reservation and be near Daddy one last time. Then she would climb over the barrier on the other side, the land beyond spread out before her. The ceaseless traffic would surge and pulse, the roar of its approach and the sigh of its departure repeated forever, but she'd know when the moment was right. When it came she'd close her eyes and walk out across the wide expanse of tarmac. Alone.

Acknowledgements

I'm hugely grateful to John Were at Xelsion Publishing, without whose creative vision and bold sense of enterprise this book wouldn't be here. Thanks also to Fiona Traill at Xelsion for endless energy, efficiency and brilliance, and to Amelia Were for infectious enthusiasm. Thanks to James Kelsall, John Hudson and Tom Benyon for sage advice; to Peter Marshall and Suzannah Lipscomb for readily dispensed kindness; and to Kathi Knapman for thoughtful generosity spread over 30 years (with a significant gap in the middle). To all other readers and sources of counsel, both before and after publication: thank you for giving your time to this book.

I owe more to my family than I can express here. Daniel le Fleming's intellectual and emotional response to my writing gave me the confidence to keep doing it, as did Henry le Fleming's assured support. Deirdre Eddy and Pamela Dixon's encouragement has been unstinting. Christie Dickason and John Faulkner have been kind and wise in equal measure. For this book especially, my debt is greatest to Morwenna le Fleming. I'm not sure the strange, solitary life of a farmer can fully be understood by any who have not lived it; but all that I do know of farming was taught to me by the Boss Lady, along with most of what I know about courage. To combine such strength of spirit with so much warmth and loving generosity is quite a thing.

I should acknowledge a debt to Matilda, through whose affections I have really come to understand the meaning of joy. Lastly infinite thanks and love to Abigail. My general belief is that words always do suffice, but for everything that I owe her, I'm not sure that's true. The best I can do is thank her for illuminating so radiantly both the life material and the life imaginative in every possible way.